Campbell Armstrong was born in Glasgow and educated at Sussex University. He and his family now live in Ireland. His bestselling novels have placed him in the front rank of international thriller writers.

DEADLINE

Successful L.A. psychiatrist Jerry Lomax receives a 'phone call that sends his life into freefall. The caller wants the confidential records of one of Jerry's clients, Emily Ford, who is about to get the President's nomination for US Attorney-General. Emily has revealed a secret to Jerry, a secret which, in the hands of her enemies, could be devastating. The caller is also holding something that Jerry holds very dear, and if he doesn't hand over the papers, Jerry will have to live with the consequences . . .

Books by Campbell Armstrong
Published by The House of Ulverscroft:

CONCERT OF GHOSTS

CAMPBELL ARMSTRONG

DEADLINE

Complete and Unabridged

ULVERSCROFT
Leicester

First published in Great Britain in 2000 by
Doubleday
London

First Large Print Edition
published 2001
by arrangement with
Transworld Publishers, a division of
The Random House Group Limited
London

The moral right of the author has been asserted

British Library CIP Data

Armstrong, Campbell, *1944 –*
    Deadline.—Large print ed.—
    Ulverscroft large print series: mystery
    1. Large type books
    2. Suspense fiction
    I. Title
    823.9'14 [F]

    ISBN 0–7089–4455–8

Published by
F. A. Thorpe (Publishing)
Anstey, Leicestershire

Set by Words & Graphics Ltd.
Anstey, Leicestershire
Printed and bound in Great Britain by
T. J. International Ltd., Padstow, Cornwall

This book is printed on acid-free paper

Thursday, 6.45 p.m.

I left my office thirty minutes later than usual. The tall lights in the parking-lot had been lit, although dark was more than an hour away. It had been one of those draining days, where each patient seemed more demanding than the last. As I walked towards my car, I tried to shed the assorted burdens I'd been gathering for the last seven or eight hours, but it wasn't ever easy — you couldn't just cast aside the torments and anxieties of those who entrusted their mental welfare to you.

Some people dumped work as soon as the clock struck a certain hour. I didn't. I took the office home with me. I grudged the fact, but I hadn't found a way around it. I tried to relax, sure; I'd bury myself in a book, involve myself in a movie or a ballgame on TV — Sondra enjoyed old black-and-white movies and basketball — but then my mind would drift mid-plot or halfway through the game, and I'd wonder about this patient or that, I'd weigh the merits of their medication or the course therapy was taking.

Increasingly I found myself thinking I

1

needed a long vacation, a break from patients and their problems; the job was too demanding, and life in Los Angeles — the American capital of psychosis, where mood disorders and high-tech pharmaceutical developments were casual dinner-party topics — unreal and vaguely unpleasant.

My car was parked directly under one of the electric lights. I set my briefcase down between my feet while I searched inside my pockets for my keys. There were only a few cars in the lot; some I recognized as belonging to other tenants in the building. Beyond, on Wilshire, traffic stop-started. I found my key and fitted it into the lock.

The man appeared out of nowhere, his face muffled by a scarf and a baseball cap pulled low over his forehead. He struck out at me with a chopping motion of his hand, a blow directed at my larynx. Startled, I moved a half-step away and his hand rammed the side of my neck instead of my throat, but the blow was still forceful enough to stun me a moment — I slid against the car, which prevented me from falling to the ground.

'Gimme your carkeys, your wallet, that nice watch, anything you got of value, and fast.'

I shook my head, tried to clear the cloudiness away.

'Fast, man. Fast. Come on.'

I didn't move. Didn't acquiesce. I stared at him, tried to bring him into focus. His eyes were very close together; weirdly so.

'Dickhead,' he said. 'You got a hearing problem?'

He raised the same hand he'd used the first time, and I watched it come down hard in the light of the lamp. And this time I saw something metallic flash, half-silver, half-black. I turned my head at the last possible moment and heard the blade hit metal. The knife, which might have pierced my cheek, went skittering out of the guy's fist and was lost somewhere beyond the reach of the light. For no logical reason, I had the feeling he hadn't intended to plunge the blade into me with lethal intent, that his real goal was to draw blood, to scar and scare. He was a thief, not a killer.

I swung at him, jabbing him hard in his left eye. Unperturbed, seemingly beyond pain, he made no noise, didn't groan, didn't cry out; he just closed his hand into a ball and brought it down yet again. This time I had sense enough to lift my right hand and smother his fist, and for a few seconds we were linked together palm to palm, and the sharp light from the overhead bulb was blinding me.

The peak of the baseball cap shadowed his eyes, and the scarf concealed him like the bandanna of a stagecoach robber in a western. Fleecy grey lining hung from his ragged military-style khaki jacket, which smelled of gasoline and tobacco and that weary odor of the streets — a brew of concrete and dank moisture of the kind that gathers in culverts, of wet paper sacks. I knew the smell: I'd done enough work among emergency psycho cases in mental hospitals — the screamers, the paranoids, the schizo-phrenics, the deranged dragged in off the violent cosmos of the streets.

But there was another scent too, one I couldn't identify at that moment; an incongruous one.

He was very strong, but I sensed his grip yielding. I thought: *one moment you're doing something everyday, you're unlocking your car, getting ready to go home. Fine, banal, civilized. The next, you're fighting off an unexpected attacker.*

I figured he was after drugs. He'd been watching me for a couple of days perhaps: he knew I worked in a medical office building, maybe he thought I was a walking pharmacy and carried samples in my briefcase. If I didn't have samples then I'd have money, which was the next best thing.

I was angry. The day had already pulverized me like beans in a coffee-grinder, my patients had depressed me, the drive home through the city was an unappealing prospect, and now I had some goddam thief attacking me. Something similar had happened in this same spot three months back, when Benny Shark, a pediatrician, was jumped as he strolled to his car. He'd been roughed up and his wallet snatched. He'd left LA a month later, and the last I heard he was working out of a small town in Oregon.

Enough, for Christ's sake. This city was a septic tank.

I brought up my knee hard into his groin. I felt bone sink into soft flesh. He stepped back, moaned. I pushed myself away from the car and kicked out, catching him on the knee. He retreated a couple of paces, then he reached down, rubbed his knee. 'So you wanna fight, huh? Tough guy. Hardass. Wants to fight.'

'I don't *want* to fight,' I said. 'I just want to go home, for Christ's sake. I just want a life without this kind of hassle.' I wondered about his pain threshold; he was probably high on something that also anaesthetized — crack, maybe some other cocaine derivative, speed. He was blinking his left eye rapidly.

'Don't wanna fight, fine. Then I'll just help

myself to this baby,' and he looked down at my briefcase.

'The fuck you will.' I bent to grab the handle of the case, a tactical mistake; he uppercut me, one of those sly blows you don't see coming. You know it's on the way, you just don't catch it in time. It jerked my head back and I heard a muscular *click* at the juncture of neck and shoulder. Furious, I kicked out at him as he reached down to snatch my case; I caught him directly in the ear, and he yelped. He dropped the case and I kicked him again; then I grabbed him by the collar of his coat and tossed him to the ground. I stood over him, my fists clenched.

I was breathing hard, too hard.

Unexpected exertion, sure. But it was more. It was the pulse of rage. I wanted to crack his head into the concrete. Raise it, smash it down. Raise it, smash it down. And again. Pulp it.

Dr Lomax, psychiatrist. Respected member of the LA medical profession. Be calm.

'I'm not carrying any drugs,' I said. 'You got that?'

He lay huddled, face concealed between cap and scarf, and he stared at me as if he were peering through a visor. 'What makes you think I want any fucking drugs?'

'Money, then,' I said. 'Whatever the hell you're after.'

He shook his head. 'You guys always think you know everything, don't you? You always think you see the whole picture in one big flash. Whoom za-zooom. The truth direct from God himself.' I wasn't sure what he was talking about. There was an unpleasant, slightly spooky nasal sneer in his voice, even though the sound came to me muffled through his scarf. The rhythms of his speech were vaguely Hispanic.

'Frankly, I just don't give a shit what you think,' I said. And I didn't. I wanted to go home and kick off my shoes. I took my cellphone from my jacket and flipped it open. 'I'm calling the cops. They can deal with you.'

He moved slightly, grimaced with pain, propped himself up on one elbow. He glanced in the direction of the office building, where a few lights were still lit, then he looked at my car. As I spoke into the phone, I didn't take my eyes off him. He didn't want dope, so he wanted money: it was either one thing or the other, because nothing lay between the poles of narcotics and hard cash. He was a rodent, he lived in alleys and doorways and abandoned buildings; I was in no mood to feel sorry for him, and even less inclined to wonder about the reasons behind his circumstances. Booze. Drugs. A childhood of abuse. What the hell did it matter? The liberal in me, the do-gooder, the bleeding-heart, was dying little by little. Once upon a time, I couldn't pass a beggar without giving him a handout, but I was through dropping coins in the dixie-cups of panhandlers. The city had immunized me against acts of charity.

I got the operator, asked to be connected to the police. I gave my name to an unsympathetic female officer, and told her what had happened, and the location. She asked me if I was in any immediate danger; I told her I thought that possibility had passed. She said a car would be along as soon as one became available; she made it sound like she worked for a cab company. What was I supposed to do — stand guard until the cops came?

She hung up. I shut off my cellphone and looked at the guy.

'You pay your taxes — for what?' he asked. He was rubbing his left eye almost constantly. 'Protection from big badasses like me, right? Well, I don't hear no fucking cavalry, Captain.'

I looked at my watch. I didn't want to hang around here; it wasn't my job to be this guy's keeper. My heart-beat slowed, my pulses returned to normal.

The guy maneuvered himself into a sitting

position. Where were the cops? I scanned the lot, looked for flashing lights on the boulevard — nothing. I turned back to look at the guy: the idea popped into my head — *run*. Why didn't he just make a run for it? Do us all a favor. Spare me time going over the circumstances of the assault, describing the indescribable. Save the cops some paperwork.

Get up, take a hike, go. I'll even look away.

But then I thought of how Benny Shark had been beaten up and robbed, and an instinctive yearning for law and order rose inside me. After me, somebody else would be a victim; and somebody after that. There was no end to the chain of violence and larceny — unless it was outright anarchy.

I had a duty. I'd wait for the cops. The good doctor.

The guy got to his feet. He was rubbing his knee. I watched him warily.

'Ouch,' he was saying. 'Ouch, ouch.' He limped in a tiny circle under the tall lamp. 'You kick like a mule,' he said. 'What are you? Six two? Hunnerd and eighty pounds?'

What did he want now? Conversation? I didn't feel like passing the time of day. Then I saw the black and white come across the parking-lot. My assailant saw it too and reacted with unexpected speed, turning, suddenly twisting past my outstretched arm, skimming me by an inch or two, then sprinting across the lot and weaving through the traffic on Wilshire with a certain wild grace, like a broken field runner. Then the black and white flashed lights and whined and ploughed into the traffic flow on the boulevard in pursuit of the guy. I heard brakes scream and horns blast.

I stood for a time, leaning against my car with my arms folded, wondering what was expected of me, if I was supposed to hang out like a good citizen until the cop car returned and an officer asked me questions. Or had I been written out of the script entirely now, an incidental character, a walk-on? What the hell. If they wanted to talk with me, they had my name.

I tossed my case onto the passenger seat and I sat behind the wheel. I tilted my head back, waited for ten minutes, then I drove out of the lot. Halfway home, I experienced after-shock, a tremor that affected my hands and legs. Sweat ran down my face.

This goddam city, I thought. I envied Benny Shark. I wanted Oregon.

9.06 p.m.

Sondra did all the talking during dinner. She was more animated than normal. She told me stories that were coursing through her office; I listened, amused as I usually was by her talent for mimicry and the enthusiastic way she launched herself into reports of scandals and affairs, who was screwing who in the world of music, the down and dirty stuff we didn't read in the entertainment pages. In full flow, she was a one-woman entertainment.

I wanted to tell her about the incident in the parking-lot; but I didn't. She hated horror stories of urban brutality. She wanted to think LA, her native city, had a heart of spun gold. It was a place unjustly maligned, it didn't deserve its reputation as a dead zone, an artificial city, a tawdry hell by the ocean where only the whacked-out poor or the grotesquely spoiled, neurotic rich lived. Besides, her humor was good: why bring her down? She was on a high, and it was clearly due to something more than just another working day at LaBrea Records.

She waited until we'd finished dinner

before she told me the real reason for her animation.

She didn't blow out the candles. She stepped through the sliding glass doors to the redwood deck, and I followed. The city, orange and vast, lay spread below like a huge foundry whose purpose was too obscure to understand. The canyons were black crevices and the air smelled of exhaust fumes and I thought of my assailant even as I tried to shove the memory away. I saw the knife come down through bright light, and I remembered turning my face to one side and how the blade had struck the car, that funny little *ping* of metal on metal. My heart shifted, boogied an extra little beat. I caught a whiff of the smell he'd left behind. And then it hit me. The bum in the scarf and cap and the greasy jacket with the stink of the city attached to him — why had he also smelled of *cologne*? I let the question drift away. What difference did it make? I was here, now, secure.

I looked at my wife. Even after six years of marriage, I had times when I couldn't read her face, when she seemed mysterious, as if she were holding something back, perhaps some aspect of herself she was reluctant to mention. She leaned against the deck-rail. A gas-scented breeze blew up and stirred her hair, which was short, dyed aubergine.

'Notice anything?' she asked.

'What am I looking for in particular?'

She smiled and turned away, and gazed out across the extent of the valley; the city was an infinite shifting arrangement of headlights on freeways. Airplanes created oases of electricity floating above LAX. She looked back at me, turned the palms of her hands over.

What did she want me to notice?

'I'll make it easy for you, doc. What am I *not* doing?' she asked. Her expression was all wide-eyed mischief.

'Let me think,' I said.

'You're supposed to be observant. People pay big bucks for your insights, don't they?' She took a couple of steps toward me, smiling. I was drawn into the enigma of her eyes. Her other fine features — the full lips and the strong structure of jaw that suggested depths of self-assurance and independence — were diminished by the unusual violet of the irises. I'd never seen another human being with eyes that shade.

'I'll give you a hint,' she said. 'What do I normally do after dinner?'

It had been staring me in the face. I clicked my thumb against my middle finger. 'You smoke — '

'And? Do you see me smoking?'

'No — '

'And do you remember me telling you the only reason in the world that would make me give up?'

'Jesus *Christ!*'

'You finally get the picture, doc?'

'Are you serious?'

'Deadly.'

'I'm . . . I'm . . . I don't know . . . '

'Like, blown away?'

'Doesn't do it justice.'

I felt suddenly giddy, the night spinning about me. *Overjoyed.* No, I didn't really have a word for this thrill, this rush of anticipation.

'How long have you known?' I asked.

'Since this afternoon.'

'And you waited — '

'It wasn't easy, believe me,' she said. 'I wanted the right moment.' She nestled against my body. 'Hold me.'

I thought of the fetus inside her, small and unformed, floating in its own cloistered reality. A child! Dear God. I tried to accustom myself to the shock of this knowledge, absorb this new fact into my scheme of the world. I understood one thing: Nothing would ever be the same again. The entire pattern of my existence had assumed an entirely new shape in the matter of a few seconds.

She said, 'According to Marv Sweetzer,

ETA's mid-January. I swear, Marv couldn't have been more pleased if he'd fathered this child himself. Loaded me down with a pile of pamphlets — dos and don'ts, drink this, avoid that, take these vitamins, remember to get exercise, you want to make sure you don't get stretch-marks, on and on.'

'And you promised to be good?' I said.

'Oh, I promised to be a saint, Jerry. And I will be.'

I pictured Sondra in Marv Sweetzer's office in Beverly Hills, Marv announcing her test results. *You and Jerry hit the spot, Sondra.* I knew Marv well, and how he operated. He was the essence of kindness and practicality.

ETA January. Six months away. I couldn't help myself — I went down on my knees and lifted her purple silk dress up to her waist and laid the side of my face against her stomach, even though I knew it was too early to feel any movement. I just wanted to be close to the baby. We'd *longed* for a child, and we'd worked at it, trying our luck on the roulette wheel of reproduction — charts on the bedroom wall, computer calculations of her cycles, the difficult math of ovulation, my sperm count, fertility tests.

I was forty-three years of age, six years older than my wife, and we were aware of our clocks running a little too fast.

15

Life had been generous to us: I was successful in my profession, and Sondra made a good income as a marketing exec for LaBrea Records. And only one thing had been missing.

The notion of a *baby* — now it engulfed me. I thought of the purity of a new life amidst the dreck of the city, and briefly my mind drifted from the elevated redwood deck, plunging down to where the hot night alleys were fetid dead-ends, and doorways were filled with the disenfranchised and the socially crippled. I imagined hearing the whispers of lunatics and addicts and the sound of a wine bottle smashing or a clip thrust inside an automatic. We'd have to move from here, and I was glad.

We'd live in a small town beyond the toxic reaches of LA, a place of good schools and clean neighborhoods where you could raise a child in safety. A place of the kind you saw on pictorial calendars or postcards, or in coffee-table books about Americana, one of the friendly little towns that still existed out there like persistent myths.

I felt Sondra's hand against the back of my neck.

'Make love to me,' she said. 'Right here.'

I drew her down to the deck carefully. She'd always been precious to me, but now even more so, if such a thing were possible. My wife. My love . . . My *family*.

Jerry and Sondra Lomax and child. Two became three.

I listened to the quickened sound of her breathing and, glancing at her, saw her lips part and her eyelids flicker. The shampoo she used was suggestive of something exotic. The breeze rose again and rattled eucalyptus leaves. The night was filled with our whispered pleasures. Even the distant scream of an ambulance — an urban distress call for a gunshot victim, somebody being rushed to die in an emergency room, who knows — couldn't intrude on this moment. The guy with the knife and the parking-lot were forgotten. And when the phone rang in the house, I didn't feel the urge to answer it. The answering-machine kicked in.

I was galaxies removed from distractions. I was elsewhere. I made love as gently as I could, imagining the fragility of the womb, underestimating how much of a strongbox it was, and how securely it contained the unborn child.

Sondra said, 'I'm not glass, Jerry. I won't break. Don't hold back.'

I closed my eyes. This intimacy with her was different from anything that had taken place before. A shift had occurred, a new level of commitment had been reached. We made love on the deck as if we were touching for the first time. Our energy was frantic. I lost all sense of my body as an entity separate from Sondra. A fusion, then a splintering, inevitable and seismic.

When I had nothing left to give, she held me inside her. 'I don't want to let you go,' she said.

'I'm not going anywhere,' I said.

'Are you happy?' she asked. 'Have I made you happy, Jerry?'

'Happy's a wimp word,' I said. 'Ecstatic.' I looked up into the sky, wishing I could see stars. But the night was cloudy.

She was crying quietly.

'What is it?' I asked.

'I don't know, I don't know. Just . . . '

I wrapped a hand around hers and squeezed. She cried a moment longer, then forced out a little laugh. 'I'm being all weepy about this.'

'There's nothing wrong with that. It's perfectly natural. This is as new to you as it is to me. You're bound to experience strange emotions. Ups and downs. Fears. Joys. You're carrying another life. I can't imagine a responsibility as enormous as that.'

Out in the dark something boomed and reverberated. A backfire. A pistol. After a

18

time, you went beyond the point of speculating about the source of such noises. They became background, soundtrack to the chaotic low-budget movie the city had become. And finally you stopped paying them any attention.

'I want to be a good mother, Jerry. I want that so badly.'

'You will be,' I said. 'Absolutely no doubt.' With the edge of my shirt-cuff, I dried the tears on her cheeks. 'Jacob for a boy. Louisa for a girl.'

'No way,' she said.

'Something you don't like about Jacob? Or is it Louisa that bothers you?'

'Jacob's sort of uncool. And Louisa . . . I don't know, I associate it with whalebone corsets and croquet on lawns. Merry old England.'

We argued about names in a good-natured way for a time. And then, because a warm rain had begun to fall softly through the canyons, we went inside, where one of the two candles had died and the dining-room was a little darker than before.

Friday, 2.22 a.m.

An electric storm over the city: thunder rolled like mortar-fire through the canyons. The noise insinuated itself into my dream, and I saw two aircraft, banked in a holding-pattern over a busy airport, suddenly collide. The planes crumpled instantly, and bodies began to fall from the battered fuselages; all at once, imbued with the kind of powers you sometimes have in dreams, I was able to zoom in on the faces of those thrown from the gashed and buckled craft. The faces — and for some reason this was the truly upsetting thing — were without expression, showed no fear, no terror. Nor were there any sounds: no screams, no cries of anguish. The victims, strapped to their seats, were unresponsive, as if they'd silently accepted the inevitability of their doom.

Falling and falling, showered by the debris of the broken airplanes, they rained down through the sky in a manner that was almost regimented, row after row of them, their lips shut, their hands resting on the arms of their seats, their posture suggestive of passengers preparing themselves for the in-flight movie.

I snapped out of the dream. I sat upright, pushed the bedsheet aside. Sondra was asleep. I padded out of the bedroom to the kitchen and took a bottle of mineral water from the refrigerator and guzzled it without closing the door. I liked the feel of cold air. The night was clammy.

I went into my office, pulled the tiny chain that turned on the desk lamp, and sat down. I put on my glasses. On a yellow legal pad, I outlined the dream before the details faded. I'd been exploring the syntax of dreams for years, searching the mysteries for meaning. I encouraged my patients to record their dreams.

Airplanes. They'd been awaiting clearance to land and disgorge their passengers. Arrivals. The baby, the new arrival. Clearly I still hadn't assimilated the fact of Sondra's pregnancy. It would play on my mind for a long time. I expected to have all manner of dreams in the coming months that could be traced to the unborn child.

But the collision of the two craft? The expressionless faces of the passengers falling out of the sky? What was that supposed to suggest to me? Obstacles to the healthy arrival of the child, say? The whole gamut of unspeakable worries that ran from webbed feet to cleft palate to Down's Syndrome to stillborn.

Or was it an echo of the violent encounter I'd had in the parking-lot? I rubbed the side of my neck, which ached.

I walked through the house. In the living-room I absently flicked the *On* button of the TV remote, and I thought of those dream people dropping, with no apparent fear, to their deaths. Not every dream yielded an interpretation. Some were obscure, wilfully so, the mind playing cryptic games. A joker loose in the head, a mischievous projectionist run amuck in the movie theater.

I opened a window because the room was stuffy. The hum of traffic never stopped. Brakes screeched somewhere, the next street, the next block. I saw a pale-blue WelCor car drive slowly past, wet and shining under a streetlamp like a pale shark. WelCor, a private security firm, patrolled the neighborhood every hour or so.

I sat down in front of the TV. The dream was already fading, even if the feeling of being unsettled still clung to me. I looked at CNN. A river had burst its banks in Louisiana; flooded streets, people paddling canoes through the floating debris of ruined households, sunken porches. Then the image changed and we were back in the studio, and the newscaster, a blond woman with unblinking eyes, was talking about something else: national events crammed into less than twenty-five minutes, everything was zap zap zap. *Moving right along . . .*

A familiar face appeared on the box. Intrigued, I leaned forward, elbows propped on my knees.

The newscaster said, 'Rumors continue to grow in Washington that the President plans to nominate Emily Ford for the position of US Attorney-General. Ms Ford, former Los Angeles County DA, and presently Chief Consultant to the West Coast Division of the Presidential Task Force On Crime, is making no comment at this time. Stories about her possible nomination have been frequent in recent weeks. Ms Ford, who has become prominent for her hard line on crime, may not prove to be a popular choice with certain elements inside the Democratic Party.'

Now the screen was filled with recorded images. Emily Ford was pictured in bright sunshine outside a courthouse, smiling thinly and brushing aside the questions of the predators who kept shoving microphones into her face. She uttered the usual cant about how she'd make a statement at the appropriate time, and then she vanished inside a waiting car.

I heard a sound from behind, and turned to see Sondra come into the room. She was yawning, and looked tousled. 'Storm woke me,' she said. She sat beside me on the sofa, one hand flat on her stomach. She nodded toward the TV.

'Your old pal Emily is going places, it would seem,' she said. Her voice was icy. She'd never liked Emily Ford, whose personality and politics were the opposite of her own. 'I'm just glad she's out of your life, that's all I can say.'

I didn't respond. I didn't want to sound as if I were rushing to the defense of Emily Ford. I didn't want to make excuses on Emily's behalf, or justify the amount of time I'd been obliged to spend with her. Almost two years had passed since Emily had last consulted me.

'She's all raw ambition,' Sondra said.

'She has goals,' I said quietly.

'Goals? Hey, goals are what ice-hockey players and kickers score. Goals are what salesmen have. Emily has this great big agenda that seems to involve the incarceration of half the population — '

'Come on, you know that's total exaggeration,' I said.

'I read about her, Jerry. And I don't like what I read.'

I wanted to drop the subject. I made a small gesture with my hand, acquiescence, *pax*. I gazed at the TV. The newscaster was going for some kind of late-night, in-depth profiling.

'During her time with the Presidential Task Force, Ms Ford has alienated certain influential Democratic congressmen, and she's also been in conflict with prominent members of her own legal profession, most notably Dennis Nardini' — here the screen was filled with footage of Nardini stepping out of a limousine. I knew the face. It appeared, albeit rarely, in social columns, always in connection with something tasteful or charitable — the opening of an art exhibit, a fund-raiser for the education of inner-city kids.

Good-looking in a dark-eyed Latino way, it was the kind of face that suggested culture, sophistication. Nardini was said to be an intensely private man, but I knew some of his background — I'd read about it somewhere. His grandfather had stepped off a steamship at Ellis Island on the first day of the twentieth century; perhaps it was this timing that had impressed the story on my mind: a new immigrant arriving on Day One of a new century, and turning himself into an American Success. He'd made a fortune importing spices. His son (Arturo? Antonio? I couldn't remember) had expanded the business — cheeses and wines — but grandson Dennis, equipped with an Anglo-Saxon first name, broke from family tradition; he'd gone to Harvard Law School, trading parmesan for the kind of prosperity a hot-shot LA lawyer could expect.

He was a man of some influence in the city, and his law firm represented an assortment of high-flying showbiz demi-gods and goddesses, as well as mega-rich clients whose occupations were less well-defined and whose public profiles somewhat murky. I recalled that Emily had subpoenaed one of Nardini's clients in a criminal case the Task Force was trying to build, but the precise details eluded me: something to do with an oil-lease scam. I remembered the term 'witch-hunt' had been bruited about in newspapers by associates of Nardini, although Nardini himself remained aloof from anything as undignified as name-calling.

Sondra was watching the screen with a look of concentration.

I said, 'I hear Nardini has some dubious connections.'

'Really? I never knew you paid attention to gossip.' She reached for my hand but she kept her eyes on the screen, where Nardini, in some library footage, was entering the offices of his law firm.

'It's just stuff you hear around,' I said vaguely. 'True, false, who knows?' What did Nardini's connections matter to me, anyway? I didn't want to talk about him; I just wanted to steer the conversation away from Emily Ford.

'He doesn't look like a bad guy to me,' she said.

'I never said he was a *bad* guy, Sondra.'

'Guilt by innuendo,' she said, and smiled.

Now commercials bounced and exploded across the screen. I picked up the remote and killed the picture. Sondra rose, walked towards the bedroom. I told her I'd be a minute; I went inside the kitchen and drank a pint of ice water. I stood for a time at the sink, thinking about the possibility of Emily Ford going to Washington. Why not? She was qualified, experienced; her bad times were behind her — correct?

I entered the bedroom. Sondra lay turned away from me, already asleep. I got into bed beside her and lowered a hand against her hip, putting my palm around the pleasing curvature of bone. I looked at the red digital numbers on the bedside clock: 3.00 a.m.

She moved very slightly, turning an inch or so on the pillow, opening her mouth with a small plosive sound, a tiny pocket of air expelled.

She mumbled, 'My love . . . ' in the flat inexpressive voice of a sleeper, a monotone I associated with messages uttered by mediums during trances.

I had never heard her speak in that lifeless way before, and it startled me a little; it was so unlike her own voice it might have emerged from a total stranger.

I wondered what she was dreaming about.

7.55 a.m.

Our working days were long, so we usually tried to spend as much time together as we could over breakfast. We drank coffee in the kitchen and ate sliced oranges and whole-wheat toast spread with Dundee marmalade from a small specialty store in Santa Monica. I liked this routine, this little clearing of peace at the start of the day. I'd almost forgotten my skewed dream.

'You were talking in your sleep,' I said.

'Bull. I never talk in my sleep,' Sondra said.

'Last night you did.'

'OK. What did I say?'

'My love.'

' 'My love?' That was all?'

I nodded. 'You remember what you were dreaming?'

'I never remember dreams.' She sipped coffee and looked at me over the rim of her cup. She smiled.

I said, 'You sounded very far away. Detached. Out of reach.'

'People are always out of reach when they're asleep and dreaming. They're always strangers in strange places.' She put her cup down and picked up a slice of orange and held it to her lips. 'I bet I was dreaming something nice about you. We were probably having a picnic by a river on a warm summer's day,' and she tossed the crescent of orange into her mouth and walked around my side of the table. She ruffled my hair. 'You look good this morning. Sort of fatherly. Proud. Pleased with yourself.'

I said, 'Life's wonderful.'

'I agree.' She took my hand, guided it to her stomach. The way she did this touched me unexpectedly. I felt an upsurge of emotion, a warmth fuse through my blood. The idea of wife and child, of family. *I'll be good to them,* I thought. *I'll be fiercely protective. I'll keep the bad things of the world away from them. We'll leave the scum of this decaying city and head for some quiet place when that time comes.*

I was surprised by the force of my feelings. It was as if the news of the baby had overjoyed me, and left me raw and vulnerable at the same time. I was already in love with this unborn, beautifully shapeless being Sondra carried. Like some ancient cave-dweller, I was already prepared to club to death anything that threatened this child's existence. Deep fatherly feelings were rising to the surface: I was nervously patrolling the front-line of impending fatherhood like countless generations of men before me. I'd get used to it as the months passed, I was sure, and my tensions would recede, but for the moment I was undergoing sensations unfamiliar to me.

'I just thought about something,' I said. 'Shouldn't I talk with Marv Sweetzer about the baby? I need to discuss my role in all this. I want to be present, you know. I wouldn't miss it for the world.'

'I already asked him about seeing you. He said to call him in a week and set up an appointment.' She carried her cup to the sink. 'What have you got on today?'

'I have a lunch date with Harry Pushkas.' Pushkas, a sixty-five-year-old wild-haired Hungarian immigrant too fond of aged brandy and infantile practical jokes, had been my mentor and advisor at UCLA. It was Harry who'd steered me towards psychiatry at a time when I was an intern unsure of my future specialty. I'd thought of general practice, but Harry had scoffed at the notion. *Don't be a mender of broken bones, my boy. Mend broken spirits.* I was fond of Harry.

'Give him my best,' Sondra said.

'I will.'

'He's an old lech.'

'But sweet,' I said.

'Which is what saves him from total depravity. You can keep his warped sense of humor, thank you.'

I watched her stand with her back to the sink. She had side-parted her hair sharply to the left, and wore small hooped earrings of plain silver. Her makeup was scant, a touch of mauve eye-shadow and pale lipstick. She wore an expensive gray-blue linen jacket, a short dark blue skirt of the same material, and a white blouse with a tiny heart-shaped brooch pinned to it. I'd given her that inexpensive piece of jewelry in the third year of our marriage, on Valentine's Day, and she still wore it now and then.

'I'll probably be home before you,' she said. 'Gerson's at some conference today, so the office is quiet.'

'When Gerson's away the mice will play,' I said. Leo Gerson was the autocratic boss of LaBrea, a strutting little man who smoked fat cigars and moved everywhere in a flurry and expected his people to work impossible hours.

'The mice rest, Jerry. They're way too tired to play.'

I got up and walked to her and placed my hands against her hips, drawing her towards me. Eyes shut, I held her in silence for a time. I was aware of her heart-beat, the scent of her

32

skin, the rich wholeness of her against me.

She said, 'Maybe I'll cook something terrific tonight.'

'Or maybe we'll eat out,' I suggested.

'We'll see. Meantime, back off or I'll be late,' and she disentangled herself from me with a couple of mock karate blows, swishing the air with small chopping motions. I heard her go out of the kitchen, walk to the bathroom, close the door. I poured a second cup of coffee and wandered into my study. I usually left the house about fifteen minutes after Sondra. I looked at the yellow legal pad on the desk; then my eye was drawn to the answering-machine, which was flashing the number 1.

I remembered now that a call had come in last night when I'd been on the deck with Sondra, but I'd forgotten to check. I pressed the *Playback* button.

A woman's voice, slightly clipped: 'Jerry, this is Emily Ford. I'd like to see you ASAP. Call me.' End of message. Short and blunt, typical of Emily.

'Who was that?'

I hadn't heard Sondra come into the office. 'Emily Ford,' I said.

Sondra frowned. 'Ah. And what did Her Highness want?'

'To see me.'

'I wonder why,' Sondra said. 'Could she be sick, do you think?'

'Am I hearing a hopeful little sound in that question?'

Sondra shook her head. 'She drained you last time, Jerry. She drank your goddam blood. Let her find somebody else if she thinks she needs psychiatric counseling.'

'She didn't say she needed anything,' I answered.

'She's always got an angle, Jerry. She's always looking for something. Refer her to Jack Carr or Phil Katz or somebody if she wants help. I don't think you ought to go near her.'

'I'll call her,' I said.

'Your problem is you're too good-mannered,' Sondra said. 'And too good-natured.'

She looked thoughtful and distant for a moment, as if she'd slumped inside some kind of mental trough. Then she obviously turned aside whatever she'd been thinking, and smiled brightly. She kissed me on the mouth.

'Gotta go,' she said.

'Drive carefully. And don't overdo things. Remember that.'

'Am I destined to hear the concerned father-to-be's nagging voice for the next six and a half months?'

34

'You can't escape it,' I said.

I heard her leave the house, then the sound of her car starting up in the garage directly below my office. She drove a gray Lexus. I heard it go down the street, then its sound was lost in the great vibrating drone of the city. I went into the kitchen, dumped what remained of my coffee, cold now, in the sink.

Propped against a crystal salt-cellar on the table was a note Sondra had written for Consuela, the stout middle-aged Nicaraguan woman who came three times a week to clean, and whose presence always caused me a mild sense of guilt. I adored Consuela, her good spirits and her helpfulness, the cheerful sound of her singing in the house, her colorful skirts and blouses and turbans; but I couldn't help remembering how all the cleaning-up in my parents' home in Buffalo had been done by my mother — with some infrequent help from my father, a big, slow-moving man whose main joy in life was his work for the railroad company. No Nicaraguan woman had ever picked up after me then, or washed the dishes, or done the laundry; my mother, an immigrant from Galway, would have hated the idea of another woman working inside the house, fussing around her territory.

An element of this blue-collar upbringing

adhered to me still, despite the big income and the expensive home and the two cars and the psychiatric practice that included a couple of Hollywood players among its clientele.

I looked at the note Sondra had written.

C, please clean up kitchen and dining-room and polish the floors in Jerry's office. Sondra

Being on first-name terms with the hired help struck me as a very Californian conceit, an attempt to infuse a situation of inequality with an illusion of parity. We meet as equals. You're poor and maybe your green card status is suspect, but you need the work, no matter how menial, so we'll be friends anyway.

The situation was natural to Sondra, born and raised in this state, a former sun-worshipper and surfer and doper, a child of sand and tide; she didn't understand my twinges of guilt. Once, when I'd brought up the subject of Consuela and what I felt, Sondra had dismissed it with the argument that we weren't exploiting the woman — quite the opposite, buster, we were helping her by giving her a job that paid well. She'd recently been widowed: her husband, a mix of Pole and Mexican named Miguel Poliakoff, had died of heart failure the day after

Thanksgiving last year. So Consuela *needed* this job. Badly.

I remembered Buffalo's sub-zero wintry mornings and my father hurriedly drinking his coffee as my mother filled his lunch-box with sandwiches, and how Dad had driven his rheumatic 1959 Olds to the railroad yards six days a week. I'd escaped that world. I'd traveled a long way from the icy wastelands.

But they were still with me and always would be, because for some reason — perhaps a sense of being grounded in a history that wasn't dominated by sand and sunshine and superficiality — I wanted it that way.

9.34 a.m.

I listened absent-mindedly to a call-in radio show while I drove to my office on Wilshire. *Yackety-yack*. It killed time and I imagined it kept me abreast of the issues that troubled the average citizen, although I was leaning towards the gloomy realization that most people merely liked whining on the phone; topics were irrelevant. We'd become a nation of people in love with our own voices. Extremists called talk-jocks to bellow their views. *Crack-smokers? Throw the switch on 'em if they use that crap. Dopers only weaken the gene-pool, so fry 'em.*

There was madness and alienation at the heart of things, and the splinters were deepening by the day. Four-year-olds shot their little buddies with pistols they'd found in Daddy's bedside drawer and didn't understand that it was *real* blood on the rug, not just Hollywood fake. Grade-school kids were forced through metal-detectors before they were allowed to enter school because too many carried guns and knives. Teachers were blown away for giving bad grades.

We're bringing a child into this menagerie,

I thought. *This freakshow.* Was it foolhardy, an act of vanity? I didn't want to think so. I had a sudden urge to call Sondra, to hear her voice. To know that some things were constant. I punched the number of her cellphone into my unit; it rang unanswered. I looked at the car clock. She was probably in her office. I tried that number. Sondra's assistant, a skinny kid called Martina, fresh out of a trust-fund liberal arts college, answered.

'Sondra Lomax's office.'

'Martina, this is Jerry Lomax.'

'Oh, hey, hi, Dr Lomax,' she said. She always sounded flustered and breathless.

'Is Sondra in?'

'Not yet. Can I get her to call you?'

'It's not important,' I said. 'I'll try later.'

'OK.'

'Bye.' I pushed the *Stop* button on my phone. I wondered where Sondra was — maybe walking from car to office at that very moment. Standing in an elevator. Stuck in traffic if there was serious gridlock or an accident.

I reached my office building, parked, got out of the car. I looked around, checking the place where just over twelve hours ago I'd been attacked. How different it seemed in bright daylight. The tall lamps were unlit and everything had a patina of the ordinary spread across it: you could never imagine being assaulted here. I remembered the blow I'd received, the glint of the knife, the guy's unexpected scent.

From the corner of my eye I was aware of somebody moving towards me, and I turned. She was dressed in a dark-gray pants suit. She looked businesslike, brisk, curt. Her black hair, lightened here and there by thin streaks of gray, was severe, uncompromising, but feminine. It hung against the sides of her lean face, in which the nose was prominent. In cartoon caricatures, the nose was exaggerated, dominating the entire face. Sometimes political cartoonists drew her as a raven, with a wickedly curved beak and black feathers. I found her attractive in her own austere way. I wondered briefly if Sondra's dislike of her was grounded in some simple but unfounded jealousy.

She moved with her characteristic long stride, always in a hurry, always a lot of ground to cover, no time to spare. She generated the impression of somebody you wouldn't want to argue with, because she'd always out-smart you. And if you were stubborn enough to go on disagreeing with her, she'd find a way of crushing you underfoot. Nobody stood in Emily's chosen path. Not for long. I liked her, I didn't like her, I wasn't sure. I couldn't get my feelings for her straight. I thought there was a softness at the heart of her, but she drew a fire-proof curtain across it. And then sometimes I wasn't sure she had any tenderness inside her, unless it was pragmatic for her to pretend she did. She'd contributed hostility and co-operation in equal measure to our therapist — patient relationship.

'Congratulations,' I said. 'I was watching you on TV just last night.'

'You've been keeping up with news, Jerry. How unlike you.' She had a clipped, declarative way of speaking, giving a kind of gravitas to the most simple statements. It was easy to imagine people being overawed by her, frightened even. 'Your congratulations are a little premature, though.'

I looked at my watch. I was already late for my first appointment. 'You want to see me, call me later. We'll set something up.'

'I don't have time for laters, Jerry. I need five minutes now. I mean right now.'

'You never stop trying to dominate, do you?'

'It's in my nature. You ought to remember that, doc, of all people.'

'Five minutes,' I said. I walked towards the entrance of the building. No matter how

41

quickly I moved, she kept up with me without any apparent effort. She was only a few months younger than me, but far fitter. She was all muscle, no trace of excess fat. She played tennis in a bloodthirsty way: take no prisoners. As LA County DA, she'd terrorized a staff of around one thousand deputies and two hundred investigators and more than two thousand support personnel. Her work was everything. She made a habit of staying in her office until eleven, midnight sometimes. She had nobody to go home to. Nor did she seem to need anyone.

I pushed the glass door open and entered the reception area. The man behind the front desk was called Grogue, and he had a slight speech-impediment. He guarded his territory like a pit-bull. When he saw me, he cleared his throat and said, 'Morning, Doctor Romax.'

The building housed a number of offices. Two other psychiatrists operated out of this place; also a periodontist, a dental hygienist, an acupuncturist, a GP, a dermatologist, and — fittingly — a health insurance company called Standfast Inc.

Emily said, 'Health Central. I always had the feeling when I used to come here that you should post a notice. Big and bold. *This building has no germs.*'

I smiled, walked past the reception desk. If Grogue recognized Emily Ford he gave no indication. But he was used to the occasional celebrity.

'I don't want to come up to your office,' she said. My suite was on the seventh floor. 'I'm pushed for time.'

I stopped by the elevator. She clutched the sleeve of my jacket and drew me to one side. 'They'll ask questions,' she said.

'Of course they will.'

'Before the nomination becomes official, they'll assemble a dossier.' *The nomination.* She uttered the word as if it were a delicacy in her mouth. She wanted to be AG. She wanted the approval of her peers and power like she'd never had before. But if she was nominated, her appointment would have to be ratified by the Senate — and now I knew why she'd called last night, why she wanted to see me.

'You are not now and never have been a member of the Communist Party,' I said.

'I don't have time for droll, Jerry. They'll dig, they'll find I was once a patient of yours.'

'They probably know all that already. They're usually ahead of the game.'

'Maybe. They've been going through my life with a fine-tooth comb. I've got a couple of suits coming down from DC this afternoon who want to 'clarify' a few things. Whatever that means. The question is — '

'I know what the question is, Emily. Here's my answer. Confidentiality. I can't tell them why you came to see me. You know that. They know that.' *I could never tell them*, I thought. And the thought was like a lead portcullis slamming shut in my head.

'Some people are against me, Jerry.'

Understatement, I thought. 'You don't have the happy knack of making friends easily,' I said.

'A bossy bitch like me is better at making enemies,' she said. 'Some people don't want me to have this post. They all have a gripe. *She's too rigid. Inflexible. She's a fascist.* You know how I affect the bleeding-hearts. I also have the same effect on certain right-wing sorts who say I don't go far enough, and certain scary elements of the criminal community who say I do.'

'I once heard you called Madame Guillotine,' I said.

'Really? I thought I'd advocated firing-squads. My memory must be slipping.'

'Politics is the art of not pleasing everybody but seeming to,' I said.

'Ho ho, Jerry. The question is, when push comes to shove — '

'I stand firm.'

'Bold words, dearheart.'

'Our sessions were confidential. I have a duty to protect a patient.'

'Sometimes there are exceptions,' she said.

'If you were a serial rapist or killer. If you were likely to do violence in the community. You don't fit. Sure, there are exceptions, but even those are muddy.'

She looked weary suddenly. She was forty-two years of age and projected a patina of youthfulness much of the time. She took care of herself. She ate sensibly. She didn't drink. She didn't take drugs. She slept well. She brushed her teeth and flossed. She was Ms Terrific, Tough on Crime. But for a second she seemed to let all this slip. Under the fluorescent strips of lighting, she looked grey and shopworn. She had a slight puffiness beneath her eyes.

'Are you sleeping?' I asked.

'Four, five hours a night. My metabolism freaks if I sleep six. All kinds of beeping sounds go off in my brain.'

'You just seem . . . tense.'

'It's a trying time, doc. It doesn't look terrific if the nominee for the position of Attorney-General of this great country has a goddam psychiatric history. Honest George McGovern dumped Tommy Eagleton from the Democratic ticket in '72 for the sin of

45

seeing a shrink. Shrink means mental problems. Mental problems mean instability. Out there in the heartland they don't like that, Jerry. Farmers and shoe-store clerks want to sleep easy, knowing the laws of the land are safe in the hands of somebody who isn't a weirdo. California — that's bad enough. We've all heard California jokes, thank you. But a shrink history could be very damaging.'

'Things have changed since McGovern showed Eagleton the door,' I said. 'There isn't anything *like* the same stigma attached to being a psychiatric patient.'

'I wouldn't bet on it, Jerry.'

'Look around, Emily. Manic depressives are outing themselves in huge numbers. Prozac and its successors are as common-place as aspirin. Bulimia, anorexia, sexual dysfunction, cross-dependence, cross-dressing, cross-this, cross-that — all this is the stuff of cocktail party conversation in the late twentieth century. Counseling, therapy, the avalanche of self-help books — how to be your own best friend, and tap your hidden creativity and, quote unquote, *empower* yourself — Christ, everybody's digging inside their own skulls for identity or understanding, or a cure for lack of self-esteem, or ways to unlock the cellar door where childhood abuses are stashed away. What I'm saying is, you don't want to think you're an easy target just because you were once a shrink's patient. That's nothing these days.'

'I don't have your confidence in the open-mindedness of our citizens, Jerry.'

'You need to relax.'

'I'll work on it,' she said.

I pressed the button for the elevator. 'What's he like?'

'Who?'

'The President.'

'I wouldn't turn my back on him. But I like his Chief of Staff, Mort Wengler. Mort's a good guy.'

'Which means he's on your side, right?'

'Of course. He's committed.'

I smiled at her. 'I'm late, Emily. If you want to talk any more, we'll meet. For the moment, be assured.'

'All right. I'm assured. But just for the moment. You have a way about you.'

The doors slid open and I stepped inside. I turned to say goodbye to her, but she'd already gone, and was walking across the reception area to the front door, her heels click-click-clicking, like the sound made by a workaholic woodpecker, as she hurried across the tiled floor.

10.15 a.m.

My secretary-receptionist was a middle-aged Londoner called Jane Steel. Patients found her comforting. She didn't threaten women, and she didn't arouse men. She was friendly but never inquisitive; she had that southern English suspicion of easy intimacies. She imparted an impression of quiet brown-eyed sympathy, and discretion. I'd chosen her for the job on account of these qualities. She also had considerable organizational skills. In the two and a half years she'd worked for me, she'd reorganized the shambles of my filing-cabinets and supervised the installation of a computer system and a patient database, with the result that now the office worked smoothly.

She looked up at me as I entered. 'Phil Stam cancelled, Jerry.'

'Did he say why?'

'No. Nothing.'

'Did he reschedule?'

'I asked, but he was vague.'

'Curious,' I said. Phil Stam, who suffered from agoraphobia, was a patient I felt I could help. I always looked forward to our sessions, when we worked together to chip away at his fears. I felt mildly disappointed.

Jane said, 'It works out, because Joe Allardyce called, asking to see you as soon as he could. I sent him into the inner sanctum.'

'OK,' I said.

I had a policy to ensure that patients didn't run into one another. The waiting/reception area, a neutral gray space, never had more than one patient waiting at any time — in theory. If I was running late, Jane ushered the patient into my private office, the inner sanctum; then, if the next patient arrived early, he or she would find the waiting area empty. Patients always left my office by a door that led them back to the elevators without having to return via reception. We were in the business not only of calming troubled souls and curing sick minds, but of sparing people embarrassment.

'He's in a jittery mood,' Jane said.

'He usually is.' I stopped at the door of my office. 'Have you had any calls about Emily Ford?'

'No.' She shook her head. 'I would have told you.'

'I think we can expect one or two pretty soon,' I said. 'You heard about this possible AG nomination?'

'On TV this morning,' she said. 'So we can

49

anticipate what — background checks? Spies from federal agencies?'

'That kind of thing. If anyone calls in connection with Emily, put them straight through to me.'

'Will do,' she said. She wagged a pencil at me. 'Meantime, Mr Allardyce needs you.'

I hesitated at the door of my office. 'Oh. One other thing . . . ' I drew the moment out; I was enjoying it. 'Sondra's pregnant.'

'No!'

'She told me last night.'

Her eyes watered instantly. She knew how long we'd been trying for a child. 'I'm so happy for you both, I can't begin to tell you.'

'You don't have to,' I said.

'I'm thrilled for Sondra. I really am.'

'Thanks,' I said, and entered my office where Allardyce was standing at the window, hands clasped behind his back. He was a small, squat man with broad, muscular shoulders. He was in his early fifties and balding. In his youth he must have been good-looking; something of a strong facial structure remained under the heavy flesh.

He glared at me with his blue eyes. He stretched his hands out in front of his body, like a swimmer testing water. They trembled. 'I'm in a bad way, Jerry. A real bad way. That prescription you wrote doesn't do shit. Look at me.'

I'd written him a script for Norpramin to counter his anxiety attacks. I had him on 50mg a day. I realized at once I'd have to increase the dosage. He was a man falling to pieces. A moderately successful movie producer who'd turned out a couple of back-to-back duds, he now found himself an exile in that tundra peculiar to Hollywood, a polar wasteland where nobody returned your calls, and old friends suddenly dropped you from their Christmas-card lists. You smelled of failure — and nobody wanted a reminder of how fast you could be an outcast in this town. A lot of desperate people wandered the tundra, all trying to get back in where the sun shone gold and deals were there to be struck and crisp dollars minted.

I told him to sit down.

'Sit? I can't sit, Jerry. I sit I get antsy. I gotta get up, walk around.' He went to the window, walked back to my desk, then again to the window. He was like a man trapped in a pinball machine: back and forward, and no control over his destiny. 'This fucking town, Jerry. This town, jeez,' and he made a sweeping gesture at the window, 'has just about destroyed me.'

'You know what to do, Joe. Leave it.'

'I can't leave it.'

I knew he couldn't. We'd discussed it before many times. I took a blue 10mg tab of Valium from a bubble-pack in the bottom drawer of my desk, where I always kept pharmaceuticals for emergency purposes, and I said, 'Take this, Joe.' I filled a glass with ice water from a small refrigerator concealed in a closet.

He stepped back to the desk and looked at the pill. 'Valium?'

'I'll write you a stronger script before you go.'

He swallowed the tab, slurped some water. 'Leave,' he said. 'That's your best advice. That's what I pay you for?'

I always ignored his barbs. 'Your life is defined by this town,' I said.

'I make my living here, Chrissakes.'

I didn't correct him. I didn't say he should have used the past tense. 'It's a dependency,' I said. 'You're as dependent on LA as any junkie strung-out on heroin. And now you've been cut off from your supply. We're not going to get anywhere unless you face that one.'

'OK. I'm hooked. You're the doc. You got the fancy certificates on the wall. I bow to your wisdom — '

'And you're destroying yourself.'

'I'm looking for a deal, Jerry. That's all I need. One new frigging deal. Don't talk to me about destroying. You know what the trouble is?'

'Tell me.' But I knew what he was going to say. Repetition was a major part of his relationship with me.

'There's people out there got it in for me. There's people out there want to see me crushed. Some high-up — and I ain't mentioning names — sent down the word from his icy fortress. 'Allardyce is washed up. Allardyce don't work in this town again. Employ him and it's on your own head.' '

'Why would any individual want to destroy you, Joe?'

He was quiet a moment, looking at me bleakly with his dead gray eyes. 'I was in Rodeo Drive day before yesterday. I see Teddy Schramm coming down the sidewalk and I say, 'Hi, long time.' He crosses the street, Jerry. Makes eye contact, but says absolutely *nothing*. Just crosses the street. I'm the invisible man. So maybe it's Schramm who put out the word. Or one of his cronies. Or all of them.'

Teddy Schramm was a producer riding the waves of a big box-office ocean. He was Midas of the Moment. Like so many people in this town, he had absolutely no discernible skills. He had charm and luck and a fine suntan and a rich wife who pushed him because she enjoyed being on first-name terms with Meryl or Mel or Michelle or Meg. Maybe Schramm had all the fluffy ingredients you needed to make a successful confection of yourself in the motion-picture industry, this business crowded with con men, hustlers, pirates, egomaniacs, and half-literate people who sat by their swimming-pools and read ill-written, one-page outlines of scripts prepared by assistants who hadn't skills enough to write a last-minute plea for leniency, even if they'd been condemned to die in the electric-chair at dawn. Greed and vanity and the lust for power fueled this commerce. And Allardyce, who'd worked the system for his own benefit, now found it had turned against him. Simply, his luck had run out.

'You didn't answer me, Joe. Why would anyone want to destroy you?'

'I broke some rule. I done something wrong. I dunno what.'

'Look it straight in the eye, Joe. Your last two pictures flopped. Nobody's got it in for you. The box-office wheel just turned in the other direction. You misjudged the market-place. And you can't accept that.'

He stared at me, not seeing me. In his

mind, he'd misjudged nothing. He preferred to construct a whole scenario of paranoia, people determined to finish him off. A freemasonry had blackballed him. Now they were after his blood. I wanted him to see that no such cartel existed. His last picture, *Oasis on the Moon*, had been a monster turkey, shown only once to the public.

I said, 'You're transferring your failures elsewhere. You're saying they were caused by men who want to destroy you. This group, Joe — does it meet once a month? Does it spend hours thinking up new ways to weaken you? And where does it actually meet, do you ever wonder? In the function room of a hotel? In a chalet at the Château Marmont? In the projection-room of a mansion in Bel-Air?'

'Maybe they communicate by phone,' he said.

I pushed my chair back from my desk. I was looking down the slanting, crooked, dark corridors of his mind, and I felt sorry for him. I was trained to make sure my personal feelings didn't slip through any tiny hole in the delicate net of the therapist-client relationship, but it happened. And lately it had been happening a little too often. I found myself feeling pity and sadness. I became despondent. I felt detachment erode, *disinterest* crumble. These were human beings, and they were broken, they were hurting — and I couldn't treat them as if I were wearing latex gloves and they were lab cultures I didn't dare touch for fear of contamination. Once again, I felt I needed a rest from all this. A time away. Maybe after the baby came, we'd head for Big Sur or the Pacific Northwest and take a long, long break.

The telephone on my desk rang. I picked up the handset.

'You asked to be notified if anyone called from Washington,' Jane said. 'Well, they're here, Jerry. In person.'

I checked my watch. 'Have them wait a couple of minutes,' I said.

'They're in a hurry,' Jane said. 'It's urgent. They've got meetings in LA all day.' She was keeping her voice under control, but I could tell she was quietly irritated; she regarded my sessions as sacrosanct and it wouldn't have mattered to her if the President himself had strutted inside the office, she would still have been reluctant to patch him through.

'I'll buzz you in a minute, Jane.' I put the phone down and looked at Allardyce. 'Don't think I'm a part of this conspiracy against you, Joe, but I need to cut this meeting short. Something's come up. Don't take it personally.'

'Don't take it personally, he tells me. Right. I take everything personally.' He sighed long and deep.

I removed my prescription-pad from the middle drawer of my desk. I began to scribble with my fountain-pen. 'I'm going to increase the dose of Norpramin.'

'It better do some good,' Allardyce said. He snatched the script from my desk and stuffed it in the breast pocket of his jacket without looking at it. 'You want I should exit stage left as usual?'

'Please,' I said. I walked with him to the door that led directly to the elevators, my hand on his elbow. 'Call me if the increased dosage doesn't work.'

'I'll call all right.'

I held the door open for him. I looked into his eyes, which were sad. I felt a stab of pity for him again.

'Make an appointment with Jane,' I said.

'Same time next week would suit me,' he said. 'Say, wasn't that a vehicle for Alan Alda and Carol Burnett?'

'*Same Time Next Year*,' I answered.

'Oh. Yeah. Right. See, I'm forgetting stuff.' He walked to the door, stopped, looked back. 'Hey hey, wait a minute. You're wrong, Doctor Smartass. It was Ellen Burstyn, not Carol B.'

'You sure?'

'How long have I been in this business, huh?'

'I could have sworn,' I said.

'Some stuff stays glued to the old memory scrap-books,' he said. 'I once had Alda lined up to make a movie for me . . . Fell through. What the hell. This shit biz.'

I watched him go in the direction of the elevators, back to a life where the silence of a telephone meant the end of the world. I wondered how much I could really help Joe Allardyce.

I walked to my desk and buzzed Jane. The door of my office opened almost immediately and Jane ushered two people inside. A plump, cheerful man flashed an ID card and introduced himself as James Brunton, a special investigator attached to the White House. The other visitor called herself Carrie Vasuu; she was blond and pretty in a sharp-edged way, dressed in a tight black skirt and matching double-breasted jacket. Her ID had been issued by the White House; a presidential aide. She and Brunton had bulky briefcases.

'Short notice,' Brunton said. 'I apologize.'

Carrie Vasuu said, 'Sometimes we have to do things in a hurry, Dr Lomax.'

'Apparently,' I said.

'You're unhappy with the intrusion,' she said.

'I'm less than delighted.'

'We'll be fast,' Brunton said and smiled. 'In and out. I promise you.'

I looked at my watch. 'It's about Emily Ford, I guess.'

'Yep,' Brunton said.

10.47 a.m.

They were in Los Angeles, as Brunton phrased it, 'to tie up a few loose ends', which involved going over a couple of things Emily Ford had discussed with senior presidential aides in Washington. The President, Brunton said, was 'almost certain' to nominate her for the position of Attorney-General.

'Barring a skeleton in the closet,' he added.

'We've all got a few bones somewhere,' I said. I didn't like him. I didn't like his smile, the cheerfulness that struck me as forced. He was a back-slapper, the kind of guy who forced drink on people at parties and pretended he was the spirit of generosity, dispensing largesse.

Carrie Vasuu, whose eyes were the blue of a Lapland summer sky, looked directly at me. 'I'll be straight,' she said, in a way that suggested she was never straight with anyone. 'The President doesn't want Congress to bite him on this nomination. He's had nominations rebuffed before and he doesn't like the flack. So we're here to check out a few things.'

I glanced at Carrie Vasuu's long, suntanned

legs. I couldn't help myself. Her short, tight skirt was slut couture, and expensive.

'Go ahead,' I said.

Carrie Vasuu said, 'We assume you're aware of Ford's position on crime — especially those crimes related to narcotics?'

'I don't keep up with what she says in public,' I remarked.

'You know she advocates mandatory prison sentences for the private use of recreational drugs — '

'I'd heard,' I said. 'The Dragon Lady.'

Brunton smiled at me thinly. 'Which riles some of our elected officials of a more liberal persuasion. Emily Ford is on record as saying that even a high-school kid caught with a single reefer should do time.'

'I don't believe everything I read, Ms Vasuu. In any case, I don't see how this has anything to do with me. I'm not interested in her policies.'

Carrie Vasuu held a hand up, a cop stopping the flow of traffic. 'Let me finish first, Dr Lomax. She's *also* on record as favoring mandatory life sentences for dealers, no plea-bargaining. She claims too many lawyers are doing too many questionable deals with overworked DAs in smoky back rooms.' She took a folder from her briefcase, opened it, and read from a notebook. 'Let me

61

quote her, Doctor. This is from an interview that appeared in the *LA Examiner*: 'Too many bad guys are walking free, or they're serving Disneyworld sentences, twelve months and three off for good behavior. Everybody knows the system needs to be totally revamped. I want an America that's free of dope dealers. I want the streets swept clean.' End of quote.'

'I still don't see where I come into this,' I said. But I did. I knew where it was leading. 'So far as I can tell, she's only echoing what a lot of people feel in this country: Dope pushers shouldn't be able to do deals with prosecutors. They ought to expect punishment.'

Carrie Vasuu asked, 'Is that your own view too, Dr Lomax?'

I shook my head. 'No. I don't think you can impose mandatory life sentences willy-nilly. Every case is different.'

She had found more papers and was glancing at them. 'Here's some of Ford's wish-list: More federal and state prisons, more prison guards. Border patrol increased by thirty to forty per cent. Another one hundred thousand policemen nationwide. A multimillion dollar Organized Crime Task Force controlled by the Attorney-General, with the emphasis on combatting drug trafficking. Special investigators answerable only to the AG . . . it amounts to a private fiefdom, it makes her damn near unaccountable. She can yank up the drawbridge of her little castle any time she doesn't like the sound of the rabble outside. A lot of people in Congress are going to find her desire to build her own domain a problem.'

'Which leaves the President high and dry if her nomination's a failure,' I said.

'It sure does,' Carrie Vasuu said. 'Some people in the President's own party . . . well, they feel he's made an enormous mistake with Emily Ford. They think it's a knee-jerk reaction to the anti-drug voices that come from certain pockets of the populace, Dr Lomax. Rabid voices.'

'But voters all the same,' I said.

'Exactly,' she replied. 'The Christian Coalition, the Baptists, the Mormons, the plain old Bible Belters — they all mark their ballots. I'm not espousing drugs, and I'm not indulging the drug culture we have in this country, but some influential people in the party believe you cannot have the kind of laws Emily Ford wants, because in the end they just don't work. They remember Prohibition.'

Brunton coughed into his rolled-up fist. 'I'd like to move on into other areas. More personal ones.'

I'd been waiting for this shift. This was why they were here in my office.

Brunton said, 'I'm looking for anything that might embarrass her if it became public knowledge.'

I said, 'Embarrass the President, you mean.'

'If you like,' Carrie Vasuu said, and took from her briefcase a loose-leaf binder with a red cover. She flicked a couple of pages. 'She came to see you soon after the unfortunate matter of her parents, I believe.'

'Unfortunate' was a word so timid as to be offhand, even callous, in the context of Emily Ford's parents. 'I'd have to check my appointment books from back then,' I said. 'This didn't happen only yesterday, you know.'

'A ballpark estimate will do.'

'OK. It might have been a year after her parents were killed that she made her first appointment.'

Carrie Vasuu said, 'Some people have suggested that the tragedy of her parents colored her views on law enforcement to a point beyond objectivity. That her views are rooted in a desire for personal vengeance. That her life is an obsessive vendetta.'

'I'm not sure I agree with any of that.'

'No? You don't think the experience

64

hardened her? She goes to visit with her parents. She finds them slain. A few weeks later, the cops arrest a known addict and felon called Billy Fear for the crime. Some people say she lost all her objectivity about crime and punishment when her parents were murdered by a junkie who needed ten bucks for a quick fix. Some say that event shaped her whole philosophy.'

Billy Fear. That name dragged me back into places I had no desire to go. I said, 'She wasn't exactly the soul of liberal thinking before the tragedy, was she? She was always tough on crime. Does the murder of her parents make her unworthy of the nomination?'

'It makes her judgments suspect,' Carrie Vasuu said. 'They're colored, they're not detached.'

I remembered our sessions. I recalled how Emily Ford had described her parents' ranch-style house and how hushed it had been that fall evening in 1994. The porch-light was burning, there was the scent of dead leaves smoking somewhere in the neighborhood, it had all seemed so ordinary. She'd entered by the front door; a desk-lamp lay upturned on the floor and sent light spilling weirdly across the carpet. And then she'd found her father, face down in the kitchen, surrounded by food that had fallen from the dog's dish, little brown nuggets splattered with his blood. The mongrel was curled in the corner, also shot. She had walked in dazed terror through the rooms of the house until she found her mother on the second floor, shot through the back of the head, her purse open and upturned on the bed, credit cards and driver's license spread all around, no sign of any money.

I remembered how difficult it had been to draw this out of her, and how deeply she'd buried the whole sequence of events. I recalled her rage, the resistance of her memory to my probing, the struggle it had been for her to accept hypnosis. And I remembered the breakthrough, even if I preferred to consign it to the dead-letter office of memory.

'What kind of treatment did you give her?' Brunton asked.

'You know better than to ask that,' I said.

Carrie Vasuu had the eyes of an interrogator; polar bears might have frolicked in her arctic inquisitor's heart. 'Drugs? Electrotherapy?'

'I taught her the best way I knew to deal with shock. I taught her some relaxation techniques. That's all I'm prepared to say.' I saw it clearly: Carrie Vasuu wanted to believe

Emily's mental state was still fragile. She wanted this nomination to be withdrawn and forgotten. She was protecting the President.

'Did she talk about how she behaved when Billy Fear was gunned down by some fellow junkie after he'd been acquitted on a technicality?' Brunton asked.

'I don't remember. I don't want to seem rude, but are we finished?'

'Can you give us some assessment of her mental condition now?' Carrie Vasuu said. 'Or do your *ethics* prevent you?'

I didn't like the snide emphasis she gave the word ethics. 'I haven't seen her professionally in several years.'

'In your opinion, is she fit to hold high office?'

I hesitated. I wanted to say *Without doubt*, but I couldn't hurry the words from brain to mouth.

Carrie Vasuu asked, 'Well? Is she or isn't she? I'm holding my breath.'

Before I could answer, the telephone on my desk rang. I picked up the handset, glad of the interruption.

The voice on the line wasn't Jane's. It was Sondra's and it was strident with panic. Her words ran together, a collision of sounds. I'd never heard her talk this way, and my heart lurched inside my chest like a great bird leaping suddenly upward. 'I don't know where I am, Jerry. Come get me. Can you come get me, please, oh please — '

'Sondra, what's the problem? What's happened? Where are you? Take your time, go slow, talk slow. Has there been an accident? Are you hurt? Is it the baby?'

The line was dead.

I dropped the handset on my desk and hurried into the reception area, shutting my office door behind me.

Jane was staring at me. 'She sounded in a bad way, Jerry. What's wrong? Is she sick? Is there something I can do to help?'

'Did she say where she was calling from?'

'No — '

One of the telephones on Jane's desk rang and she picked it up, then handed the receiver to me. The voice I heard was that of a man I didn't recognize. 'You want to see your wife again, go outside, take a right, walk three blocks. Go inside a bar called The Punch Bowl. Got that? You'll be contacted at eleven-thirty.'

'What is all this?' I asked. 'A joke — '

'A joke? What kind of world do you live in, Lomax? Just do what I tell you and skip the dumb questions. And one other thing — keep this to yourself. Remember, we've got your wife.'

'You've got my wife? What is that supposed to mean?'

'What does it sound like to you, Lomax? You open your mouth in the wrong place at the wrong time, and I can't guarantee her safety. Clear?'

'Who the hell are you?' The line was dead. I was railing at nothing, nobody.

Jane wadded a Kleenex nervously in her fist. 'What's going on, Jerry? Has something happened to Sondra?'

I looked at my watch. It was just after eleven. 'Cancel my appointments for the day. Also my lunch with Harry Pushkas. Tell those White House goons I was called away. Emergency. I don't care what.'

'Where are you going?'

I didn't answer. I moved out into the hallway, walked to the elevator, pressed the *Call* button. My mind was upside-down. It was a joke, it had to be, what else could it be? Old Harry Pushkas, practical joker, had dreamed it up: *Let's knock Jerry sideways, keep him from getting all smug and complacent and shrink-like. Play with his head a little.* But I couldn't see Sondra going along with a joke like this. It wasn't her style.

And yet it had been Sondra on the phone, different-sounding, sure, but Sondra all the

69

same. Panicky, scared: *Please oh please come find me.*

I tried to stay calm while I waited for the elevator, but then I realized from the light-panel that it was stuck way below on the second floor. I hurried to the stairs and took them two or three at a time, my feet clattering on stone; when I reached the foyer I was hyperventilating, and sick to the bottom of my heart with dread.

11.11 a.m.

The man who came across the foyer towards me was about six feet tall and wore his hair thickly gelled and flattened back against his skull, a style that had been popular in the late '80s and early '90s, usually accompanied by a double-breasted linen suit.

'Dr Lomax?' he asked, and introduced himself as Detective Petrosian of the LAPD, flashing his ID quickly in front of me. At first I imagined he must be here on account of Sondra, that he had some information to relay, that he was going to tell me she was safe.

But that wasn't it at all.

'You reported an incident last night,' he said. He had very thin lips, almost like two lengths of purple twine. 'An attack.'

'Look, I'm really pressured for time right now,' I said. 'Can't this wait?'

I was thinking about the voice on the phone and the cocktail bar where I'd been commanded to go, and I longed to be outside in the smoggy sunlight. Petrosian didn't seem interested in what I said.

'You left the scene before anyone could

question you,' he said. 'The perpetrator managed to get away.'

'I'm not a cop, it's not my job to arrest people.'

'It took the patrol car four minutes to reach you,' he said. 'Which I consider a fast response time. But you didn't hang around, did you? You didn't wait.'

I stepped past the detective, moved towards the doors. 'Talk to me later. Call my office. Make an appointment.'

'You always in a hurry, doc? I appreciate you're a busy guy, but this is only going to take five minutes tops.'

'I'm in . . . look, it's an emergency,' and I kept moving.

I thought of saying: *It's like this, Petrosian, a stranger's voice on the phone tells me my wife has been kidnapped, get the picture? Please help me.* But I said no such thing. I stepped outside, and he came after me.

'You get a look at the assailant, doc?'

'No, his face was concealed.'

'How?'

'He had a scarf wrapped round his mouth.' I couldn't keep the impatience out of my voice.

'And he assaulted you in what way?'

'This is going to have to wait, Petrosian. I mean that.'

'How did he assault you?'

'You don't take no, do you? OK. He punched me here,' and I pointed to the side of my neck. 'Then he tried to knife me.'

'You fought him off?' Petrosian said.

'There was a confrontation, sure.' I moved along the sidewalk through the thick air. The details of an assault, for Christ's sake — what did they matter? Petrosian kept coming after me; he had the persistence of a force of nature.

'You'd say it was a straightforward attempted mugging,' he said.

'I can't imagine what else it would be. Money. Drugs. That would be my best guess.'

Petrosian scribbled in a little brown notebook. 'This knife. Did you disarm him? Or did he run off with it in his possession?'

'I remember he dropped it.' I looked across the parking-lot, trying to recall the precise spot where I'd had the encounter last night. 'It fell under my car. Maybe it's still lying in the same place.' I pointed a little vaguely to one of the tall lamp-posts.

Petrosian held my elbow and said, 'Show me the spot, doc.'

'Jesus, I keep telling you, I don't have time. Anyway, I'm not sure I remember.'

'Try. One minute is all I ask. Support your local cops. Remember, we're the only thing that stands between you and outright anarchy, doc.' The lips extended into a smile.

I half-ran, half-walked to where I thought I'd parked last night. So many parking spaces, so many lamps — how could I be certain?

The knife was on the ground, lying at the center of an old oil stain that looked like a blackened map of Scandinavia. Taking a plastic baggie from his pocket to avoid direct contact with it, Petrosian picked up the knife and examined it. I noticed the weapon had a dark rubber handle.

Then Petrosian unexpectedly pressed the tip of the knife firmly with a finger; the blade disappeared inside the handle and there was the faint sound of a spring being compressed. He laughed. 'A prop,' he said, and looked at me. 'A stage dagger. I'll be damned.'

'I was threatened by a *toy* knife?'

Petrosian said, 'Hey, this is LA. You expect every mugger you see to carry a *real* weapon?' He dropped the fake knife into the plastic baggie. 'I'll check it for prints, anyhow.'

A fake knife. A whiff of cologne. What was I supposed to make out of that? 'Can I go now?'

'Sure. If we need to talk again, I'll be in touch.'

I walked away from him quickly. I was

aware of him watching me. I turned once to look back and saw him examining the toy knife in the baggie; he had an odd little smile on his face. He may have been thinking: *Hotshot LA shrink spooked by dummy knife.*

When I was out of his sight, I broke into a trot, a run. The idea of Sondra in trouble was burning like a brush-fire inside my head, and I was impatient to get to the cocktail bar — where, God willing, I'd find that the kidnap was as authentic as the mugger's weapon.

11.29 a.m.

The Punch Bowl was a dim, old-fashioned little cocktail bar, an anachronism I'd passed thousands of times without ever really noticing it. Red naugahyde booths lined the walls and signed photographs of old prize-fighters hung everywhere: Marciano, Graziano, Sugar Ray Robinson. Hence The Punch Bowl, but I wasn't in any mood for cute.

A couple of guys sat on stools at the bar; late morning drinkers, maybe two men having a hair of the dog, or just getting a buzz before lunch. They turned to register me when I came through the door, then went back to their conversation, which was low and mumbled. I caught a few words — *she's way too skinny . . . she's been doing coke, you ask me* — and I wondered, *What am I here for?* It must be a hoax, something dreamed up by Harry when he'd had too much cognac one night and his brain was churning out idly elaborate notions.

Why was I playing along with it?

Because it's serious. You're not treating it as a bad joke, are you, Jerry? You want to.

But you can't. Something tells you not to.

The barman appeared, a muscular young black guy wearing a navy-blue T-shirt with a sparkly logo that read *The Punch Bowl* on the chest. 'Help you?' he asked.

'Scotch,' I said.

'Ice? Soda?'

'Yes,' I said. Ice, soda, it didn't matter.

I watched him pour. I took a long drink, tried to still my hand. I looked around the bar, which was long and narrow and receded into impenetrable shadow at the rear. So far as I could see, there were no customers other than me and the two guys on the stools. I sat down in a booth facing the front door.

My hand still shook. Outside traffic rumbled past, all very ordinary — people making deliveries, going to offices, running errands, whatever it was the human race did in the mundane slipstream of life. I couldn't see through the opaque glass panes of the door, I could only hear noise: wheels, the squeak of brakes suddenly applied, mechanical splutters, gears grinding. I sat inside a dark box listening to a world of noise. At the bar, one guy absently tapped a coin on the counter, his companion breathed with a slight whine through congested nostrils, the barman ran a finger round the rim of a glass.

The world roared at me. I was floating on a

great ocean of noise.

I looked at my watch. It was eleven-thirty now. OK, I was here, I'd been punctual, what happened next? The door would open — light would penetrate the gloom, and Harry would come through with Sondra, and they'd be laughing. *Oh, look at Mr Serious and 'ow long 'is face is,* Harry would say in that European-accented English he'd never lost. Then, sounding like a Nazi in a low-budget war-movie: *Vee have given de poor doktor somezing of a fright, my dear Mrs Lomax.*

But the door didn't open and the second-hand of my watch kept marking the time until eleven-thirty became eleven thirty-five, then forty. And still it kept moving. Heraclitus had got it all wrong. Time wasn't a river. It was a torturer's rack. The motion of the second-hand was like the old Chinese water-drip. The watch vibrated in my vision.

I'd been here for more than ten minutes. I took a couple of very deep breaths and tried to relax, but my muscles felt padlocked.

'Willie, the same again,' one of the guys at the bar said. He turned to look at me a moment, then lost interest.

The telephone rang. I heard Willie pick it up and say, 'Punch Bowl. What can we do for you?' He listened a moment, then looked in my direction. 'Say, are you Jerry Lomax?

Somebody here wants to speak with you.'

I got out of the booth, trying not to hurry. I took the cordless phone from Willie's hand and walked away from the bar, turning my back on the three men. They were listening. They'd fallen silent, unintentionally or otherwise. Maybe they wanted to hear what I said. Maybe the guys on the stools were involved in this — but that was a crazy tapestry I didn't want to start working on, a mad design with no end in sight.

'This is Lomax,' I said.

'You keep good time.' It was the same man who'd spoken to me in my office.

I said, 'Put my wife on.'

'That's not possible at the moment.'

'Put her on the line or I hang up.'

'You hang up and I might not call you again. And then you'd never find your wife, would you? You'd look and you'd look. All the days of your life. And you'd never find her.'

He was goading me, cruelly correct. 'What do you want?'

'You leave The Punch Bowl. You head for home.'

'Then what?'

'Then I send you somewhere else. Call it Point B. You get to B and perhaps I'll send you to C. That's how it works, Lomax. You go here and there, and when I'm sure you're following instructions, I decide it's time to tell you exactly what I want.'

'And what the fuck *do* you want? Spell it out, for Christ's sake. I hate this cloak — '

'Just do what you're told and we'll get along famously. Go home. Go back to your house. Wait there.'

'I want to speak to my wife — '

'Realize something, Lomax. You're dealing with some serious people. And if you want to see your wife again, you better grasp that fact damn fast. Oh, one last thing, at the risk of repeating myself: You don't talk to a soul. You got that? Not a living soul.'

Then the connection was severed abruptly, and the receiver in my hand became a purposeless lump of plastic. I passed it back to Willie, who hung it up and then asked, 'You OK?'

'I'm OK,' I said.

'You need another drink?'

I shook my head. He shrugged and wandered to the other end of the bar. I picked up the handset and gazed at the numerical pad.

Willie looked at me. 'That a local call you're planning to make?'

I said it was.

'It's just that we get assholes phoning Peru and New Zealand, sticking us with tabs.'

'No Peru. No New Zealand. Just LA.'

I punched in the number of Sondra's office. I knew she'd pick up. I would have bet good money on it. She'd say *Hi, Jerry, what's happening?* or, *Hey, Daddy-to-be, what's up?* and all the pieces of the world that had splintered in the last thirty minutes would come together again. Everything would be whole. This entire kidnap scenario would be a big unfunny gag.

I just goddam *knew*.

Martina said, 'Sondra Lomax's office.'

'Martina, let me speak to my wife.'

'She didn't come in this morning, Jerry.'

'What does that mean exactly, Martina? Did she call and say she was sick? Is she taking a meeting somewhere? What does it mean, 'She didn't come in'?'

'Uh, just that, Jerry. No phone calls. I don't see anything in her appointments book either. She didn't come in.'

'Could she be someplace else in the building?'

'If she is, I haven't seen her,' Martina said.

'Page her,' I said. 'It's important.'

'Hold a minute, Jerry.'

I closed my eyes. Waited. I heard an ice-cube crack in a glass.

Martina came back on the line. 'Nobody's seen her, Jerry,' she said.

'And nobody knows where she is?' I asked.

'Apparently not. Look, if she comes in or if she calls, I'll have her contact you. OK?'

'Do that,' I said. I kept my eyes shut because I felt them fill with water and I didn't want the guys at the bar to see I was upset. I didn't want questions, I didn't want interference, I didn't want people to say, *Jesus Christ, he's in a hell of a state.* Guys from blue-collar Buffalo didn't cry.

I cut the connection. I wondered who else I might call. Her hairdresser? Her masseuse? Goddam, I couldn't remember their names, anyway. And she hadn't mentioned anything at breakfast about a haircut or a massage.

I went outside just as a dark cloud in the shape of a clenched fist drifted across the sun, and the city was immersed in momentary shadow. Then there was a vague tremor underfoot, a quake in the earth so mild it would barely register on the Richter scale; in a seismic recording-station somewhere a needle would tremble on graph-paper, a blip signifying a mild disturbance in the earth's crust.

I wondered what that needle would record if it could measure the turbulence in me.

12.05 p.m.

I drove homeward. My head throbbed. Pain burned behind my eyes. I needed to anchor myself, drag myself up out of this whole terrifying swampland into which I'd been sucked. OK: a few hours ago I'd said goodbye to my wife, my *pregnant* wife, and I'd driven to my office. I'd talked with a patient and then the two characters from DC — and then the telephone rang, and I'd spoken to a man I didn't know who had uttered a few words that had stuck a sharp shaft of cold steel into the heart of my whole world.

I pressed buttons on my cellphone. Consuela answered. I'd half-hoped to hear Sondra; but no.

'Consuela, is there a message from Sondra?' I asked.

'Nope, no message, nothing,' she said. She sounded suspicious. Did she detect in my voice that something was wrong? 'Why?'

'Take the rest of the day off. Go home. Relax.'

'I got plenty stuff to do here,' she said. 'I got laundry and things like that.'

'Forget it, do it tomorrow.'

'What's up with you? You sick? Gotta flu, somptin like that?'

'Nada. I'm coming home and I want the place to myself, OK?' I didn't want her to see me this unnerved, and I didn't want her to watch me hovering anxiously by a telephone and willing the goddam thing to ring, and I didn't want her to hear what I said the next time the man called.

If he called.

No if. He'd call because he wanted something. But what? Money? If I sold the house and cars and cashed in insurance policies and emptied bank accounts, I could probably come up with a million at a stretch. If the kidnapper wanted a load of cash quickly, he could have chosen somebody in a better position to oblige.

The police, I thought. That's where I ought to go. I had a few connections in the LAPD; I'd worked with a couple of their psychological cases, victims of the stress of imposing law and order. I had only to dial a number and I'd find a sympathetic listener. But I discarded that option, because the voice on the telephone had instructed me to tell nobody, and the tone had left me in no doubt that if I spoke to anyone in authority about Sondra I'd never see her again.

I was alone in this. It was me and the man on the telephone.

Consuela said, 'OK. I go home. But you explain to Sondra. This is your decision. No my decision. Yours. OK. You tell Sondra.'

'Leave it to me,' I said.

Twenty minutes later, when I reached my street, I parked outside the house. I tried to focus and be calm. I went inside.

I half-expected Sondra to be sitting on the brown leather sofa near the window in the living room, legs curled up under her body, a book or magazine in her lap.

You're home early, my love, she'd say.

Yes, I needed to see you.

The sofa was unoccupied. She was somewhere in the world, but she wasn't here. So now all I could do was wait.

I thought back to when we'd met, and how quickly that easy friendship had changed to love. She'd been doing PR for a local radio station and I'd been a guest on a late-night talk show, one of those quasi-serious programs where the host went head-to-head with the guest; basically it was fluff dressed-up as intelligent conversation. I didn't remember a word of it now. All I could recall was how Sondra had been standing on the other side of the glass booth, a cigarette in one hand, webby little smoke-drifts creating an impression of mystery about her. Her hair then had been long, down to her shoulders, and was lighter in color than it subsequently became.

She had a way of pouting slightly when she was looking serious, a faint forward thrust of the lower lip. Kissable — my mind kept wandering to those lips on the other side of the glass booth. That mouth. Later, when the show was over, I invited her to have a drink, a coffee, anything, what did it matter as long as she agreed to spend some time in my company?

Her first words to me were: *You're really nervous for a shrink. How do you get your patients to relax?*

And I said something like, *I drug them copiously, of course.*

. . . And now this intelligent, funny, lovable woman I'd married was gone. She'd disappeared out of our world.

I stood at the window and shut my eyes. I tried to make-believe I was psychic, that if I concentrated with all my strength I'd receive pictures transmitted across mystic space, I'd know her location and I'd go there without hesitation and rescue her. How naïve desperation makes us: loss renders us vulnerable to crazy notions. I squeezed my brain until my head felt as if it were about to come off my shoulders —

And, yes, I saw Sondra, I saw her as one might see a long-dead young woman in a faded daguerreotype. She was in a pale-green room; the door was locked, and the window had a view of what looked like a field of purple grass; she was touching the pane with her fingertips, but she couldn't break the glass because there were others in the room, people who watched her every movement —

I was being ludicrous, trying to make my mind zoom across this great city like a heat-seeking missile programmed to detect my missing wife. I saw her only because I wanted to see her; I could no more make my brain produce a map to Sondra's location than I could dial a phone number on Mars.

I looked from the window: the city lay under a gasoline sun. I thought of the unborn child. And suddenly I hated the man who'd telephoned — I hated him in such a way that the feeling swarmed my mind like a black flurry of iron-filings hurrying towards a powerful magnet.

The telephone rang. I picked it up.

'You're home. You run like a Swiss clock. That's good, Lomax. That's very good.'

I tried to picture this man. I tried to imagine the face behind the voice, but I couldn't get any images. Tall, short, dark, fair

— the voice gave little away. It was deep: the guy was maybe in his late forties, early fifties. The accent wasn't one I could identify. Midwest maybe. He spoke in complete sentences; he rarely slipped into unfinished phrases. His slang expressions were sparse. He was educated, no street gangster. He gave me the impression that in any kind of negotiation he'd be utterly inflexible.

'Tell me what you want from me,' I said. 'Tell me exactly what it will take to get my wife back.'

A pause. 'This is what I want you to do, Lomax. Go inside your bathroom.'

'My bathroom? Why?'

'This is lesson number one, Lomax. Always do exactly what I say.'

I took the handset and walked out of the living-room. Why did he want me to go inside the bathroom? I paused, stood very still, listened to the way my pulses beat.

'Keep going,' he said. 'It's only a few yards down the hall from your living-room.'

Only a few yards.

He knew the house-plan.

Had he been here when we were out? The thought spooked me. A stranger or strangers going through the rooms. The place had been violated. Our home. Entered and explored.

I stepped into the hallway that led to the bathroom.

'You there yet?'

'Almost.' I looked along the hall at the half-open bathroom door.

'Keep going.'

I heard it then, the sound of water running quietly into the bathtub.

'Open the bathroom door. Go inside.'

I nudged the door open with my hand.

'You inside now?'

I crossed the threshold. 'Yeah. I'm inside.'

'Look in the tub.' My eye had already traveled to the bathtub, where both faucets trickled water.

The tub was filling up very slowly.

She lay, flat on her back, duct-tape strapped across her mouth. Her hair and clothes were sodden, her eyes shut. The water had risen above her lips. In a minute, maybe a little more, she'd be drowning.

I dropped the phone on the floor, reached inside the tub and turned off the faucets and yanked the plug. Then I raised her body up to a sitting position, and as gently as I could I tore the tape from her mouth. Straining, I got her out of the tub and spread her on the floor. I searched for a pulse, any sign of life. It was weak, hard to find. I wrapped her in dry towels, and she moved her lips, but the only sound that emerged was a sing-song little moan.

I caught her face between the palms of my hands. I forced one of her eyes open. The pupil was dilated. But she wasn't seeing anything. What had they done to her?

Then I saw the bottle on the floor near the washbasin. I picked it up. It was a small plastic 100-tab container from the Sandoz Pharmaceutical Company. It had contained about twenty-five tabs of Restoril, a sedative; I'd kept it in the medicine cabinet where I stored a small selection of drugs in the event of weekend or after-hours calls from insomniac or panic-stricken patients. I picked up the container and tipped what remained of the contents into the palm of my hand. I counted quickly — ten maroon and sky-blue capsules. I understood. Christ, oh yes, I understood. She needed the hospital. She needed her stomach pumped before it was too late.

I grabbed for the phone and the man on the phone said, 'You found her all right?'

'This is monstrous. She's not involved in whatever this thing is. This is just downright . . . ' I couldn't find the word I needed and I didn't have time to hunt it down.

The voice said, 'I want you to have absolutely no doubt in your mind, Lomax.

We're serious. And that's how you'll treat us — seriously. Understand?'

My throat felt dry and constricted. 'She's our housekeeper, for God's sake — '

'She's just the hired help,' the voice said. 'Go get yourself another one. LA's full of them. Meantime, enjoy the thought that you just saved the woman from death by drowning.' He was silent a moment, then he added: 'Think of this, Lomax. It could have been your wife you found in the tub.'

'You're a fucking miserable piece of shit,' I said.

'I'm breathless, Lomax. That's hardly the language of a respected professional in the health field.'

'For Christ's sake, for the last goddam time, just tell me what you want.'

A pause. 'You had a patient.'

'I've had lots of patients.'

'I'm thinking of one in particular.'

12.50 p.m.

Consuela was in a coma. Someone had forced her to swallow between 300 and 400mg of Restoril; the normal dosage was 30–40 mg at bedtime. She was limp and heavy, and I maneuvered her downstairs with considerable difficulty. I made it into the street, hoisted her into the passenger-seat of my car, and buckled her seat-belt. Her long damp hair was glossy in the sunlight.

I drove fast down through the canyons where trees blocked the sun and threw occasional twilights across the day. I ignored speed limits. I was operating on automatic; instincts pulled all my strings. I'd do what I needed to do, what I'd been *told* to do, and in a few hours I'd have Sondra back. The ethics of my profession, the concept of confidentiality, didn't enter my thinking. I *wasn't* thinking. I couldn't afford to. If I paused to analyze the situation, I'd find objections to what I was planning to do, so I didn't contemplate anything, I just drove, just kept an image of Sondra in the front of my mind.

The way she'd looked on the deck. How

we'd made love under the sky. Her tenderness. How she'd cried so unexpectedly afterwards. *I want to be a good mother, Jerry. Yes, love. You will be. I know you will.*

I used my cellphone to call a young physician I knew at Valley Samaritan Hospital. His name was Kit Webb; I'd treated him for stress a year or so ago. I told him I was bringing a woman to emergency, a drug OD, but I couldn't explain the reason for her condition; I also told him I needed him to be discreet and 'forget' about filing an incident report for the next few hours. He agreed. One physician's favor to another; the freemasonry of doctors.

When I got to the hospital, I backed the BMW up as close as I could get to the Emergency entrance. Kit was already there, tall and lean and white-coated, clipboard in hand, red hair flopping down over his forehead. He helped me get Consuela out of the car and into a wheelchair and we pushed her inside the building.

He examined her face quickly, gently. He had long white fingers. He pushed her eyelids open. 'What did she take?'

'Restoril,' I said.

He looked at me. 'You just came across her on the street, huh?'

'That's good enough.'

'For the moment,' he said. 'Are you in trouble, Jerry?'

'I can't talk, Kit. Sorry.'

'OK. But I can't overlook this forever. You better call me.' He wheeled Consuela, whose head hung loosely to one side, along the corridor, past other casualties of the great metropolis — broken people who sat in chairs and waited their turn, people with gunshot wounds, a biker with a shattered leg, a pretty Thai woman holding a handkerchief to her face, which had been cut. Blood slid down her wrist, stained her white blouse. Her eyes were shut; I noticed the delicate sky-blue veins in her eyelids.

Another victim of the city.

Another outrage.

I walked hurriedly to my car, drove out of the hospital parking-lot. I reached my building on Wilshire, rushed inside, rode the elevator to the seventh floor. Jane Steel was behind her desk and she looked at me with concern as I entered. She didn't say anything — she was too discreet to ask questions — but if I wanted to talk, she'd listen. I touched her briefly on the back of her hand, a gesture meant to convey normality, that nothing was wrong, everything was functioning.

'It's going to be fine, just fine,' I said.

'Mrs Lomax is all right?'

I said, 'Yes. Take a lunch break, Jane.'

'You're sure?'

'Positive.'

I went inside my office and closed the door. I pushed a chair away from a spot at the center of the Persian rug, then I rolled the rug back. I removed a square section of the wooden floor, under which the safe was concealed. It was made of steel, and measured about twenty-four inches by twenty; I went down on my knees and looked at the combination lock and for a bad moment I couldn't remember the sequence of numbers — my mind quit, my memory lapsed, the numbers were lost in the soup of my brain.

What in God's name were they? I concentrated, tried to remember when I'd last used the safe, the numbers I'd turned: lost, lost, lost. On hands and knees, gazing down into this secret space under the floorboards of my office, I felt like some dumb animal, an ox whose progress had been halted by an unexpected obstacle. I felt shackled.

Numbers. There was a four, a six, a nine, something else, some other goddam number. I watched a cockroach scurry across the face of the safe, climbing over the lock before disappearing into the darkness of the struts that supported the floor. Four . . . six . . . nine . . . then what?

I was sweating, the air in the room was warm, the smell that rose from beneath the boards suggested a long-shut attic opened for the first time in years, everything inside dehydrated, rotted old clothing destroyed by moths. I'd written the number down on a scrap of paper and stuffed it inside a book someplace at home, but now I couldn't even remember which book —

Four, six, nine —

What the hell was the other number? Why wouldn't my mind yield it up to me?

The answer was easy: I was doing something that was nowhere permitted in my code of ethics. My conscience was playing moral dictator. All the files stored in this floor-safe contained the most sensitive secrets of my patients, their dreams and fears: a collection of bones. These were the private files I'd written up late at night in the hushed privacy of my own home, material that wasn't stored on the computer, records that even Jane Steel knew nothing about. I was the only repository for all this stuff, much of it potentially damaging to the patients involved; I was the curator of confessions and desires and murderous urges, and sexual material that in criminal hands might lead to extortion.

But now I was prepared to take a detour around my conscience and give up one of these highly confidential files to an unknown party, so desperate they'd kidnap one innocent woman, and seriously assault another. I wanted my wife and unborn child back more than I could possibly have wanted anything on the face of the planet, and even if I *knew* it was wrong to sacrifice the records of one of my patients for that purpose, I'd come to a place where I couldn't afford the luxury of qualms; I'd closed down that part of myself where scruples took root.

I had an image of Consuela in the bathroom, the tape strapped across her lips.

It could have been your wife you found in the tub.

Yes, yes, it could have been. So easily.

I'll call you in your office at two and it would cause me great pleasure to think you'll have what I want, doctor. Everything works out, you'll get your wife back intact.

And if I didn't do what I'd been told, if I didn't deliver — but he hadn't elaborated on what might happen if I failed, and it didn't bear thinking about anyway.

Three. I had it.

Four, six, nine, three.

I put my hand on the dial, turned it forward to four, heard a click. Then to six, another click. Nine, click. And back all the way to three. I reached for the handle, and the door opened. I looked at the cardboard boxes inside, about twenty of them. I'd arranged them as you would arrange books in a library. The side of each box was labeled with the number I'd allocated to each patient.

I scanned the labels. I reached inside the safe and withdrew the box marked *2567*. The box didn't feel right in my hand, something was wrong. Just as the phone on my desk started to ring, I realized what it was. My vision became fuzzy. My brain was all static bewilderment.

I set the box on the desk and picked up the handset.

'Got what I want?' he asked.

I removed the lid. Looked inside the box.

I didn't need to look. I knew.

'Well, Lomax?

I felt wasted. I undid my tie, opened the top button of my shirt. My skin prickled.

'Well? Is there a problem?'

'No, no,' I said. 'Everything's fine.'

'You have what we want?'

'Of course I have it.'

'Delighted to hear it.' He laughed softly, pleased. 'I'll be in touch about the exchange.'

'When?'

'Just stay close to your phone, Lomax.'

He hung up.

I let the lid fall to the floor. I continued to gaze inside the empty box, my hands clammy. I wondered, with a raking sense of fear and panic, self-control draining rapidly out of me, what had happened to the contents.

2.25 p.m.

In Otto's bar I was gazing at a photograph of
Fred Astaire and Ginger Rogers, in a 1940s
world of tuxedoes and clinging silk dresses,
when Emily Ford arrived from her downtown
office. She told me at once she was rushed,
she didn't have much time, she'd interrupted
a meeting to come here. I put my hand on her
elbow and led her to a corner of the room.

I set my Scotch on the table and said, 'You
better sit down.'

'OK. I'm sitting. What's this all about?'

'Look me straight in the eye and tell me
you don't know.'

'What is this, Jerry? *You* phoned *me*. You
ask me to get my ass over here. I'm in the
middle of being grilled by these two
characters from Washington, Attila the
Hunette and her jolly sidekick. I've got about
nine minutes before I have to get back and
face them again.'

'I met them already,' I said. 'They paid me
a call.'

'What impression did you get? Do they
want to bury me and protect Caesar?'

I ignored her questions. I had another

agenda. 'You really *don't* know why I was so persistent about meeting you, do you?'

'Mind-reading isn't one of my talents, Jerry. What is it I'm supposed to know?'

I skipped the story of Consuela. I told her about the demands for her file.

Then I told her that her records were missing from my floor-safe.

Finally, I told her about Sondra.

Emily stared at me. 'Sweet Jesus, Jerry. I don't know what to say.'

'Just be honest with me, Emily. Tell me you have nothing to do with the theft from my safe.'

'You think I *stole* my own *records*? I don't even know where you *store* them, Jerry. God, you're being absurd. You're also being extremely naïve. Even if I had my own file, do you think I'd *admit* it? Or were you counting on your intuition? You'd look at me and you'd just know? Anyway, why would I steal my own records?'

'Emily, you have a great motive. You think you're vulnerable because of what your records contain, so you want them — '

'I've never read my file, Jerry, I don't have a clue what you've written about my sessions with you. How damaging could it be?'

'It depends on who's reading the files, and what they're looking for. Somebody searching for evidence of a certain mental instability in the past — OK, he'd find that. Somebody looking for evidence that these episodes are *not* behind you once and for all, well, he might find what he needs too. Somebody else would say your mental health was just tickety-boo, first-class.'

'The material is wide open to interpretation,' she said.

'Right. It's not an exact science. The files could be used one way or the other. In a court of law, they'd be just as useful to the defense as to the prosecution, OK? Let's put that to one side, Emily. What it boils down to is this: You have this exaggerated notion that because you were once a psychiatric patient, you'll be crucified when it comes to the big job in DC. You hear the sound of all your ambition going down the toilet. So, you don't want to take any chances with your file, you just feel it's safer in your hands than somebody else's. So what do you do? You arrange to have it stolen. I don't know how. I'm the only person with the combination to the safe, and so far as I could see, nobody jimmied it.'

'Jerry, *I did not steal my own fucking file.* What you're really telling me is *somebody* has my private psychiatric records. Some guy's walking around out there with the inside of my mind in his hands, for Christ's sake. All because you didn't have my file secured. That's criminally irresponsible of you. And it's a wholesale disaster for *me*. And you don't know *who* — '

'Emily, my wife's been seized. And if I don't find your file and hand it over . . . ' I didn't complete the sentence. It led into narrow black areas, clefts of fear.

'This is outrageous,' she said. 'You don't take security measures? People come and go as they please, they just traipse in and out of your office?'

'People don't just come and go,' I said. 'Jane's always at her desk. Nobody gets in to see me unless they have an appointment.'

'You got any reason for suspecting sweet, reliable Jane of this theft?'

'None. Even if she knew the combination of my safe, she wouldn't have taken anything out of it. I trust her one hundred per cent.'

'Maybe somebody has some kind of hold on her, only you don't know it. Maybe she's been threatened by somebody. She's scared.'

'OK. Let's imagine she's *been* threatened. She still doesn't have the combination.'

'If you rule her out, who does that leave?'

'If I rule out both her and you, then we're looking for somebody who wants information about you. Why? Let's imagine he's exploring ways of destroying you. He doesn't like the idea of you being the next AG. You have too many axes to grind and one of them is swinging a little too close to his head.'

I drew the tips of my fingers across my eyes. A current of apprehension ran through me, a tiny little shock. I wondered if Emily was lying, if she had the file, despite all her protests. I wasn't sure. I couldn't read her face.

I said, 'At the same time, the mysterious party who abducted Sondra *also* has the hots for this file, and maybe for the same reasons. How many goddam enemies have you got?'

'I've got them in Washington, and right here in LA. I've got them in the exalted ranks of organized crime, and in refined private clubs where certain kinds of lawyers drink ancient port and pretend they don't have scum for clients. I mean, some of these guys' client-lists read like the executive boards of organized-crime syndicates, for Christ's sake. Then there are dope dealers who probably burn me in effigy. And the civil liberties people don't always like my attitude. It's a big catalog, Jerry.' She was quiet a second. 'Has it crossed your mind it may have been a professional job? Somebody hired especially to get their hands on my file?'

'I hadn't considered a professional. Even

so, it was my responsibility to secure your records, and I'm sorry. I assumed the safe was impregnable.' I'd assumed the same thing about my life.

Emily was quiet a moment. 'You want Sondra, I want my file back. The idea of any old sonofabitch waltzing around out there with my private records is goddam unacceptable to me, Jerry.'

'Maybe I should go to the cops,' I said.

'Oh, not very bright,' she said. 'Cops have a tendency to bungle really sensitive things, believe me . . . Have you considered the possibility that one of your patients might be involved? Somebody who infiltrated your office because he wanted my file, someone you took on as a patient and who turned out to be a thief?'

An infiltrator. A phony patient. The notion worried me — the idea that somebody had convinced me they were mentally sick or unbalanced, that I'd opened my door to him or her. It angered me to think that one of them might be a fraud plausible enough to deceive me. I considered my list of patients; I hadn't taken on any new ones recently. Besides, it was unlikely I would have left any patient alone in my office long enough to roll back the rug, open the safe, take out the box marked *2567*, remove the contents, return the box, shut the safe, replace the rug, and *then* smuggle the file out without being seen. More likely, it was somebody who'd come when the office was closed; and since there had been no sign of a forced entry, the person who'd stolen the file had a door key *as well as* the combination.

There were three keys to the office. Jane Steel had one, I had another, and the security guard, Grogue, had a third. But keys were easily duplicated. Maybe somebody had stolen Grogue's, copied it, then returned the original before he noticed it missing. Maybe my key was the one that had been taken and duplicated. Or Jane's. And then the thief had come quietly in the dark, unlocked the front door, walked into my office and, with all the time in the world, had picked open the safe, removed Emily Ford's records, then slipped away. *Somehow.*

'Forget the cops, Jerry,' Emily said. 'Frankly, I think you'd be better off making a check of your patients' records, see if anything strange turns up. But all your patients are a little strange, aren't they Jerry?' She looked at me curiously. 'So what do we do?'

'*We?*'

'Don't you trust me?'

'Should I? You only want your records. You

don't give a damn about Sondra.'

'You think you can work this thing alone? Fine, Jerry. Fly solo. See how much gas is in your tank, buddyboy.' She turned away from me, looked in the direction of the bar. She said, 'I have access to a FBI database so vast it would blow your mind. I could run a check on your patients in the blink of an eye.'

I must have looked hesitant, because she said, 'You're quite prepared to trade my file in return for your wife, right? Don't even try to deny it, Jerry. It's written all over your face. So I don't want to hear any guff about you having this ethical need to protect your patients. Just print me up a list of them and I'll feed it through the database, nobody will know I've done it except you and me. And I'm not telling.'

She was right, I had no claim to the moral high-ground. 'Tell me what you'd be looking for,' I said.

'Anything that stinks like a long-dead fish. Anything that's off-center. Maybe I'll find a name that has some connection with me. Somebody from the past. Somebody I'd forgotten. Some kind of bell that rings. It would take me about thirty minutes to run the names, Jerry. And if you're still queasy about it, you don't even have to hand the list to me personally. Print it out. Leave it on

107

your desk, turn your back.'

She was persuasive, I had to give her that; she spoke quietly, creating an atmosphere I found unsettlingly intimate.

'What will you do *without* this wonderfully generous offer of help I'm holding out to you? I'm talking about a computer that has everything. Supersonic bells and whistles, and faster than Superman on his best day.'

'Let's say I cooperate, and by some amazing stroke of luck we locate your records. What happens then? Are you going to hand them over to me so that I can trade them for Sondra's life? For the baby's life?'

'*Baby*? Sondra's *pregnant*? Ouch. I have a feeling you just punched me below the belt.' She tilted her head back and appeared thoughtful. I looked at her; in repose, she was lovely in an angular way. She'd never married. She'd had lovers, but her work had always taken precedence. Ambition had overruled her heart. She was on a fast-track and she'd been traveling that way for a long time; she'd never allowed anything or anyone to stand in her way, and now there was a chance that her career might crash and burn. But she wasn't about to be thrown off that particular locomotive without a serious fight to stay on board. She'd inherited her father's cast-iron determination: Robbie Ford, public prosecutor, didn't understand defeat and knew even less about compromise. Emily had inherited his virtues and flaws, his steely obligation to the law as well as his pig-headedness, his focus as well as his inflexibility.

My mind raced to the kidnappers — and suddenly I had one of those little flashes that illuminate the darkness which clouds our brains much of the time. It was either the flare of an inspiration — or the small candle-flame of my desperation.

I said, 'Something just occurred to me. They want a file they've never set eyes on. They don't have a clue what it might contain. They don't know what it looks like. Typed, handwritten, the kind of paper — they don't know anything like that.'

'And?'

'So — I write one for them. From scratch.'

'And you think they'd go for that?'

'It's worth a shot,' I said. 'I can make it look good. I can give it authenticity. OK, granted it sounds crazy, but I'm not thinking in a straight line at the moment.'

'It doesn't sound crazy to me. How long would it take to dummy something like that?'

'An hour. Maybe more. If I type like I'm demented.'

'How close to the truth will it have to be?'

'Very close. Otherwise, these people will smell a fake as soon as they read it.' *And goodbye, Sondra,* I thought.

'Give me some idea what you'll write.'

'Simple. You came to me as a patient for grief therapy. You were having nightmares about your parents. I had to put you on some heavy-duty medication. Then I toss in some vague technical jargon: Generalized anxiety disorder. Post-traumatic stress. I can paint it on thick. I'll say that the treatment was a success.'

'It's a sanitized skeleton of the real file,' she said.

'Basically.'

'And there would be nothing in it that could be damaging to me if it fell into the wrong hands?'

'I'll make sure of it,' I said.

'Swear,' she said.

'I swear.'

She touched my knuckles with her fingertips. 'And if it works, you get your wife back.'

'Wife and baby,' I said. My world was black and white, my focus narrowed down to where it could only encompass Sondra and the life of the child she carried.

'So, at the very least we buy enough time for you to provide me with your patient list, and I see if I can make anything out of the names.'

I was still hesitant about this part. I said, 'On the condition that you destroy it when you're through.'

'Deal. Straight into the shredder, Jerry. My word.'

I walked her back to her Mercedes. She unlocked the door of the car and turned to look at me. 'I want that nomination. And I want it ratified. I want it so bad, Jerry.'

'And I want Sondra.'

'Two goals that don't necessarily have to conflict,' she said. She studied my face a moment. 'Been in an accident? Your neck's badly bruised,' and she touched the contusion gently.

'Yeah, I tripped, lost my balance,' and I left it at that.

She didn't look convinced. She had the kind of eyes that could sometimes penetrate the best defenses. Sharp, flinty. 'Let me get rid of these Washington characters. You go print that list. I'll call you.'

She got inside the car and as I watched her drive away, I thought: *She really has no idea that the material stolen from my safe was already laundered, already sanitized.*

3.09 p.m.

Out of nowhere a car slid up close to me, a grubby old Pontiac, dust-streaked and rusted-out, paint cracked. The windows were mud-caked, almost opaque.

It came in against the curb and an arm emerged from the window on the passenger side and a voice said, 'Hey, Lomax.'

I flinched, thinking instantly of assassination, a gun in the hand that protruded from the window. In my imagination, I heard a shot and felt myself blasted backwards to die slowly on the sidewalk, the whole mystery of things unresolved; I'd enter eternity with a conundrum I could never work out — and then silence and darkness. I thought of the trajectory of the bullet, the explosion of skullbone, the leak of brain fluids. *LA Psychiatrist Gunned Down in Daylight.*

I stepped back, one hand held out in front of my face, as if this might shield me against the bullet when it came.

But there was no gunfire, only a small, innocuous, brown-padded envelope tossed towards me. I picked it up and the car, gathering speed, squealed away from me. I pulled the tag that opened the envelope — it was light, almost weightless — and I tipped its contents into the palm of my hand. I halfway expected it to be something gruesome, something I couldn't name and didn't want to see.

It was a lock of hair the color of aubergine. I stared at it. I raised it to my face. It smelled of Sondra. In different circumstances and another age, the hair might have been a token of love to be enclosed in a locket.

The Pontiac came back again, braking halfway up on the sidewalk. The passenger door was thrown open and I found myself looking into the curiously bland face of a fair-haired man in a blue denim shirt. A second man emerged quickly from the passenger side. He was large-skulled, hair-cropped as short and sharp as new-mown Bermuda grass. Large eyes protruded from his head like a couple of ping-pong balls cut in half and placed in each socket. He gripped my shoulder and pushed me against the car.

The fair-haired man slipped on a set of brass knuckles and rubbed them against my chin. A silver and turquoise bracelet hung at his wrist. He smiled. 'A word of advice, Lomax . . . Do yourself a favor, give the man what he wants. Or it's gonna get real hairy. I promise you.'

I couldn't help saying, 'Fuck you.'

The fair-haired guy brought his face so close to mine the motion might have been a preamble to a kiss. His breath smelled of cow-slurry. 'What am I hearing?'

'Simple. I said, 'Fuck you.' ' I felt a tightness in my chest. I didn't need to alienate this pair, but I couldn't blunt the sharp antagonism I felt, the awareness of outrage. One more push and the dam of myself would crack.

The big-skulled guy said to his associate, 'You want me to kick the living crap outta him?'

The other man said, 'Yeah, I'd like that. Except it wasn't no part of the job-description.' He rubbed my chin with the brass knuckles again, a circular motion, slow and menacing. I could have pulled my face away, but I didn't. I wasn't going to be stared down either.

'You think you got *huevos*, buddy,' he said. 'Doncha?'

'Yeah, that's what he thinks,' said the big-skulled one. 'But is he smart enough to keep them getting all fucking scrambled into an omelet?' He made a crushing gesture with his huge hands, as if he were pulverizing a couple of stone orbs. 'Crunchy crunchy, crunch crunch. Here's your balls in a blender, Lomax. You smart enough to save yourself from that fate, huh?'

The man with the sour breath said, 'Just do what you been told to do, doc. Don't take no detours. Listen to me. Be obedient. And don't play tough guy, because it don't impress me and my friend here. OK? Whatever you can do, we can do a whole lot better.'

So: it wasn't enough that Sondra was being held captive; I needed extra pressure too.

I heard them drive away. One of them shouted, 'Keep what we said in mind, doc,' and I sensed the world darkening around me and something half-visible vibrating on the edges of my vision.

3.27 p.m.

The hair had shocked me, sent me into a deeper downward spiral. And the appearance of the two men had given the situation a hard reality it had lacked before. Finally there were faces, belligerent and cunning, behind the abduction of my wife. Real people — more than a disembodied voice at the end of a phone.

Give the man what he wants.

I sat in my office in front of the keyboard. I struck the keys hard and sweat ran down my face. I tried to remember the sessions I'd had with Emily, the areas we'd explored; my memory kept shorting out, dates escaped me, particulars of our interviews, those concrete details that would give a sense of indisputable reality to the counterfeit. This had to be convincing beyond all doubt, but I felt like a man forging a document the original of which had been lost, or somebody applying chemicals to a brand-new parchment to make it look and feel antique. Solvents, dyes, toxic substances.

I had the feeling the formula was eluding me, that I'd end up with nothing credible.

This wasn't going to fool anyone. And then there would be repercussions I didn't want to think about.

The letters on the screen blurred as I pounded . . . *the subject expressed great concern over the limitations of justice . . . the subject wondered if she might have gone into a different profession, and believed that she'd developed a scepticism about the practice of law . . .*

. . . She is obsessed with the burdensome influence her father had on her life, his intellectual bullying . . .

. . . He was constantly hypercritical of her in childhood . . .

. . . She was often the target of his anger . . .

. . . His personality dominated the family. When she qualified as a lawyer, a serious competitive edge entered their relationship . . . In my opinion, her feelings for her father fitted the classic love-hate matrix . . . perhaps with more hate than love . . .

. . . My judgment is that although his death was a tragedy for her, she feels an unconscious relief that he can no longer pressure her. This induces feelings of guilt . . . She wishes she had been able to settle the differences between herself and her father before he was killed, and now that the

opportunity to do so is no longer available to her, she feels even more guilt . . .

. . . I have taken her off Serax and prescribed 4mg daily of Ativan for anxiety. The effects of Serax were too short-lived . . .

I typed and typed faster than I'd ever done in my life. I fudged the dates and times. I couldn't remember them with any precision, anyway. Then I wondered if I should mention our hypnosis session, at least in passing — but no, I didn't want to introduce that into the report. For reasons of authenticity, I might have done: but I couldn't. I walked round the office, thinking, trying to remember. There was gridlock inside my head, a pile-up of stalled thoughts.

I'd placed the lock of Sondra's hair beside the keyboard, and now I picked it up and caressed it between thumb and forefinger. I had to sit down and type more, harder, churn out the words, keep them coming. I knew the telephone would ring soon enough.

And it did.

'Santa Monica, Lomax,' he said. 'The pier. Go there now. Bring the file and your phone. You'll be contacted . . . and do us all a favor by staying away from Emily Ford. You got that?'

They're following me, I thought. They saw me go inside Otto's, saw me walk Emily Ford to her car. I wondered about the surveillance, when it had begun, and the extent of it. I felt a tiny shadow cross my mind, such as a genuine paranoiac might feel: I sensed unseen faces behind the sun-glossed windows of parked cars, I wondered about a guy standing at a bar with an absent expression, a woman sucking an ice-cream cone on a street-corner, a face in a phonebooth — everything was charged, everything loaded, with the menace of the invisible observer. I might have been the subject of a lab experiment, shunted through a maze, my movements charted and recorded.

'What did you talk to her about anyway, Lomax?'

'This and that.' I stared at the screen. I still hadn't written enough; I had eight pages. Jesus. Eight pages was nothing. I needed double that. I needed length, density, an infusion of technical jargon.

'Don't give me 'this and that,' ' he said. 'You just *had* to tell her somebody wanted her file, right? Feel free to stop me if I'm wrong, Lomax. You and she tossed a few names back and forth, candidates who might want her psychiatric records, scoundrels with underhand motives. You wanted her to know that somebody's looking for a way to crucify her. You still feel a responsibility towards her.

Dare I say a fondness, even? Or is that simply speculation?'

I didn't respond. A note in his voice scared me: supreme authority. *I have your wife and I own you. You obey every command I issue.* How could I even *consider* the idea of telling this voice that the records he demanded had been stolen, for God's sake?

He said, 'I'll say this for the last time, Lomax. You're alone. You don't have any allies. You don't have friends, you don't even have acquaintances. The universe you live in is very big and very empty. There is no God. Like it or not, I'm your best friend. Understand? Say so.'

'OK, I understand,' I said. 'Incidentally, I'm not enamored of *your* friends — '

'Get used to them. They're never very far away from you. You might even say they're more close to you than anyone else in this situation, including *moi*. Their manners leave something to be desired, but they were raised in bad neighborhoods, underprivileged, alcoholic homes, abusive fathers, you know how it goes, bla bla . . . Now, if Ford calls you, or contacts you in person, tell her you've come to the conclusion that the 'kidnapper' was just some loony, some kind of phone-freak playing with your head, and that your wife's OK. Say something like . . . she had to go out of town on business. It was unexpected. OK?'

I said OK. I was tense. I scanned the screen, the words I'd written. I felt my heart drop and go on dropping, a stone down a well. He was never going to buy this half-assed mock-up. He'd see through it like a transparency. He didn't sound like a stupid man.

He was quiet for a moment. 'By the way. Get the hair?'

'Yeah,' I said.

'You should be grateful. Considering.'

Considering what? Considering what I *might* have received in that envelope? I had images of butchery, dismemberment. I shoved the pictures away. My saliva felt like silt in my throat.

'I want to speak to my wife,' I said.

'You speak to her when I decide, and only then,' he answered. 'Now go to the pier.' And he hung up.

I sat down, hammered out a few last sentences, then printed up what I'd written. Dear Christ, it was as thin as consommé. But I didn't have time to embellish or expand it. Eight pages, double-spaced in Univers Condensed 12 point. It didn't feel right.

The paper looked and smelled too new, that was it.

I rummaged in a closet in search of some

old paper and found a box that had been opened a while back; I took some of these sheets and stuck them inside the printer, then I printed the file again. Better, but not much.

I slipped the pages inside a manila envelope and licked the gummed flap and sealed the thing shut.

Then I brought up on-screen the file that contained the names of my patients. Attaching it to an e-mail, I sent it to Emily Ford, with the message: *I'll contact you.* After I'd sent it, I wondered if my computer was secure, or if my electronic mail was being illicitly monitored.

I picked up the lock of Sondra's hair and stuck it in the breast pocket of my jacket, as if for luck. I passed Jane Steel on my way out. She was updating computer data: housecleaning, she called it. Making copies. Deleting out-of-date material.

'I may not be back today,' I said.

She gazed at me. Her mouth had a slight downward twist that suggested concern. 'Is there anything you want me to do?'

'If I can think of anything, I'll call.'

'Take care,' she said.

'I'll do my best, Jane.'

4.29 p.m.

In Santa Monica I parked a couple of blocks from the pier, then I walked past the carousel and the hot-dog concessions. The tide rose and fell sluggishly against the pilings. I'd come here with Sondra on our second date, and I remembered, with a measure of pain, the slow-running calm of the ocean, the first kiss, the first connection, that almost unbearable contact of flesh, my hand on her naked breast beneath her white cotton shirt. The image shimmered, the water slipped over the sands beneath the pier.

I remembered telling her, with brazen certainty, that I was falling in love with her. She'd laughed lightly, a little surprised. *Do you usually give your heart away this fast?* she'd asked. No, I'd never committed myself so quickly to anything before, but I'd known that it was right to tell her what I felt. I was like an adolescent afflicted by love's first assault. I trembled even now to think of that intimacy.

A dozen sailboats moved listlessly about half a mile from shore. A distant freighter plumed the air with dense brown smoke that rose into the sun. Two freckled, red-haired kids, probably brothers, carried fishing-poles towards the end of the pier. I'd fished creeks around Buffalo as a boy. I remembered nylon and reel and float and the splash of a hooked fish breaking the surface. I could almost hear it now. A lost world, innocence capsized. I thought of the route my life had taken, and how it had turned suddenly into a series of fiendish switchbacks.

What was I supposed to do now? Wait for somebody to contact me? Or was this a dry run that had been devised, a chance for me to prove that I'd come to the designated place alone? My senses had altered. The disappearance of Sondra had colored everything. I ached for her. I might have lost a limb. Or the will to live. My goals — but I couldn't recollect specific goals. What had I wanted, anyway? A different car, a house in a quiet place out of the city, my office refurbished, walls painted? God knows, none of it seemed of any importance now.

I touched the lock of her hair in my breast pocket, and pictured the battered Pontiac from which the envelope had been tossed. I could have described the two men easily, but I couldn't recall the license number, because my attention had been focused on the idea of violence and the way sun glimmered on the ugly brass knuckles. I should have been more alert, but my first impulse had been fear, the idea that somebody was going to shoot me down on the sidewalk in cold blood; you don't think straight in these situations, you don't look for peripheral details — I reached the end of the pier. I checked the people strolling in the afternoon sun. Couples, solitary men and women, some teenagers, two old guys playing chess on a bench with a miniature set. The air smelled of brine and something else, a scent like that of dead fish. The ocean was polluted. I sat down, my back to the sun, the crisp manila envelope on my lap. I felt like a student whose final exam lay in that envelope, and whose whole future depended on this paper receiving a high grade. An A, a B-plus. A simple Pass would be enough.

When my phone rang I took it out of my pocket immediately.

'You're on the pier,' he said. 'I can see you.'

I turned my head, looked the length of the pier, back through the entrance as far as the avenue that ran parallel with the beach.

'You're wasting your time, Lomax,' he said. 'You can't see me.'

Was he in one of the white-faced buildings on the far side of the avenue? Or was he closer than that, standing in a concealed place on the pier itself? The thought struck me that maybe he was offshore, a passenger in one of the yachts, a guy with binoculars or a telescope.

'Get up, start walking,' he said. 'There's a trash-can on your right just as you step off the pier. Drop the envelope in the can. Got that?'

'I've got it,' I said.

'Then you go to your car and you drive away,' he said. 'If anyone impedes the person picking up the envelope from the can, if you've brought anyone with you as back-up, if a single goddam *thing* goes wrong, the consequences are on your head. I hope I'm making myself plain.'

'Plain as day,' I said. 'When do I get my wife back?'

'You'll hear from me.'

And the line was cut.

I walked towards the exit. A flock of black-headed gulls flew overhead, shrieking. Ten yards from the trash-can stood a couple of homeless characters, a barefoot guy in an old plaid poncho, and a skinny waif of a teenage girl with a tie-dyed bedsheet drawn around her shoulders. She had matted hair and gazed at me pleadingly, holding a hand out for change. She smelled of unwashed flesh, and she was shivering.

'Got a quarter, mister? Fifty cents? Please?'

'Sure,' and I fished out a bunch of coins, dropped them in her palm.

'Thanks a lot,' she said in a plaintive little voice.

Then I wondered: how did this transaction look to the man observing me? Might he interpret my contact with the girl as a sign? Might he think that this thin urchin was an undercover cop and the guy in the poncho her partner, and that I'd just imparted vital information, passed on a prearranged signal? An innocent gesture, coins dropped in the dirty palm of a wasted young woman — but how did I know he'd see it that way? I didn't. But the notion had a reverse side: how did I know that the pair weren't the kidnapper's people, his gophers, messengers, part of his scheme?

I was crushed by questions. And no answers.

I dropped the envelope into the trash-can surreptitiously. I glimpsed a half-eaten burger, alive with buzzing flies, and a condom wrapper. I kept moving. I was nervous, and curious to turn my head, but I didn't look back. Would the file convince? It had to, otherwise I was lost, everything was lost.

I reached my car, drove away. I kept an eye on the rearview mirror. How could you know if you were being followed in a world filled with traffic flowing endlessly? You couldn't. It was an effective trick of one person tracking another: you didn't have to be a constant watcher, you only needed to plant a single seed. The victim's troubled imagination did the rest, imbuing the follower with omniscience. Or maybe in the mind of the hunted the follower was multiplied — one, two, four, eight, a platoon, a whole goddam battalion.

I knew all this, I knew how easy it was to succumb to paranoia. I knew it, sure, but that didn't make it any easier to overcome.

My head felt like a pod about to burst open.

I wondered where they'd seized Sondra. Maybe she'd been snatched at a *Stop* sign, her door jerked open, hands grabbing for her, a chloroformed handkerchief. But she always drove with her doors locked. Unless something had persuaded her to unlock the car and step out, a rigged accident, say, or a vehicle blocking her way. I thought of the gloomy parking garage at LaBrea Records, another possibility. I wondered if her car was parked there, if she'd been abducted at her place of work.

I passed the park on the bluff that overlooked the Pacific. The homeless congregated here with their shopping-trolleys and kids whizzed past on skateboards and people threw Frisbees for their dogs. I chewed on my thumbnail so hard I gnawed it down to the quick, drawing a little blood.

I turned right off Ocean Avenue. I glanced at a surfboard sales and repair shop, and a tea-room that was a replica of something you might find in an idealized English village — scones and clotted cream and pictures of royalty. I had the impression these places were unreal. They were movie sets. This entire city existed only in some movie-maker's mind. Fake knives. Fake patients.

My cellphone rang.

Sondra. Her voice was distant. She was trying to speak through tears. I didn't understand anything she said. She seemed to be in pain. It was as if somebody had forced her arm up her spine to an impossible angle. I imagined the bone held at breaking point, the distorted expression on her lovely face. I felt her pain inside myself, a stake.

'Sondra — '

Whatever she was trying to say was incoherent, choked back in her throat. I pulled the car into a narrow alley and parked among dumpsters, old wood crates, and cardboard boxes heaped outside the rear door of a restaurant. 'Sondra . . . take your time, talk to me . . . I love you and I'm trying to get you back and it's only a matter of time, I promise.'

Then there was silence. I said her name over and over. Why was she quiet now? What were they doing to her?

The man came on the line and said, 'It seems that she's not entirely herself, Lomax.'

'Put her on again!'

'You're not hearing me, Lomax. She's not herself. She's not well. She can't come to the phone again.'

I said, 'Look, I left the file where you asked me to leave it. Now just tell me where my wife is and I'll come get her. I kept my end of the deal — '

'Really, Lomax? You really kept your end of the deal, did you? Let me read you something. '*Subject reports a series of bad dreams. In some of these, she is being chased through the corridors of a house that resembles the one she grew up in, but in the dream it is bigger, with many more rooms and unfamiliar passageways. She wakes breathless and covered in sweat. She cannot identify the figure that chases her in the dream.*' This ringing any bells?'

'It's from Emily Ford's file,' I said.

'OK. Here's another. '*Subject has been dreaming of Billy Fear. In her dream, Billy Fear is a male Caucasian of about forty. In* reality, *Billy Fear was an Afro-American of twenty-three. She says that in her dreams Billy Fear wears a cloak covered with the signs of the zodiac, or something similar . . .* ' You remember writing this?'

'Yes.'

'I've got a real problem with it, Lomax. Let me explain. It's a yawn. It's an eight-page yawn. I could hardly keep my eyes open when I was reading it, which took all of ninety seconds.'

He knew. He goddam *knew*. 'I don't have anything else I can give you — '

'Do not fuck with me, Lomax. The point I'm making is I'm not going to be fobbed off with these notes, which are total shit. They're about as bland as a rail-road timetable. This is the kind of stuff that belongs in Psych 101 or some prerequisite class for kiddy shrinks. It's boring and useless, totally useless, Lomax. What did you do, decide you'd try to con me with the *Reader's Digest* condensed version? Jesus, Lomax. One thing I seriously hate is being underestimated. I can smell crap from a long way off, and crap is what I'm smelling from these pages. I want the *meat*, Lomax. Are you with me? I want the blood, the rich, marbled flesh. I want this woman's eternal soul in the palm of my hand. I want everything, godammit. And you know what

131

I'm talking about.'

'No, I don't know.' I'd failed the test. I hadn't had a chance from the start. The idea had been dumb and hopeless and fueled by my despair and anxiety.

'Oh, *please*, Lomax. I'm not one of your patients, whacked-out on funny drugs. I'm angry. And I have your lovely young wife sitting a few feet from me. Your lovely young *pregnant* wife. And all I want in return for this precious cargo is everything you ever learned about the inside of Emily Ford's head. You understand that?'

The connection was broken suddenly.

I struck the handset against the dash. I smashed it hard in rage a few times until I heard the plastic casing break. What was I doing? I couldn't shatter this device, it was moronic to do so, I needed it, I needed to be connected, a telephone was the only thread I had to Sondra.

I put it back in its slot under the dash.

Precious cargo, I thought. *On a perilous sea.*

4.46 p.m.

I drove to my bank.

Do it now, I thought, *before you change your mind.*

I got out of the car. I entered the bank, a place of glossy marble surfaces and steel, and a sense of money hoarded in bomb-proof vaults. I told a sullen woman at the Customer Service desk that I wanted access to my safe-deposit box. She asked for ID, ran me through her computer, then escorted me down a flight of stairs to the safe-deposit room. She didn't speak. She liked being aloof. She'd probably done a college course in Aloof, maybe even obtained a certificate. I had a deep, instinctive dislike of her.

We inserted our keys, I removed the box, took it into a small private room, opened it, looked at a rectangular white envelope that measured about six inches by four.

I didn't touch it. I didn't want to touch it. I wanted it to stay right where it was.

Take it, Jerry. You're going to need it.

I lowered my hand, pressed my fingertips against the envelope. I felt the hard, flat object it contained.

I thought: *Don't give in. Not yet.* And I was angry again. Angry with the abduction, sure, but it was more than that now — it was the manipulation, the way I was being followed, the threat of the two guys. Fuck them. I wasn't giving up this envelope just yet. Its contents were a last resort. I closed the box — I had the thought: *You may live to regret this* — then returned the box to its drawer. The woman and I turned our keys, then I rushed up the stairs ahead of her.

In the foyer, I encountered Bo Sonderheim, the bank manager. He was an open-faced, kindly man I knew socially. He was from New York State and we shared a mild interest in the fortunes of the Buffalo Bills. He wore a short-sleeved taupe shirt, a brown necktie, and brown pants. He smiled, genuinely pleased to see me.

'Jerry, long time, too long,' he said. He grabbed my hand, shook it hard.

'I've been busy. You know how it is.'

'LA's a great town in your line of business,' he said. A banker's quiet joke; a slight wink. 'How's Sondra?'

'Expecting,' I said. I felt cold. I shivered very slightly.

Bo Sonderheim clapped my arm. 'That's terrific, Jerry.'

'We're excited.'

134

'So you should be,' he said. 'Listen, call me when you've got some spare time. We'll get together. You look like you could use a night on the town. You're pale, Jerry, way too pale.'

I said something inane about recovering from flu. He nodded his head in sympathy. 'A bug's going round,' he said.

'There's always a bug going round,' I replied. We smiled, shook hands, I promised I'd call him. It was all very pleasant in a superficial way. I waved, hurried to my car.

I was half-tempted to go back inside the bank and get the goddam envelope. Why leave it in its steel box? Why not give them what they wanted? I thought about the phone call. The guy holding Sondra was good at cruelty, at twisting the knife. The way he'd said *pregnant*, the menacing spin he'd put on the word —

No, *goddam* them. I wasn't going to be pushed around. There was something of Buffalo in me even now — something of the small hard-assed, working-class streets, of the raw neighborhood taverns where men smelled of sweat and iron and smoked cigarettes down to the last possible strand, of a city where winter lasted for five months. Yes, it was still there — I hadn't surrendered that upbringing entirely in this Mickey Mouse State.

5.05 p.m.

I ran a red light on my way to the Pacifica center on La Cienega Boulevard, where LaBrea Records had its offices. I sailed through an intersection illegally, swerving to avoid a truck. I wasn't giving my full attention to what lay ahead; I was more interested in what might be traveling behind. The old Pontiac somewhere at my back, maybe, or a different vehicle occupied by a different pair of guys — either way, I couldn't know. I felt a strange, numb terror. I was moving through a world that had the consistency of molasses.

I reached the Pacifica Center, a smoked glass and weathered brass building fourteen stories high. Navajo symbols had been embossed in brass panels — stylized feathers, eagles, horses. A huge twenty-four-hour video and music store called *Look & Listen* occupied the ground floor. The first floor housed a number of small fashion boutiques that came and went in flurries of bankruptcies. I passed below the unlit neon sign that read *LaBrea* in fashionably illegible script; after dark, it glowed red and purple, hanging halfway up the building as if it were some kind of gaudy electric spider attempting to reach the summit.

I thought of Sondra going inside this tower five, sometimes six, days a week. I thought of her office on the tenth floor, in the marketing department. The posters. The CD covers. The buzz of the music biz. Phones forever ringing. Petulant musicians, trumped-up by sycophantic press items, demanding to know why their albums hadn't hit the *Billboard* Top Fifty. I'd always found these characters dull and inarticulate the few times I'd accompanied Sondra to a LaBrea promo party. They played at being deeply cool; they had no idea they were ineluctably heading towards their own obsolescence, fickle as the public was. Sondra was good with these narcissists and their frail egos.

Had she made it as far as LaBrea before she was abducted? I circled the building, found a parking-slot, idled for a couple of minutes and watched traffic go past. I was looking for the Pontiac, sure, but I was also keeping an eye open for any vehicle that looked . . . what? Suspicious? What the hell would constitute a 'suspicious' vehicle, anyhow? I was traveling up the paranoid escalator. I had to take a chance and move. And if the watchers were watching, I couldn't see them; and even if I could, what would it take to avoid them?

I drove back round the block and into a five-level parking garage, where a sign read: *Free Parking for LaBrea Records Employees and Retail Customers Only.* I inserted a five-dollar bill into the automatic dispenser. A ticket slid out of the slot and I plucked it just as the yellow-black striped barrier rose like an arthritic arm.

Blinking in the sudden dimness of the place, I drove up through the levels slowly. If she'd come this far before vanishing, then maybe her car was here. I drove to the upper level, but saw nothing, no sign of the Lexus. Then I swung my car around and started down again, checking each parking-slot as I drove. A few of the cars were ostentatious — an old pink Caddie convertible, a bug tricked out in retro Dayglo, a white Packard hearse. The vehicles of wannabe rock stars.

On Level 3 I spotted a gray Lexus parked between an old Corvette and a low-slung, two-door MG sports. I'd missed it on the way up. I got out of my car and walked to the Lexus, thinking: *It can't be Sondra's, it's a commonplace car in LA, it could be anyone's.* Then I saw in the rear window the tiny logo of the car supplier, *Marco Motors of Brentwood*, where Sondra had bought the

138

Lexus. So what? A lot of people probably bought their Lexus cars at Marco Motors.

I moved around the front of the vehicle.

A St Christopher medallion, fashioned out of copper, hung from the rearview mirror. I recognized it at once. I'd bought it for her two years ago when we were vacationing in Verona. She'd liked the detail in the face, the benign look. She was superstitious about religious medallions.

I wanted to break the glass and haul the thing from the mirror, hurl it off into the gloom. It hadn't protected Sondra. It hadn't done her any good. The car was unlocked, so I opened the door on the driver's side. The interior light clicked on. I didn't know what I was looking for — evidence of a struggle? Something her abductors had carelessly dropped? How goddam convenient that would be, and about as likely as her having the time to scribble a quick description of her assailants even as they dragged her out of the car. I imagined it that way — people pulling at her, perhaps her arm painfully twisted up behind her back, a hand clamped around her mouth. I could picture her kicking, resisting, as she was hauled off inside a waiting vehicle.

There was a copy of *Billboard* on the passenger seat. A couple of work files. And there, stuck between the seats, her wallet. I picked it up; it was wine-colored leather. It contained her driver's license, employee ID, Social Security card, a photograph of us snapped last year in San Diego, a picture of her parents.

And this, which brought me to the edge, which made me feel I was taking a step out into bottomless dark — a blank square of clear plastic she said she'd keep vacant for a baby. Whenever we had one.

If we had one.

I slumped behind the wheel, lowered my head, dropped the purse to the floor. My throat was dry. The roof of my mouth. My lips.

I opened the door, I slid out. I kicked the door shut. This gray space yielded nothing, and the car was a mute witness. I paced around the Lexus, gazing at the ground, looking for what — clues? The butt of an obscure foreign cigarette — fortuitously dropped — would that establish the identity of one of her assailants? A credit-card receipt that had slipped out of a pocket, a laundry ticket?

In what goddam world of fancy? Not this one. Not where I lived.

I gazed up at the row of pale electric lamps spread at about twenty-feet intervals. I wondered what strength of lighting they used here. Forty watt? Less? The place was pocked with shadow, shadowy corners. Dire. The air smelled of burnt oil. I wanted out of here, back into the sun, the world —

Then I saw it. It hung approximately fifteen feet from the ground, and was fixed to the wall. Barely noticeable, it moved on a short stalk slowly from side to side. The lens scanned me, then moved past. *Yes,* I thought.

I walked until I stood directly under the security camera and I wondered where the videotapes it created were stored. In this building someplace, I guessed — but where?

I parked my car in a vacant slot and walked from the parking-garage through a door that led to an elevator. I was on Level 2. I pressed the *Call* button, and when the car came, I rode down to the ground floor. I entered *Look & Listen,* where I was immediately assaulted by a violent fusillade of noise — videotapes playing on a hundred enormous TV screens, music issuing from scores of speakers. It was babble, it was the future where you were assailed simultaneously from so many directions that your focus was shattered and concentration became an act consigned to history. You could go mad in these vast institutions of pictures and sounds; how did employees survive this attack on their senses? I walked through the store,

141

under MTV clips of a rap group, a German techno-rock band, an old Sid Vicious punk video, tapes of the Marx Brothers in *A Day At The Races*, Bogart in *Casablanca*, James Dean dead drunk in *Giant*.

The store clerks were mainly young women who looked like zombies, glazed and indifferent to the whirl around them. They had dark fingernails and glossy lips and clunky shoes. They didn't approach and ask if you needed assistance. That would have been uncool, if uncool was still a word in use. There was a form of consumer Darwinism at work here — if you couldn't find what you wanted on your own, you were doomed to do without.

A security guard stood at the exit to the street. He looked uncomfortable, conspicuous in his stiff maroon uniform. I made my way towards him between displays of CDs and videotapes. He was in his late forties and had the look of an ex-cop miles off his turf. His face was scarred. One side of his neck had evidence of skin-grafting, a map of puckered flesh. He'd been in a fire, probably pensioned from the force, and he supplemented his pension with private security work.

Guesswork.

He looked at me as if the appearance of

somebody normal was the high-point of his day. Somebody in an ordinary suit, everyday shoes, and a necktie. Hallelujah. I wondered if his dreams were loud and raucous; when he slept, did his mind flash strobe-lights?

'I need some information,' I said. 'I wonder if you can help.'

He had a sweet smile, despite the scar that ran under his eye. He wore a badge with the words *George Rocco, Gardall Security*. 'Go ahead,' he said.

I mentioned the security cameras in the parking-garage. I asked if he knew where the tapes were kept, and how I could gain access to them. I tried to restrain any desperation in my voice, but George Rocco must have detected something, because his smile evaporated and the light in his eye went out.

'The control room is the place you're looking for,' he said. 'It's on the fourteenth floor. But it's not exactly a place where you can just go and poke around, know what I mean? You need a real good reason for going up there. You got one?'

I took out my wallet and handed him my card, and while I tried to think up an excuse — something to do with a kleptomaniac patient who specialized in stealing from parked cars — George Rocco said, 'Hey, I *know* you! I know your name!'

I waited for him to say he'd read it in connection with a certain aging actress who'd tried to commit cocaine suicide, and who'd come to me as a patient when she'd failed. The matter had generated publicity — which was what the actress had wanted all along — and invariably my name was mentioned as her therapist. It wasn't the kind of attention I sought. Still, the exposure helped the actress, who went on to land a few choice roles. And, for myself, it brought me a couple of Hollywood neurotics whose basic problem lay in the fact that they had more money than they knew what to do with; they suffered more from economic ennui than any existential malaise.

'You helped *Bobby Stone*,' he said.

'You know Bobby?'

'Hey, Bobby was my partner in the LAPD, man,' George Rocco said, seizing my hand, shaking it with such vigor I thought he'd block the flow of blood in my veins. 'We were together the night it all went to hell. You turned him around, I got to hand it to you, doc. You turned him around real good.'

'Small world,' I said. And so it was: if you worked in the LAPD, you were part of a big fraternity, whether you'd been pensioned off or not.

Bobby Stone. I hadn't thought about

144

Bobby in a while. He and his partner — Rocco — had been working a stakeout on an abandoned house in East LA in the summer of 1993. They'd been doing it for days, and they were both fatigued. And maybe they grew careless in their weariness, or they were bored by numbing inactivity — whatever, they decided to enter the house. It was an elaborate trap. The Colombian dealers had been inside all along, waiting. In the gun battle that followed, George Rocco was shot in his left lung, Bobby Stone once in the thigh, a second time in the stomach. The dealers didn't finish them off. They devised an alternative plan of greater cruelty.

They tied George and Bobby together, doused them in gasoline, and then set fire to the house which, bone-dry in that hot, arid summer, had blazed immediately. The intervention of the fire department had saved both men, but not before they'd sustained serious burns.

Rocco apparently bounced back to health, but Bobby Stone had been sent to me by the LAPD. He was frightened of sleep, beset by nightmares of flame and falling rafters, dreams that scalded and smothered him. He was also terrified of daylight and spaces. He'd tried suicide twice and failed narrowly both times; his wife and daughter had gone.

145

Bobby was a mess, a hard road to travel. Slowly, we'd worked at his fears; we glued him together with therapy and hypnosis, chemicals and patience. He'd returned to the LAPD where he was given a desk job. He didn't dream of flames any more, and I was proud of how the therapy had succeeded. But it would have failed if Bobby had lost the will to live. It was one of those rare times when cooperation between therapist and patient had been seamless; difficult, certainly, and time-consuming, but both Bobby and myself wanted the same thing, his restoration.

I looked at George Rocco, who'd clearly decided he was going to be helpful. He felt an obligation to me. 'I'll take you up to the control room if you like,' he said, and he clapped my back, as if I was a star he just wanted to touch in the hope that some stardust might rub off.

A chance meeting with somebody happy to be helpful, no favors required. All breaks were usually chance affairs, and this was the first break I'd had since Sondra's abduction.

I followed Rocco back to the elevators. He was saying how he didn't see much of Bobby any more, they'd gone their separate ways. I wasn't really paying attention. I was anticipating the recording, I was already seeing it in my head. And when we stepped inside the cab and rode upward to the fourteenth floor, Rocco's voice had become a background drone.

We walked along the corridor, past the accounting and personnel offices of LaBrea Records. Throughout the building, the latest LaBrea releases played all day long on a looped tape: it was background fuzz.

We turned left at the end of the corridor.

Ahead was a room with a small, reinforced window and a gray door. The word *Private* was stenciled on wood. Rocco took a key from his pocket and opened the door. He beckoned for me to follow him. I stepped inside the room, which was long and narrow and smelled of cigar smoke.

'Hey, McGloan,' Rocco said. 'This is Doc Lomax.'

McGloan, a tall, angular man in a maroon Gardall uniform, looked up at me from his desk. He'd been reading a paperback novel. I noticed the title. It was one of those forensic thrillers filled with dug-up corpses and hanks of hair and maggots tunneling through rotted flesh. He had a dead cigar between his lips.

He said, 'Zup?'

George Rocco said, 'The doc wants to see a tape.'

McGloan waved a hand at the bank of monitors. They had scraps of paper stuck to them. Each scrap had writing on it. I looked closer. *Level 1. Level 2.* Ten monitors total, two to each level. 'Against company rules,' he said. 'You know that, George.'

'Doc's a friend of mine, McGloan.'

'Don't matter if he's the Queen of the Silver Dollar, bubba. Company policy is company policeeee.'

'Come on, McGloan. The doc's a good guy.'

'I'll pay,' I said. 'I don't mind.'

Rocco said, 'You don't need to pay.'

'The man says he wants to pay to scope out some cars coming and going, Rocco. It's his money.' McGloan looked at me. 'A hundred bucks gets you a look at what you want.'

Rocco said it was an insult to me. I told him it didn't matter. It was a transaction, capitalism, that was all. Everything had a price. I took two fifties from my wallet and gave them to McGloan.

'OK,' he said. 'What do you want to look at?'

'Pictures from Level 3.'

'Which camera? East or west?'

East or west. I didn't know.

McGloan looked irritated. 'East is on the right when you come in. West is left.'

'Then I want east.'

'Any special time?'

How was I supposed to know? I'd have to guess. 'Between nine-thirty and ten this morning,' I said.

McGloan moved to a shelf where video-tapes were stored. He ran a finger over them, then removed one. It was labeled with the day's date, with the time-frame scrawled on in green Biro: *8 a.m. — Noon.*

'We make four-hour tapes here. We only store them for a day, then we record right over them until they're fucking useless,' he said. 'I'll put this in the VCR for you.'

'I want privacy,' I said.

'Ah, a private viewing,' McGloan said. 'That's different.'

'That's against company policy too, I guess,' I said. I gave him another fifty and he folded it in his breast pocket.

'This is goddam extortion,' Rocco said.

McGloan slipped the tape into a VCR unit and gave me a remote-control. 'Use fast-forward,' he said. 'Don't waste your time. I used to look at the monitors when I first started this job. I was fascinated. I used to imagine I'd see something, like, *real weird* down there. But nothing ever happens. Now I read books. I gulp down them forensic detective yarns. Larva literature.'

He stepped out of the room. Rocco looked

at me and shrugged. 'Sorry about McGloan,' he said.

I said it wasn't important. I was impatient for him to go. I pressed the *On* button just as he left the room and closed the door. I looked at the monitor. Black-and-white pictures, poor quality, grainy, too much shadow, some slippage. Cars came in, parked, people got out, walked out of shot. More cars, more people, everything moving through the gray light; it was as if I was seeing the world in an aquarium whose dank water had never been changed. Cars and people. Periods of lull. Just the angle of perception changing slightly as the camera moved. I picked up the remote and fast-forwarded. An old silent movie.

I stopped the tape. Backed it up.

I saw the Lexus emerge into view. I saw it slide into a parking-slot. Irritatingly, the camera panned away from the car, and when it tracked back Sondra was already stepping out of the Lexus. I felt a strange shock seeing her. I felt that I was spying on her, but more than that: it was as if I were looking — not into the past — but into some dread future, where the only animated record of her life would be these images trapped on gritty videotape. I wanted to tell her to get back in the car — *Turn round, Sondra, drive away now, just get the fuck out of there* — and I raised my hand to the screen to touch her, warn her.

And then a white van moved into the shot, backing up towards her as she stood by the open door of the Lexus. She made a move to reach inside the car, presumably because she'd forgotten to gather up her purse and the files on the passenger seat, but she was distracted when the rear doors of the van opened and two men dressed in white overalls clambered out.

They wore dark stocking masks.

She turned to look. She seemed surprised, uncertain, snapped out of her own preoccupations by the sudden appearance of the men. Maybe she was immune to sights like this — masked men in parking-garages, gun-fights on sidewalks; a child of LA, she was accustomed to movies being shot around town. She was blasé. And maybe she half-expected to see a camera wheel into view, and a director shout 'Action!' Maybe she thought it was one of those *Candid Camera* kind of TV shows.

Whatever, it was clear she didn't feel any danger at first, because she didn't run. And when she did feel it, it was too late.

The men approached her in a quick, flanking action. She finally stepped back from them. She held a hand forward, palm facing out. *Don't come any closer*, that was what the gesture said. *Stay away from me.* The smaller of the two guys lunged at her and she eluded him, ducking under his outstretched arm. But she lost her balance, and went down on one knee. I watched her try to rise again, but the men had already pinned her arms back. One of them caught her hair in his fist and yanked her head back. I watched her mouth open in pain, and I wanted to shut off the videotape, I couldn't absorb her look of hurt and fear. But I continued to watch in a state of paralysis as her assailants dragged her across the floor to the van, forced her to her feet, thrust her inside the vehicle, and slammed the doors. And then they were gone.

I didn't move for a minute. I thought of how she'd opened her mouth in pain, and I was glad that the poor quality of the picture prevented me from seeing the expression in her eyes. I pressed the *Rewind* button and ran the tape back to the point where Sondra's abductors shut the doors of the van.

I pushed the *Stop* button and looked at the vehicle until my head ached. I couldn't make out the number on the licence-plate, which was caked with mud. I pressed *Eject* and the videotape slid out. As I stuck it in my pocket, I thought: *I deserve this. I paid enough for it.*

I left the room and walked back the way I'd come.

I saw no sign of either Rocco or McGloan. I rode the elevator down to Level 2. I went into the parking-garage and got inside my car. A shadow fell across me.

5.28 p.m.

My passenger door was yanked open and I saw the guy with the turquoise bracelet smiling at me. Immediately, the driver's door was hauled open with such force I thought the hinges would snap, and the big-skulled guy grabbed me by my shoulders and dragged me out of the car. I fell sideways, and Big Skull kicked me in the chest. I rolled over on my side, trying to deflect the full force of the blow from my ribs, but it hurt like a cattle-prod, anyway. As I tried to get up, the fair-haired man grabbed my neck and hauled my face back, allowing his companion to take a free shot at me — a clubbed fist straight to the side of my head, at that fragile junction where hair met ear. I felt like a wire that had fused into meltdown, dizzy, disoriented, brain scrambled by shock therapy. Deafened, I half-rose, sinking my teeth into the upper thigh of the guy who'd punched me. He roared — 'Fuckensonfabitch!' — and cuffed me hard on the back of my head. I lolled forward and the light in the parking garage turned a strange color, like steak blackened on a barbecue. I lay quiet, trying to gather up the threads of myself, as the two guys walked round me. I thought: *I could fight back, if only I could get up, if only I could reassemble myself. I could take them one on one, if I had my senses together. If I was nineteen, and this was Buffalo.*

'Fucker bit me,' the one with the skull said.

'He's one brave dude,' the fair-haired guy said. 'Aincha, doc? Aincha one brave big dude?'

My mouth felt numb. I stared up at the ceiling. I wondered if this scene was being recorded by a security camera. Big Skull frisked me, found the videotape, and said, 'He's a downright nosy bastard. Goes around poking into stuff where he don't belong.' He stuffed the tape in the pocket of his brown cotton jacket.

'And I warned him,' his associate said. 'You can't say I didn't warn him. You heard me, doc. Right?'

'You warned me,' I agreed, and my voice was coming out all wrong.

I coughed and my ribs hurt. I labored not to show it, but I must have grimaced because the fair-haired man said, 'I don't think he looks too good.'

Big Skull said, 'I seen better.'

'Maybe some internal bleeding. What do you think, doc? Feel like that to you?'

'Your concern touches me,' I said.

'Hey, we're human beings,' said the fair-haired one.

'No man's a fucking island,' said Big Skull.

The fair-haired man stuck a hand in the pocket of his jeans. He said, 'You're a bigtime disappointment to us. You didn't produce what The Man asked for, did you? You let him down badly. And then you turn to this . . . this *snooping*. You are one tricky customer, man. What are we supposed to do with you, huh?'

I maneuvered myself into a sitting position. It was disconcerting to see the two men loom over me; their faces seemed strangely elongated from my point of view. I wanted nothing more than to get to my feet and meet them on eye-level, but I couldn't face the embarrassment of trying to rise and having to grab their hands or arms for support. At the same time, I couldn't just sit where I was, so I made an almighty effort to get up; my gestures resembled those of the Frankenstein creation taking his first steps. I was almost at full height when Big Skull kicked my legs away from me and I slid back to the ground. I rattled my head against the concrete floor, which smelled of years of exhaust fumes and rubber.

I felt sick, my mouth flooded with saliva.

The fair-haired guy bent down and said, 'Doc, The Man has power. He has life in one hand, death in the other. It's neat how he balances them. It's up to you to decide. You have merchandise he needs. I don't know what it is, and I don't give a good goddam, all I know is he wants it. So . . . hey-ho, I hate to do this, friend . . . ' and he brought from his pocket his hand fitted with the brass knuckles. As he raised one arm up to strike me, and even as the arm began to fall, I could anticipate the crack of brass against forehead or cheek-bone or teeth. The advance party of impending pain, hard-ridden horses kicking up dust on the horizon, hoofbeats.

I raised a hand to divert the blow if I could.

'Hey-hey, what is *this*?'

The brass froze in descent. The fair-haired man turned his face in the direction of the voice, and Big Skull fumbled for something hidden in the flap of his jacket. I raised my head just enough to see George Rocco coming running towards us. He was taking his pistol out of its holster.

'What are these fucks doing to you, doc?' Rocco shouted, as he ran to where I lay. He fired his pistol into the air, a warning shot, and he kept coming.

The man with the big skull had a gun in his fist, some kind of automatic, and he fired it a couple of times at Rocco, whose uniform appeared to explode. I thought: *Hollywood — chicken blood in plastic bags strapped to tiny detonators hidden under the uniform, somebody will shout 'Cut!'* I was thinking the way my wife might have done. As George Rocco took a few steps back, I was still waiting for the director's voice.

This is how we deal with reality we can't face: we place it inside another frame of reference that is only tangentially connected to the world we inhabit. Or maybe not connected at all. George Rocco was still alive. Even as he lay there with his blood oozing out of him, his life flying away, there was a place in which he was still alive.

I'd lost it.

I was thinking lunatic thoughts. I was stunned. How casually George Rocco had been shot. Like he was a nothing, a sub-human, worthless. An inert target.

The gunman stuck his weapon back inside his jacket. He looked at the fair-haired guy, shrugged and said, 'It was him or it was me.'

'It sure was.' The guy's bracelet rattled. It reflected dull light.

'Let's blow this place,' Big Skull said.

'And the doc?'

'The doc can get in his car and just drive the hell away. He didn't see anything, anyhow. There was nothing to see. Right? Right, doc?'

I gazed at him, didn't speak. Couldn't.

'What about the security camera?' the fair-haired guy asked.

Big Skull said, 'We'll just go locate the fucking tape. Whatever it takes.' He stared at me. 'Hey you, doc. Move it. Drive. Now. Let me hear you burn a little rubber. Nothing happened here. Remember that.'

I watched the two men hurry away. I thought of McGloan bent over a paperback tale of old corpses and pathologists, the detectives of death; in a couple of minutes his door would be kicked down and his novel would drop out of his hands. And then —

I didn't want to project. I hauled myself towards my car, dragged myself up, got in behind the wheel, turned the key in the ignition. I glanced at George Rocco. I thought of stopping, I wanted to stop — but I couldn't help him. No mouth-to-mouth was going to bring him back, no crazy rush through the city in the back of an ambulance, his body hooked up to tubes — he was beyond all that.

5.52 p.m.

In the lobby of my building, I asked Grogue: 'You still have a key to my office, John?'

'Always do, doc,' he said. He surveyed me; he must have noticed the oil-stains on my suit, observed the awkward way I was holding myself. But he said nothing. My ribcage ached as if the bones were held together by wire. I felt like a prehistoric skeleton, reconstructed for a natural history display. I couldn't get rid of George Rocco's image. When I closed my eyes, I could still see him. He was dead and it was my fault for asking questions. If I hadn't spoken to him, he'd still be alive.

If I'd just handed over the goddam envelope from the safe-deposit box. But I hadn't. And why not? Was it some underlying macho turbine that drove me? Some skewed sense of ethics that lingered still? I remembered the voice on the telephone. *You still feel a responsibility towards her. Dare I say a fondness, even?* Was that what it came down to finally — that I cared, in my own fashion, in a manner that wasn't absolutely professional, for Emily Ford?

'Mind if see it?' I asked.

'No problem.' Grogue unlocked a drawer in his desk with a silver key attached to a chain of keys, and took out a small envelope marked *Dr Lomax*. The key to my office suite was inside. He showed it to me, a little grudgingly.

'Have you ever mislaid this key, John?'

Grogue looked at me as if the idea of him losing a key indicated a suspension of natural law. 'Never.'

'So there's no chance somebody could have taken it and made a copy?'

Grogue laughed, a kind of rattling sound, pebbles loose in his throat. 'They'd need the key to my drawer first. And that never leaves this chain.' He flashed his chain of keys. I looked at his uniform. Dark blue serge, the Sunset Beach Holdings logo — a gaudy orange half-sun sinking behind a bed of blue — stitched to the breast pocket. Sunset Beach Holdings owned a dozen office complexes in the city.

I leaned over, glanced at Grogue's drawer. It was filled with keys, paperclips, Bandaids, postage stamps, rubber bands. The lock looked flimsy; anyone with some expertise might open it in twenty seconds with a metal pick.

'What's all this about, anyhow?' Grogue asked.

I came up with an excuse that struck me as feeble. 'I'm thinking of raising the insurance on my office and its contents, John. You know how it goes. The insurance company will send a guy out to check the existing security. I was curious, that's all.'

Grogue looked halfway convinced. 'No Tom, Dick or Harry comes here and walks straight past my desk to the elevators without stating his express purpose to me. That's what I call security, doc.'

I told him he was doing a good job and thanked him. I heard him slam his desk drawer shut as I walked to the elevator. I stepped inside the car and rode up to the seventh floor. Jane was at her desk when I entered my suite. She looked at me in a grave way. She was too polite to ask, but I could hear her questions, anyway: *What's going on, Jerry? Why do you look like something the dog dragged in?*

I asked if there had been any messages. Harry Pushkas had called a couple of times.

'Where do you keep your office key, Jane?'

'It's in my purse,' she said.

'And it's never out of sight?'

'Most women don't stray very far from

their purses, Jerry. You should know that. It's a security thing.'

'When you go home at night, the key stays in the purse?' I was sinking into a morass of keys and possible duplicates and locks.

'Correct,' Jane said. 'And the purse sits on the bedside table.'

'Has anybody ever broken into your home?'

'No,' she said, and she looked at me. 'Jerry, what's going on here?'

I wasn't sure how much to tell her. I skipped over her question and asked one of my own. 'Has anybody ever threatened you in any way?'

'*Threatened* me? I'm not sure I follow.'

'Has anyone ever said they'd hurt you if you didn't do them a certain favor?'

'I don't know where this is going,' she said. 'Nobody's threatened me. Besides, I can look after myself. I carry a pistol everywhere I go. At night I keep it beside the bed.'

A pistol? I was surprised. I couldn't imagine Jane having a gun. But there was an ocean of guns in this land. Guns were part of our culture, our birthright. They were the major icon of our democracy. Why shouldn't Jane have a pistol? A woman who lived alone needed a handgun in a climate of violence.

'It's a Jennings J-25, six-shot magazine,' she said. 'I go target-shooting a couple of nights

163

a week. I've also developed a social life with other gun-owners. You'd be surprised. They're nice people. They're not all rednecks.'

I speculated on how little I really knew about Jane, what she did when she left work, how she lived her life. I knew she had an apartment in one of the canyons, and that was all. Now I had to start filling in blanks, and imagine a life that included target-practice and — what? Line-dancing? Barbecues with fellow shooters? Did they discuss the relative merits of Heckler & Kochs and Glocks, or how much they approved of Emily Ford's position on gun laws and law enforcement? I was brain-dead when it came to pistols. I couldn't work up an interest in them.

I heard the echo of the automatic in the parking-garage, remembered how George Rocco had expelled air as he dropped to the ground. I loathed guns, that whole killing culture.

'Speak to me, Jerry,' she said.

'OK. A file's missing from my office.'

'Are you sure it hasn't just been mislaid?'

'I'm sure. It was in my floor-safe, now it's not.'

'You sure you didn't take it home with you?'

I said I hadn't.

'You think it's been stolen?'

I shrugged, then I went inside my own office and shut the door behind me before Jane had time to ask me if I'd thought about calling the cops. I walked around the edges of the rug, trying to imagine an intruder here. Somebody rolling the rug back. Opening the safe. Plucking out Emily Ford's records. Walking away. Easy as that. I tried to put a face to this thief. One of my patients? I scanned their faces in my mind. It was absurd. How could I imagine Joe Allardyce in a clandestine role? Or Teddy Newberg, a schizophrenic scriptwriter, or Callie Wronk, an angelic twenty-year old obsessive-compulsive from Venice Beach, or any of the others who came to me for therapy — how could I ascribe this theft to any of them? And yet —

I looked at Sondra's photograph on my desk, taken two years ago. She was smiling into the camera. She was carefree and lovely and the world was filled with promise. I felt a stab of bitterness, anger. Why hadn't I built an elaborate high-tech security fence around our whole life? Something capable of charbroiling anyone who tried to intrude? We'd have been secure behind it, Sondra and I. We'd have stayed home in our sealed enclave and made love behind steel shutters that snapped shut at the slightest sound. And life, cocooned, protected by electronic sensors, would have gone on. I was suddenly weary, enervated — what was I doing, playing detective, asking questions about locks and goddam keys and wondering who to trust? I was a trained psychiatrist, for God's sake. I was living in a world I hadn't chosen for myself. But I'd been forced into it, hammered like a nail into a plank of hard wood.

I fingered my ribs lightly, then I went inside the bathroom and put my head under the cold-water faucet. I took a towel and dabbed at the soiled spots on my jacket and pants. Then I ran a comb through my hair.

Presentable. Up to a point.

I needed to move. Forget the goddam keys. Forget who had one and who didn't, and whose might have been stolen and copied. I thought of the list I'd given Emily Ford. I imagined her going through the names, feeding each into the brain of the computer, links and connections and buzzing in cyberspace . . . But how did I know she was *really* doing that? How did I know she didn't want the list for some other inscrutable purpose? What if she somehow contrived to get her records back and didn't tell me?

I needed to know what Emily Ford had

discovered, if her wonderful computer had spat out anything that might bring me nearer to Sondra.

Problem: how did I contact Emily if I'd been forbidden by people who thought nothing of murder? While I was thinking my way around that, I called Kit Webb at the hospital. I asked him about Consuela.

'She'll be fine,' Kit said. 'Gastric lavage to the rescue. She's pretty dopey right now, but she'll be *compos mentis* in a couple of hours. You going to give me some details of her OD?'

'Later,' I said. 'I owe you, Kit.'

'I'll think of something.'

'Has she said anything about what happened?'

'She's not saying much of anything, Jerry. If she speaks, it's mainly mumble.'

I put the phone down, picked it up again, dialed Emily Ford's office. An assistant informed me she'd gone home. I knew where she lived: if I wanted to see her, I'd go to her house near Sunset. The trick was to make sure I wouldn't be followed there. I stood by the telephone and wondered about this for a moment — how could I make myself invisible? How could I avoid detection?

I stepped into the reception room.

Jane looked at me, but didn't ask anything.

'My car's busted,' I said.

'Don't tell me,' she said. 'You need mine?'

'Does that cause you a problem?'

'Not really.'

'Take money out of petty cash for a cab home,' I said.

She opened the middle drawer of her desk and removed a carkey attached to a bright red Goofy keyring. I thanked her, told her I'd call her later at home to make an arrangement for returning the car, then went down to the lobby. I could have traded her my BMW for her car, but there was a chance she'd be mistakenly followed if she was driving my vehicle, and I didn't want her dragged into this. I didn't want to think of her and George Rocco sharing a common destiny.

I stepped into the elevator. On the way down, I had a moment of dizziness, tidal drift, as my ribs flared with pain. By the time I reached the lobby it had passed.

As I walked out of the elevator, I saw Harry Pushkas coming towards me. He had his arms extended in a friendly way, and when I got within touching distance he hugged me. His breath smelled of cognac. His black hair, which he dyed, stood up from his scalp as if he'd received an electric shock.

Harry stepped back and looked at me. 'You tell your secretary to cancel lunch with me?

You can't tell me yourself, hot-shot? This I find an insult. Old friends cancel their own lunch dates.'

'I'm sorry, Harry. Something came up.'

'Something came up? What? You had a fight with your dry-cleaner?' *Some-zing.* He fingered the lapels of my jacket, like a concerned father assessing his son's clothing. He shook his head. 'You got a stain here, another here.'

'Harry, I'm pushed for time. Maybe we can get together later.'

'What's going on, Jerry? You don't have a moment for your old professor, your friend and your former tormentor? May I remind you that without me — ach, where and what would you be? A GP in Bakersville? Bandaids for little boys? Flu shots and nosebleeds?'

'Probably,' I said. When Harry drank brandy, he liked to take credit for whatever success I'd achieved. Usually I didn't mind. But today was different.

'You look half-dead,' he said, and punched me lightly on the shoulder. 'What's the trouble? Are you ill?'

'Later, Harry. I'll call you when I have a minute, I promise.'

'What? I should sit by the phone and wait?'

'That's not what I'm saying.'

'Now I'm deaf. I'm not hearing things

properly.' He placed his hands on my shoulders and gazed into my eyes. 'I'm worried with you.'

'*About* me.'

'Whatever. Stupid sonovabitch prepositions. I never mastered them, all the years I been here.'

I had the urge to tell him about the sudden fissures in my life. I wanted to put my arms around him and hold him as if he were the only reality in the world; an anchor, a safe harbor.

'You need to slow down and smell the brandy.' He nudged me with his elbow and winked. His mouth opened in a sly expression. I noticed he'd lost one of his bottom teeth since I'd last seen him. 'Promise me for later, OK?'

'I promise you,' I said. 'We'll open a fresh bottle and we'll get sloshed.'

'I like sloshed. Sloshed sets the mind free. I'll hold you to that promise,' he said. 'I go home now, and you call me.'

We embraced again.

'I need to piss,' he said.

'Over there. The men's room.' I pointed across the lobby.

'Old men need to piss all the goddam time, Jerry. The bladder becomes like a colander.'

I watched him walk slowly away from me. I

couldn't let him go like this, I couldn't leave him without a word of explanation, even if I couldn't tell him the whole truth; if he knew too much, he might be endangered. I followed him into the men's room. He stood with his back to me, unzipping his fly.

'OK,' he said. 'Whatever's on your mind, get rid of it. You'll feel better.'

I didn't know what to tell him, how much to leave out. He urinated, walked to the sink, soaped his hands and ran them under the faucet. A tuft of his shirt protruded through his zipper.

He glanced at himself in the mirror. 'I look at my face for some sign of recognition, Jerry. Who is this old geezer I see every day in the mirror? What has become of the bold young man who treated all the bourgeois neurotic families of Budapest? Gone, gone, gone.' He looked at me. 'So, speak.'

So, speak. I remembered my student days. I remembered Harry's lectures. When a student had a question and raised a hand, Harry always said the same thing. 'So, speak.'

I saw a certain loneliness in his face, a quality that had become the condition of his life since his retirement, and the death of his wife Hattie, whom he'd met during the Hungarian uprising in 1956. They'd been devoted to each other for more than forty years of squabbling and making up. Some-times they'd seemed to me like a double act throwing pies in each other's faces. Three years ago Hattie had died of a heart attack, and Harry had never really recovered. It struck me that I was perhaps the human being closest to him since Hattie had gone.

'It's an ethical matter,' I said.

'Ethical? Ah. How serious you sound. Tell me more.'

'I may have to provide a list of my patients to a certain party.'

'A certain party? Do you mean the law? Is that what you mean by this coy expression? The police want your patient list?'

I didn't answer his question about the police.

'You have made a decision already?' he asked.

'I think so.'

'And now you have the armed peasants of conscience swarming your castle, is that so?'

'Yes.'

'With musket and cannon-fire,' he said. 'And what is it you wish? Advice from me?'

'Maybe. Maybe I just wanted to run it past you.'

'How can I advise you if I don't know the details, the circumstances? You believe there is some general principle involved here?' He stared at me hard. 'OK. You asked. I will answer. Nothing, absolutely *nothing*, would make me give up my clients and the details of their sicknesses and treatment.'

'If it was a matter of life and death, Harry?'

'Pah' — he waved a hand vigorously. 'A man or woman comes to you and asks you to explore the sickness in their soul. They confide in you. They lay their heart open for you. And you probe, you explore, you go gently. You make them better if you can. The last thing you do is betray this man or woman.'

'If you could have saved Hattie's life, if somebody had said to you that he'd spare your wife's life in return for the secrets of your patients — would you have let Hattie die?'

'That is the worst question I have ever been asked.' He looked crushed, as if his face were a creased old flower that had just been flattened. 'How do you expect me to answer it? It's hypothetical. It's unreal. Hattie is dead. I cannot travel back down time to make bargains with the devil. You don't make sense, Jerry.' He stepped closer to me and laid a hand on my arm. 'Is this about your wife? Is this something to do with Sondra?'

'Perhaps,' I said.

'She's in danger, is that it?'

'I can't tell you any more, Harry.' I turned away from him. 'I'll call you later. I promise.'

'Wait,' he said.

'I can't wait,' I said.

'Let us discuss some more, Jerry.'

'I don't know what else there is to discuss,' I said.

'Then why waste an old man's time asking advice?'

I stepped out of the men's room into the lobby. Harry came after me. 'We should talk some more,' he said. 'We've barely scratched the surface.'

I looked back at him. He had his hands held out towards me in an imploring gesture. 'Do the right thing,' he said.

6.10 p.m.

I left the building by the back door. I knew Jane parked her bottle-green Honda in the same place every day. I hesitated before I moved towards it, scanning the lot, looking for a sign of the Pontiac, but I didn't see it. I walked quickly to the Honda, unlocked it, and drove into the traffic on Wilshire. Harry's words echoed in my head: *Nothing, absolutely nothing, would make me give up my clients and the details of their sicknesses and treatment.*

I thought: *It's less complicated for you, Harry, it's an abstraction, a philosophical game.* But I was dealing with flesh and blood. My wife was alive. The child inside her was a living thing.

I took out my cellphone, intending to call Emily Ford to tell her I was on my way. I raised the instrument to my ear, but before I had time to punch in the number, the phone rang.

It was Sondra. I fumbled the handset in surprise, and it slid into my lap. I picked it up and spoke her name, hoping that in the few seconds it took me to recover the phone she hadn't been disconnected. She was still there.

'Hi, Jerry, talk to me, tell me stuff.' Her voice was distant and strange, a dreamer's voice. I remembered how she'd spoken in a similar way, twelve hours ago when she'd been asleep: twelve hours, a lifetime. 'My love,' she'd said in her sleep. *My love.*

'Where are you? Are you free to speak?' It was a dumb question, born out of hope. Her captors wouldn't allow her unsupervised access to a phone.

'Jerry, Jerry,' she said. 'I feel so damn good.'

'*Good?* What is there to feel good about? I don't understand — '

'I'm just floating, Jerry. I'm totally mellow. Mellow yellow. Wasn't that an old song? How do the lyrics go, Jerry? Do you remember? It was way before my time.'

Floating. Mellow. The draggy tone of voice. Somebody had given her drugs. Downers, I wasn't sure what. And her abductors had allowed her this call as part of their strategy. *Turn up the heat under Lomax, fill his head with more and more static, cram his mind until there's nothing but a universe of white noise. Let him hear his wife's drugged-out voice.*

'Concentrate,' I told her. 'Give me a little hint. A clue. Anything that'll help me find you. Try. For me. Try.'

She was singing that dumb old song in a husky voice. I wanted to reach down through the mysterious avenue of power that connected us, through the invisible signals that bounced around in the ether, and grab her by the hand and drag her back to me. I felt as if she was lost in space. She was circling the planet, only I couldn't see her.

And then she was quiet.

'Sondra? *Sondra?* Are you still there?'

'Yeah, I'm here, Jer. I'm here.'

'And where is here? Tell me, Sondra.'

'We'll sing lullabies, Jerry. We'll sing 'Hush Little Baby.' ' That little-girl voice: it was breaking my heart.

'And we'll take the baby to the ocean. Oh-oh. Here comes the man and he wants my arm and — '

I thought I heard a man say, 'Come to Daddy for goodies, sweetie.' It sounded like that.

And then the line was killed and she was gone again. Her captors were playing games with her, a little pain, a little pleasure. I clenched the hand holding the phone. I saw my knuckles change to the color of bone, as if the flesh were peeling back, layer by layer. I stared through the traffic. *Here comes the man and he wants my arm.* I imagined a needle sliding into a vein, her flesh

177

punctured. 'Talk to me, Sondra.' I spoke into the phone, although I knew there was nobody at the other end of the line. I uttered the same sentence again. 'Talk to me.' I shut off the phone: madness lay that way.

I stopped at a red light. A middle-aged woman with heavy makeup and dyed blond hair walked in front of my car. She looked at me. What did she see? Some pathetic bastard talking to himself? Just another LA breakdown? It seemed that the gods that had pampered me for years, that had supported and advanced my career and brought me here from drab old Buffalo, had abdicated the heavens. The skies were empty and I was alone. I'd had my share of good fortune. Now it was over. I'd been ostracized by the gods, just as Joe Allardyce had been exiled from Hollywood.

What fucking sin or crime had I committed?

Maybe it was all random. You had good luck sometimes. Then you had bad. And there was no rationale, no logic. The driving force that shaped our lives was Whim.

The phone rang again.

I answered, expecting Sondra.

But it wasn't her.

'This is what comes of trying to con me, Lomax,' he said.

I loathed the self-assurance in that voice. The smugness. The murderous weight of his authority. 'What are you doing to her? What kind of dope are you giving her?'

'That's beside the point. The only important thing for you to keep in mind is what I want from you. I'm tired of reminding you, Lomax. Weary, weary to the bone.'

I pictured again a needle going into a vein, and I wondered what drug they were using on Sondra. Maybe it was one of the benzodiazepines, or Thorazine, possibly even heroin — and then the idea of an overdose ran through my mind. I could see Sondra, stretched out and pale, in a morgue; her eyes were shut and a man in a white coat was exploring her flesh for puncture marks.

'She's pregnant, for God's sake,' I said.

'I know, I know. Congratulations.'

'Please don't shovel any more dope into her system,' I said. 'That's all I ask.'

'Coochy-coo,' he said, his voice flat and bored.

'Jesus Christ, you can't keep pumping dope into her — '

He ignored me. 'You're obviously having some difficulty in bringing me what I need. I wonder about this. Does the good psychiatrist think he can buy a little time and use it to save his wife? Is he a brave man? Does he want to fight? Does he want to outsmart me? Is he just plain goddam stubborn? Or does he perhaps worry needlessly about giving away his patient's secrets? Or could it be some other reason I haven't yet fathomed? Whatever. I reached a conclusion, Lomax. You know what it is?'

'Tell me,' I said.

'This is the thing: I don't give a *damn* about your reasons. They don't interest me. I just don't *care*. I'm single-minded, I'm highly motivated, I'm a missile zoning in on its target, and your wife is an innocent bystander. If she gets in the way of the missile, too bad. It's now six-fifteen, Lomax.'

I looked at my watch.

'I'm going to give you a gift. I'm going to give you a little time to produce. Let's say you have until nine o'clock . . . no, wait, make that ten, which is about three hours and forty-five minutes away. That's getting on for four hours, which ought to be more than enough time for you to sort out whatever delicate problems you're having concerning the material I need. In fact, even if I say so myself, I think that's a truly *generous* wad of time. I'm an understanding guy when you get to know me. But remember this. I don't want any half-assed documents. I don't want any undergraduate nonsense. I don't want an introduction to psychoanalysis for dummies. I want the prime cut. The genuine article . . . I used the word 'soul' before, didn't I?'

'Yes, you did,' I said.

'Then deliver that soul unto me at the appointed hour,' he said. 'I want it for my collection.'

'What happens if . . . ' I let the question fade.

He jumped on it. 'What happens if you don't or won't or can't deliver? Oh, bad stuff, Lomax. Stuff you don't want to hear about. Obviously, I'd prefer if you produced the material within the next ten minutes or so, and then we'd put all this unpleasantness behind us quickly — but I'm being munificent, Lomax. After all, I hold the better cards. I'm also being patient. You should be thankful.'

'Jesus, you're all heart,' I said. 'Like your two murderous hired hands, you're a walking charity.'

'Every now and then there's a little tone creeps into your voice I don't think I like,' he said. 'It's smartass. It's sarcastic. You deliver sentences from the side of your mouth like tired old vaudeville gags. Play the game the way I drew up the rules, Lomax. Don't cheapen yourself with unworthy comments. I like refined people.'

'Such as yourself?' I suggested.

'There's that tone again,' he said. I heard him sigh.

'Who are you working for?' I asked. 'Or are you self-employed?'

'These are *verboten* areas. You should know better.'

'You want power over Emily. Maybe you want to ruin her. OK. But where are you coming from? A political angle? A criminal one? Or are you a middle-man who just wants information so that he can sell it to the highest bidder?'

'Are you trying to rattle me, Lomax? I prefer self-control at all times.'

'You hate chaos,' I said.

'I hate chaos, yes,' he said.

'You're a law-and-order sort,' I said.

'Who or what I am isn't your concern, Lomax.'

I kept pressing, thinking I might force him to reveal something inadvertently. Or maybe I just wanted to irk him. 'You like hiding away from me, don't you? You couldn't stand the idea of meeting me face to face, could you? You couldn't look me straight in the eye, because you don't have what it takes for that kind of contact. You're cowardly. You lack guts.'

He laughed. 'You're a card, Lomax,' he said. 'But we have business to conduct, a clock is ticking in the background. And you're beginning to drag on me . . . Here. Speak to your wife. And keep this in mind: Unless you cooperate, this may be the last time you'll ever talk with her. Quite a consideration, my friend. Quite a possibility. Months of total quiet. Years of silence. An eternity. A place where all the clocks are frozen and stopped.'

'We'll meet one day,' I said.

'I doubt it, Lomax.'

'We'll meet and — ' but before I could finish my sentence and whatever threat I was trying to formulate, Sondra came on the line again.

'Sweetie. Is that you?' she asked.

'Are you OK? Are you feeling OK?'

'I'm just cruising, honey.'

'Hang in there.'

'I think I felt something, Jerry.'

'Like what?'

'Like the baby kicking.'

'It's a little too early for that, love.'

'There. There it is again. Ooooeee. Jerry. It's spooky.'

I heard her laugh as if somebody was tickling her, and then the line went dead. I thought of Sondra and the phantom kick of the fetus in her stomach and I wondered how much dope was running through her blood.

And then I thought of Emily Ford's soul.

It was six-twenty on the dashboard clock and I'd made a deal with the devil.

6.30 p.m.

The street where Emily Ford lived was one of large houses on large lots. It lacked architectural unity: the homes here had come into existence before the demands of planning permits. Ranch-style, neo-plantation, a couple of stabs at truly stark modernism — it was like a street of architectural samples: pick the one you like and builders will replicate it on the lot of your choice.

I phoned her just before I reached her house, which was a two-storey redbrick surrounded by palms; I watched the rearview mirror, which had become now as much of a habit as blinking an eye. Nobody had followed me, I was sure of it. Nobody had seen me in Jane Steel's car. I felt a little jolt of victory. I'd skipped out on my guards. I was free of them.

It took Emily about thirty seconds to answer the phone. I told her where I was, asked her to open her garage for me. She sounded surprised to hear from me. A little guarded, maybe, as if she had a rule that no visitors were allowed without an invitation, and I'd just broken it.

I turned the car into the drive as the garage door slid upward; then it shut behind me and I got out of the Honda. Emily stood in the doorway that led into the kitchen.

'Traded down?' She nodded at my car.

'For the sake of necessity,' I said.

She turned, went inside the kitchen, and I followed. It was a large room with old-fashioned pine cabinets; sliding glass doors led to a patio area where a parasol with the word *Absolut* printed on it shaded a table. Beyond the table was the swimming-pool. There was a sky-blue stillness about the yard, like a California postcard. I followed Emily out, and we sat under the parasol. My bones ached as I lowered myself into a chair; when I sucked in air, there were little flickers of pain through my chest.

Emily poured lemonade from a pitcher. I drank hastily; I was ash-dry. Also I was faintly hungry, but the idea of food sickened me. I hadn't eaten since . . . when — breakfast? Breakfast was ancient history, another life. I saw Sondra pop a segment of orange into her mouth. I heard her say: *Maybe I'll cook something terrific tonight.*

I heard her say: *I'll probably be home before you.*

I remembered holding her against me and

feeling the rich warmth of her. I remembered saying I should contact Sweetzer about the role I'd play in the birth.

I heard her say: *Gotta go*.

And then she'd disappeared, and the doorway was just empty space. Her car started up outside the house. Our home. She drove down the street.

She vanished on a videotape inside a parking-garage.

I set my glass down and looked at Emily. I told her about the delivery of the lock of Sondra's hair. I mentioned the fact that I was being followed, and that we'd been seen leaving Otto's.

'Did anyone see you come here?' she asked.

'I don't think so.'

'But you don't know.'

'Not one hundred per cent.'

'This isn't your kind of game, Jerry. This is something you've never played before. You think by driving a different car you can fool these people? It isn't always that simple. They might be watching my house. If they know that you and I have met, why wouldn't they detail somebody to keep an eye on my home? Didn't that cross your mind?'

I hadn't considered the possibility. Maybe I didn't have the instinctive cunning of self-preservation, that cutting sense. Maybe I'd had it once, years before in New York State, but it had softened or withered here in the sun.

She picked up a cordless phone and punched in two digits. I assumed it was some kind of walkie-talkie system. She spoke in a quiet tone. 'Sy, I want you to take a walk down the street . . . Yeah, just be casual, make like you're strolling . . . If you see any guys sitting in a parked car, anything unusual, let me know.' She shut the phone off, looked at me. 'My police protection. I have two guys that watch round the clock. Sy Lancing's one of them. It's a perk of the job. Probably the only one.'

'Makes you feel secure?' I said.

'Nothing makes me feel secure, Jerry.'

I finished my lemonade, then told her about Sondra's car and the videotape of the abduction in the parking-garage at LaBrea; and the murder of George Rocco. She stared in a gloomy way at the swimming-pool. A bee drifted close to her eyelids and she smacked it aside. It fell into the pitcher of lemonade and skidded around on the surface, buzzing furiously.

Then I raised the subject of the dummy file and how it had been rejected.

'So you didn't fool them,' she said.

'No.'

'What now? What do they want now?'

'The original,' I said. The lie came easily to me. I wasn't ready to tell her the truth. I thought of the envelope in the safe-deposit box in Santa Monica. I should have collected it when I'd had the chance. Now I imagined the bank shut, security sensors activated, the place empty.

'And I've got until ten o'clock in which to provide it,' I said.

'There's been an ultimatum?'

'If you want to call it that.'

'Ten o'clock. Why?'

'Why what? Why ten o'clock, do you mean?'

'No, why an ultimatum of any kind? I hate to say this, but in his position I'd start by sending you Sondra's ear in a cardboard box. I wouldn't waste my time on locks of goddam *hair*, Jerry.'

I pressed the palms of my hands together. My hands were cold. 'He's so damn determined to get his hands on what he wants that he makes allowances, cuts me some slack, makes a little leeway. Maybe he's got a lot to lose if he doesn't produce. And just maybe, in his heart of hearts, he doesn't really *want* to harm Sondra.'

'Dreamtime, Jerry,' she said. 'Ding-dong.'

'Probably. But I have to believe she'll be returned to me.'

Emily was silent. She looked stressed and pale. I'd seen her this way before — a couple of times during our sessions, and once or twice when she was under hypnosis, speaking in a stilted way about her slain parents, and the overpowering feelings of hatred she'd experienced when she'd seen Billy Fear in court. The urge she'd had to stand up and shoot him where he sat, just like that, pop-pop-pop in the direct center of his face. *If only I'd smuggled a gun into court*, she'd said.

I remembered one time I'd had to slap her gently on the face to bring her out of a hypnotic trance. She had seemed unwilling to surface, a resistance almost unique in my experience. Billy Fear roamed her dreams. Billy Fear was everything that had ever scared her. His name was engraved on her like a black tattoo.

Did you want him dead? I asked.

More than I wanted to go on living, she'd said.

She got up. 'Let's go indoors.'

I followed her into the big living-room of her house. It was furnished in a traditional way, matching sofa and armchairs, framed diplomas on the walls. A caged finch banged its head into a tiny mirror, time and again. I sat on the sofa, hunched forward.

She said, 'You look crummy, Jerry. Shop-worn.'

'I had a confrontation,' I explained. 'I was provoked by a couple of passing thugs.' I wanted another shot at them, I realized. I wanted to make a violent response; maybe that chance would come one way or another eventually.

'You handled yourself well, I assume?'

'Well? I was like the goddam Terminator.'

Emily smiled in a weary way; it lasted a couple of seconds. Then she said, 'Those Washington characters didn't like me, Jerry. I got the feeling the little blond number wanted to eviscerate me with her eyebrow tweezers. She had this smug I-see-where-you're-coming-from-look. I think I'm hanging by a goddam thread. Thinner than a thread. Christ knows what they'll take back to the White House. I have a feeling that my nomination is sinking into troubled waters. And I'm not sure how to save it.'

Her nomination. Did anything else in her life really matter? She hadn't asked for details about the death of George Rocco, she hadn't wanted to know the particulars of Sondra's abduction, nor had she inquired about the encounter I'd had with the two thugs. It was

191

as if these things took place in a world that ran parallel to her own; external events were shadows on the wall, and not all that important to her.

I thought of Carrie Vasuu and Brunton.

I thought of how I'd protected Emily when I'd talked to them.

How I'd misled them.

There was absolutely no doubt that the experience of murder had seeped into Emily's belief-system, shaping and cementing her views on crime and punishment. And the death of Billy Fear had filled her with elation, a weird glassy-eyed joy I'd never seen in her before. She might have been richly stoned on a satisfying narcotic. I remembered the day after Billy Fear's shooting, when she'd entered my office and said, in a sing-song way, *The motherfucker's dead. The motherfucker's dead. Ask me if I'm ecstatic, Jerry. Ask me if I'm happy.*

Now I didn't know how I could continue to protect her.

I looked across the yard, the trim grass, the shrubbery. The sun over the city was a faded ochre color, and weary-looking, like the eye of a man numbed by the repetitions of rising and falling. I thought of the list of patients I'd given Emily; I wondered what she'd learned by running the names through her supercomputer. I wondered if she'd tell me everything, or if there might be some nugget she'd conceal for reasons of her own.

Trust her, Jerry. Take her at face value.

But which of her faces? The shattered woman who'd found the bodies of her murdered parents and who'd come to me for treatment? The individual so tormented by her past that she'd built impenetrable walls around it? The ambitious, hard-driven former LA County Attorney who'd caught a tantalizing whiff of the power that drifted out of the White House like so much smoke from the Vatican? The helpful soul who'd offered to enter into a partnership with me because she wanted me to get my wife back?

I asked, 'Did you check the names?'

'Yeah.' She gestured to a manilla folder that lay on a coffee-table. I had a sense she was holding something back, but it would come out eventually, whatever it was.

'And?' I was impatient. I could hear it in my voice. Time had become a hawk on my shoulder. Claws hooked into my skin, I could hear the ruffle of its feathers, and I knew if I looked sideways I'd see a malevolent eye glint.

'You're not going to like this.'

'Try me,' I said.

She reached for the folder and removed the

list of names, which she gave to me. I ran my eye down it to where she'd drawn a small red asterisk.

'The one I marked,' she said.

I gazed at the name. 'What about it?'

'He doesn't exist, Jerry.'

'What the hell is that supposed to mean?'

'*Phil Stam does not exist*, Jerry. He has no social-security number. No driver's license. The address he provided you is a fake. The IRS doesn't know him. He's never paid income taxes. There's no record of him ever having been born.'

I shook my head. 'This is a mistake. I *know* Phil Stam. He's scared of his own shadow. He hates going outdoors because he thinks the goddam sun is going to fall on his head. He has fainting spells in supermarkets. He pays people to buy his groceries for him.'

'Phil Stam does *not* exist, Jerry'

'He's a tall young man with a kind of hollow-cheeked look and he wears his hair back in a ponytail and he suffers from agoraphobia. He's basically a very nice guy, a kind of neo-hippie. I know about his childhood in Santa Cruz, I know about his father dying of cancer and his mother's OD, I know all about his divorce from a cocktail waitress called Lydia, and how he gets to see his daughter one weekend in four. I've been prescribing him Nardil for the past three months, Emily . . . OK, so he gave me a fake name. Maybe.'

'Maybe he gave you a fake *everything*, Jerry. Maybe he's a damn good actor and he fooled you. This town is full of good actors who can't get legit work.'

I pressed my hands to the sides of my head. I had an ache, and I tried to massage it out of existence. Phil Stam, one of life's victims, a man who found total screaming terror in places like shopping-malls, auditoriums, and beaches, a man in conflict with the space around him — no, I didn't believe he'd been coming to see me four times a month for the last three months under false pretenses. I didn't believe he'd spun out fictional yarns just to fool me, or gain access to my office, or whatever his motive might be.

'Some people detach themselves from their real names, because that creates a distance between themselves and the psychiatric problems they have. It's a defense mechanism.'

'You're whistling in the wind, Jerry.'

'I believe he was telling me the truth about his problems. He just didn't want to give me his name — '

'You can't stand the idea of being taken in, can you?'

Maybe she was correct. Maybe the idea of an impostor deceiving me was a blow to my self-esteem. I didn't respond. I didn't have the energy to argue with her.

She said, 'I think if we locate this Phil Stam, we find the missing material. He was scoping out your office all the time he was seeing you.'

I thought of how Phil Stam sometimes undid his ponytail and nervously spun strands of hair around his fingers. And now Emily Ford was telling me he was a counterfeit.

She said, 'The other patients are on the level, which may be a small consolation to you, Jerry. Now the problem is — how do we locate Phil Stam . . . or whoever he is? Do you have a photograph of him?'

'I don't keep photos of my clients,' I said.

'Pity. I could have circulated it through the LAPD. I still have a few friends there.'

I couldn't handle the fake Phil Stam scenario. It jammed my brainwaves. It sent out messages in a code I couldn't break. 'I just remembered. Phil cancelled his appointment this morning.'

'Is that unusual?'

'It's a first. Also he didn't reschedule. Which is weird, because I had the feeling we were making progress — '

'I think you've been well and truly conned, dear-heart.' And she patted my arm. She might have been saying, *Poor Jerry, there, there* . . . But she wasn't patronizing me. We'd been through too many things together for that. We'd taken a trip through the strange terrain of her psyche. I'd seen the demons that stalked her world. I believed I knew her as well as one person can know another. Her instinct for self-preservation, the depths of her willpower, the tenacity with which she held to her beliefs — maybe I knew too much. Maybe I liked her more than I wanted to admit to myself, maybe I was drawn to the dark history in her head, fascinated by the energy she'd thrown into creating a self that was partly illusion.

Her hand now lay still, palm down, on my arm. Her expression was suddenly grave. I realized that whatever she'd been holding back had nothing to do with fake patients. And she was about to tell me. I felt a weird tension.

'By the way, Jerry. Why didn't you mention this? Did it just, uh, slip your mind?' And she took a sheet of paper from the manila folder and handed it to me. I picked it up and read it, read it again, then again, and all the time the typewritten letters were slowly turning to a liquid that ran down the surface of the page like rain-smeared black mascara.

6.55 p.m.

The sheet of paper seemed to wilt in my hand. I shivered because I felt suddenly cold, raw. I saw through the sliding-glass doors the figure of a man move among shrubbery. He was present only a moment, then he was gone.

I looked at Emily and said, 'A trespasser or a protector?'

She walked to the glass doors, and stood in front of them, as if to obscure my view. 'That's just Danny. One of my police shields.'

'Like bodyguards.'

'On the taxpayer's nickel.' She came back to where I was sitting and flicked the paper in my hand with a fingernail. 'Sondra didn't tell you about this, did she?'

'No . . .'

'Why not?'

'I guess maybe she was ashamed. She'd also be worried about bad publicity and how it might affect my practice.'

Emily Ford said, 'Are there secrets in good marriages?'

'We've never had any secrets until now,' I said.

'I guess some stuff gets hidden in every relationship,' she said. 'Partners keep one another in the dark.'

In the dark, I thought. *Like the submerged bulk of an iceberg.*

Like Emily Ford's own life.

'Why the hell did you run my wife's name through your computer, anyway?'

'I ran everyone who has had access to your office, Jerry. I did the same with Jane Steel who, incidentally, has sixteen unpaid parking-tickets. And her gun license is out of date, and her work-permit expired last year — '

'This is ridiculous, it's petty,' I said.

'The efficient secretary who overlooks something as important as a work-permit, Jerry? Really?'

'So Jane has forgotten to fill in a couple of goddam forms, what's the big deal?'

'This is where we differ, buddy. I believe the big picture's hidden in the tiny details. But you think the details are just too tiresome, don't you? You're a guy that jumps right into the lake without testing the waters.'

Emily Ford's need for order and thoroughness, her desire for exactitude, annoyed me. I glanced through the glass doors. A sparrow rose off the diving-board. I wished Sondra would just materialize in front of me with a surprised smile: *Oh, Jerry, I was thinking about you! What a surprise! Let's have a drink and dinner.* We'd embrace. I'd kiss her. And life, as we'd once known it, would go on. The baby would grow inside her and we'd move to another town. Our new home would have a stained-glass window and a porch and a terrific attic and a couple of acres where we'd grow tomatoes and green beans and oranges and whatever else people cultivated in one *Stop*-sign towns. The rooms would smell of fresh paint and baking cookies, and on Thanksgiving turkey juices would scent the air.

Emily Ford was watching me carefully, as if she expected me to explode like a firework and shower incandescent bits and pieces of myself all across the room.

Cocaine. Goddam coke.

I'd never tried the stuff. I'd been in the presence of it, of course, I'd seen it razor-chopped and carefully laid out on mirrors, and I'd watched people bend over powdery lines with a straw pressed to a nostril. I'd heard the garrulous talk at parties that always followed cocaine, the bright-eyed energy that lasted only so long before people vanished again inside bathrooms to recharge flickering batteries.

'All right, sure, I knew Sondra had done drugs as a kid,' I heard myself say. 'She was born and raised in LA, she hung out at the beach, she surfed, she was into all that when she was a teenager, skinny-dipping and healthy, unashamed sex in the sand. She'd smoked pot. Who hasn't? It's no big deal. She told me. She told me everything.'

'Except this one thing,' Emily Ford said.

I looked at her hard. 'So she never mentioned doing cocaine. But it's natural she'd come in contact with it. It's the fuel of the business she's in. Musicians and their entourages use it. So Sondra is in this loop, the promo parties, the receptions, and maybe one night when she felt depleted . . . '

I quit talking. My voice seemed to come, not from myself, but from a stranger. Why hadn't Sondra mentioned this tawdry business to me? We discussed everything, it had always been our way. But this one time she'd failed to do that. She hadn't taken me into her confidence. It prompted the question: *Did she keep other things from me?* I had to let that one go. I had no time for that kind of exploration, that entanglement.

'Using coke and buying it are two different things,' Emily said. 'She was busted for making a *buy*, Jerry.'

'My bet is that she was only doing a favor for Gerson. He owns LaBrea Records. He probably snapped his fingers and told her to find him some blow for one of his musicians. I can imagine it happening that way. He shouts, she jumps. His whole staff jumps. Look, the fact that Sondra was picked up by an undercover cop for buying cocaine doesn't alter this situation. Nothing's changed. She isn't free. I have a few hours to find her and fuck all to go on except a patient who gave me a fake name — *maybe*. So what difference does it make that she bought cocaine from an undercover cop, who then dragged her off to jail?'

Emily said, 'OK, maybe it doesn't have any relevance to her present situation, but here's the odd part. She walked, Jerry. She was held for an hour and released, and that was the end of it. No bail. No follow-up. No court date. The report I showed you said she and a man named Timothy Dole were collared by an undercover officer called Lawrence Nimble on the night of March 7 at a place called Joolie's on Sunset. And that's where the matter just died. She and this guy Dole were sent home and nobody bothered to slap her wrists with a fine or some nominal community service. She wasn't even photographed or fingerprinted, Jerry. Neither was Dole . . . Do you know him?'

'Never heard of him,' I said. 'Maybe Gerson pulled a string or two.'

She said. 'Tod Resick was the one pulling strings. You know that name? Resick's a shill for my old pal, Dennis Nardini, one of whose clients I recently subpoenaed. Resick is Nardini's trusted lieutenant and doesn't dare *breathe* unless The Man tells him to suck air. *Nardini*, for Christ's sake. This is no ambulance-chaser, Jerry.'

'I can't see a guy like Nardini coming into Sondra's orbit,' I said. 'Unless it was through Gerson. Maybe he's Gerson's lawyer.'

'Dennis Nardini, Jerry, is one hundred per cent monster. Oh, he comes across as your well-oiled charmer with his Harvard degree, his imported shoes, his handmade suits, but he's still linked to the old ways. The main difference is that he knows some ten-cent words and how to schmooze influential people and he goes to *Giselle* instead of *The Godfather*. He prefers ballet to bullets. When we run into each other, it's smiles and backslapping. But he knows I'd sling his ass in jail if I could. Intimidation of witnesses. Bribery of judges. Jury tampering. Wholesale corruption. Dennis doesn't care how he gets his clients out of the shit . . . ' She hesitated before she added, 'I just can't see a guy like Dennis Nardini dealing with this in the middle of the night, Jerry. I can't see him getting out of bed and ordering Resick to

204

spring your wife and her companion for something so banal as a cocaine rap.'

I was quiet for a moment, then I said, 'I guess it's safe to say Nardini isn't fond of you.'

'An unassailable truth.'

'He represents people who'd prefer you didn't go to Washington. His associates. His clients. People who have sleepless nights when they think of you sitting up there in the hot-seat in DC. People who don't want Emily Ford trawling through crimes and issuing subpoenas like they were inflated currency in a Third World republic. People who are very happy with the *status quo*.'

'Hold it there, Jerry. If you're suggesting Nardini's a factor behind your wife's abduction, I'd have to draw a line. If he *is* behind it — and that's *truly* slim, Jerry — he's so far removed from the action you couldn't trace it back to him in a hundred years. You'd never get through the chain of command, who ordered who to do what, et cetera. I think we've got a better chance of trying to track down the guy who passed himself off as Stam than we have of dumping Sondra's disappearance anywhere near Nardini's doorstep. Believe me.'

'Did Resick pressure the arresting officer . . . what's his name?'

'Larry Nimble.'

'What did Resick say to him?'

'Jerry, let's leave Nardini and his patsy out of the picture. Concentrate on the phony patient. Stam.'

'Have you talked to Nimble?'

'Dear Christ. You're dogged. I tried to reach him. Apparently he's on leave of absence. He's ill. Ulcers or something. Satisfied?'

No, I wasn't satisfied. I couldn't imagine Sondra in a holding-cell. I couldn't imagine Nimble or any cop handcuffing her. And who the hell was Timothy Dole? Maybe he was another lackey at the record company, and he'd gone with Sondra to make the coke buy. And now Dennis Nardini had come into the frame, and suddenly the picture had altered, but I wasn't sure how.

I said, 'What if Nardini owed Gerson some big-time favor, and that's why he sent his gopher to deal with the coke situation? Maybe Gerson's a major client.'

'It's possible,' was all Emily said, but in such a way I knew her mind was elsewhere. She had the look of a novice highwire artiste, withdrawn in concentration, alive to the fear of slipping.

I thought about Gerson. I'd been to a party at his ostentatious home once, but I didn't have any special insights into his world. For all I knew, he could have connections in the same dank places as Nardini allegedly had them. I thought: *Fine, intriguing, but none of this is taking me closer to Sondra.* She was slipping further and further away, as if she'd been dragged out to sea by a hungry tide and I couldn't do a damn thing except watch from the shore.

I wondered if she'd fallen into a drugged sleep, if she was dreaming, the baby still and motionless in her womb. And then I was rushing into a place of dire possibilities, that space in the head where you imagined only the worst. Sondra had tried to escape and they'd shot her. She'd tried to climb from a window and lost her hold and fallen, and her neck was broken. She'd overdosed on drugs and slipped into a coma. The time-frame was a sham, a scam. She was already dead.

I thought: *Godammit, enough of this pressure, this anxiety and dread.* I'd get the man what he wanted, I'd give it to him after his next call. *I have the goods,* I'd say. I'd make the arrangements, and they'd give me Sondra back.

And I'd trade Emily Ford as if she were a baseball card I didn't need in my collection.

What would happen to her world then?

I looked at her face, and then away. I didn't

have the heart to stare into her eyes. Suddenly, she leaned towards me and put her arms around me. I felt her hair against my eyelids, her cool hand moving to the side of my face, where it rested. The gesture touched me, even as it disturbed.

'We'll work it out just fine in the end,' she said.

How could she sound so goddam confident?

I gazed back towards the garden, the shrubbery, and I saw one of Emily's private guards. For a moment I was stung by surprise, and upset; was it a coincidence, or was it something else, something of more sinister design? The man didn't know I'd seen him. He moved back into the shade of the shrubbery, it parted before him, he disappeared. It was the same man I'd glimpsed so briefly earlier, the one Emily had called Danny. I hadn't seen his face clearly at the time, but now I knew who Danny was.

Detective Petrosian.

Emily moved back from me, as if she were embarrassed by the spontaneity of her embrace. She pushed a strand of hair from her forehead in a brisk way. 'You still don't really trust me, do you?'

The word 'trust' was like a plum-pit in my throat. I wondered about Petrosian. Did he combine his regular cop duties with a little overtime protecting Emily? What were the chances that the cop investigating last night's assault on me would also be detailed to guard the home and person of the Chief Consultant to the West Coast Division of the Presidential Task Force On Crime? How many cops were on the LA payroll? How many thousands? What were the odds against Petrosian being involved with both me *and* Emily?

'You didn't answer me,' she said. 'About trust? Remember?'

I felt a certain tumbling inside, questions spinning wildly this way and that. What if she'd invented the cocaine story? How did I know she was telling the truth about Phil Stam? But why would she fabricate these things? What did she stand to gain?

Truth, falsehood, half-lies. I wanted to trust her, dear God, how I *wanted* to trust her. I wanted to trust somebody. I felt very alone, lost in a place where people and the words they uttered were prisms that distorted the purity of light. Now I wished I'd told Harry more, confided in him, because what you saw with Harry was what you got, there was nothing hidden, no rage of unfulfilled ambition, no empty office waiting for him in the justice department. I contrasted that with Emily's burning appetite for Washington, and it seemed to me that she might be capable of anything in her drive to get what she wanted.

'I trust you,' I said quietly.

'You lie so goddam badly, it's totally pathetic.'

'I'm not having the best of days,' I said.

'Yeah, and all this is a walk in the park for me too, Jerry. I don't think you can even begin to grasp what I stand to lose.'

'You're not the only one that loses, Emily.'

'Then let's have a little more faith here, huh? You think you can come up with just a wee bit more belief in me?'

She was asking *me* to trust her.

She'd never asked if she could trust *me*. We were in different playing-fields.

The things we plan to do with other people's lives. The little treacheries that sicken us.

I looked through the glass doors. The yard was empty. Maybe I'd never seen Petrosian. Maybe it was a case of mistaken identity. And if it *had* been Petrosian, so what? It didn't have to mean anything sinister. It was an accident, a coincidence, Petrosian was sent wherever his superiors wanted to dispatch him, he didn't pick and choose his duties. It was my head playing sick games, looking for connections, little flashes of insight in the murk of things. But I felt choked, panicked, and I was under the pressure of time. I wondered if my anxiety showed on my face, or if I'd become good at hiding my feelings. Pain rippled suddenly through my chest and I clutched the area and sucked in my breath quickly.

'You OK?' Emily asked.

'Heartburn or something.'

I needed to get out of this house. Get away. I didn't want to sell Emily Ford. Not yet.

I knew where I had to go next. And I knew I had to move quickly. Time, what was the time? But I couldn't look at my watch, didn't want to, didn't want to think of seconds elapsing and hours rushing away from me, and the idea of a void at the end of it all. I'd been given less than four hours, and a part of that span had been devoured; the collapse of time was a kind of torture.

And he'd known that only too well when he'd given me what he called a 'gift'. He'd set the clock running in my brain. He'd turned my life into pie-shaped segments of time, each slice dwindling all the time. *I'm an understanding guy when you get to know me*, he'd said. But not in any sympathetic way. No. What he understood was the nature of pain, and how to inflict it. He might just as well have touched me with a cattle-prod. The 'gift' he'd given me wasn't one of time; it was of fear. He'd imposed upon me a timetable, a schedule that would eventually run out.

I walked to the door that led to the garage. 'Where are you going?' Emily asked.

'I'm not sure yet.'

'You're lying again.'

I wanted to say: *Forgive me for what I might have to do. Forgive me if I have to trade your world for somebody else's. And even if it doesn't come to that, forgive me for thinking these thoughts.*

'Can you stay out of trouble?' she asked.

'Who knows.'

'Try,' she said. 'As for me, I'm going to find Stam.'

'How?'

'Some people in this town owe me, Jerry. I'm not a complete pariah.'

'Nobody ever said you were, Emily.'

'Hey, I read my press. I don't have too many clippings I'd save. Some people think I'm the founder member of a local coven that meets every full moon to cast spells.'

'Spells? What I heard was you don't do anything more harmful than test-drive new broomsticks.'

'Malicious gossip.'

I walked into the hot garage, got into the Honda. The automatic door slid open. I saw Emily standing in the doorway that led to the kitchen. She was watching me but I couldn't see her expression.

'Call me,' she shouted. 'Use the cellphone.'

I backed into the driveway. Emily went into the kitchen, and the door swung shut behind her. I wondered what she'd do now, what contacts she'd work, what kind of juice she had.

I backed onto the street, and the garage door descended behind me.

A man in a stylish, lightweight powder-blue suit stepped around the Honda and moved towards the side of the house in a proprietorial manner; it wasn't Petrosian, but it was somebody vaguely familiar to me only I couldn't place him until he turned his head a fraction just before he vanished — with some haste, as if I wasn't meant to spot him — under the deep green fronds of a palm.

Then I knew.

7.36 p.m.

I sat in the passenger seat of Bobby Stone's treasured '67 Olds Cutlass in the parking-lot of a Ralph's market a few blocks from Sepulveda. Planes roared overhead, flying out of LAX or landing. The skies were crowded. I remembered my dream of planes colliding. How long ago that seemed. I checked the parking-lot. I was sure nobody had followed me here. As sure as I could be. I'd driven a circuitous route, even as I was conscious of the fact that I didn't have time to take a labyrinth of back streets, or drive through a maze of suburbs.

I thought of the guy stepping round the side of Emily Ford's house, the parting of fronds: *You're mistaken,* I told myself. *You're off the wall.* But there was no mistaking the eyes that were too close together and the memory they evoked of the scarf that muffled the mouth and the baseball cap and the knife that had turned out to be a prop.

Bobby was rolling a cigarette, filling a ZigZag paper with tobacco. His black hands, big and fire-scarred, worked at this task with the skilled patience of a craftsman.

I said, 'Thanks for coming.'

'No problemo,' Bobby Stone said. He stuck the skinny cigarette in his mouth and flicked flame from a gunmetal Zippo. 'I owe you, Jerry.'

'You don't owe me,' I said. 'We did it together.'

'What a team we made back then, hey?' Bobby Stone sucked deeply on his cigarette and his cheeks hollowed out. He was bald. After the fire, his hair hadn't grown back. A few scars crisscrossed his scalp, but they'd been diminished by cosmetic surgery and were hardly noticeable. His back, severely burned, had required twenty or more grafting operations. I tried to imagine the physical pain he'd undergone. I knew enough about the other scars, the ones inside, the ones we'd healed.

'I was a wild sonofabitch,' he said. 'I wanted the world in a goddam sandwich, so's I could chew it and spit it out. Funny how a guy changes.' He laughed, coughed, spluttered. Smoke came out of his nostrils. 'I'm OK now. I'm getting along real well. The desk job keeps me outta mischief.'

'You don't want to go back on the streets?' I said.

'Naw, the streets are for younger animals.

I'm pushing forty, doc. I did my time out there.'

I looked across the parking-lot. A few scattered cars, the lights in the market windows burning even though the sky wasn't dark yet; the sun was slipping down towards nightfall, but for the present it was a California dusk, pale-blue deepening to navy, here and there a splash of pink. Darkness was next. I suddenly wanted everything to stay just as it was. The sun frozen. Eternal twilight. I didn't want night and streetlights, that other world on the far side of daytime.

I didn't mention George Rocco's slaying. Bobby hadn't raised the matter; it was possible he hadn't heard of it yet. Another murder in LA, a security guard shot in a parking-garage; news at eleven.

'You mind me saying you look like shit, doc?'

'Thanks,' I said.

'You got trouble, judging by the appearance of you.'

'You could say,' I remarked. 'You think he'll show?'

'He's a funny cat,' Bobby said. 'Keeps to himself. A loner. He told me he'd be here. But he was, like, reluctant . . . you wanna fill me in on all this, Jerry?'

'I can't. Not now.'

Bobby Stone shrugged. 'Holler if you need me, OK?'

'I will.'

Bobby crushed his cigarette in the ashtray. A plastic daisy dangled from the rearview mirror on a length of red twine, and he put up his hand and touched the fake petals. I thought that perhaps it had some sentimental value for him, but I didn't ask. I knew his wife had left him in the wake of the fire when he'd been drinking and shooting up and every day was a day in hell, and that she'd taken their daughter — maybe this cheap flower was a souvenir of a kind. I wasn't going to pry.

'You ever run into a Detective Petrosian?' I asked.

'Once,' he said.

'What do you know about him?'

Bobby Stone shook his head. 'He's the guy they get when it comes to, like, celebrity protection. You know, when there's a federal judge being threatened by criminal types, or some movie hot-shot's being stalked, that kind of thing. It's like he has his own private colony inside the LAPD. He picks his own personnel, he's got maybe a half-dozen operatives at any given time. You don't hear much about his office.'

'He wouldn't investigate an attempted robbery?' I asked.

Bobby smiled. 'That would be way beneath him, doc. He might get his fingers dirty.'

'The name Sy Lancing mean anything to you?'

'He's one of Petrosian's gang. How come you're asking about Petrosian, anyway?'

'Simple curiosity,' I said. I let this knowledge simmer inside. I wanted to see what shape it might assume when it was done on the back-burner.

Bobby Stone said, 'For a guy who always told me to be open, you are into some very serious mystification these days, doc.' He looked across the parking-lot. 'Here comes my man.'

I turned my face.

The man approaching the car walked with an exaggerated swaying motion; he might have been on a ship in a storm, and clutching ropes to keep his balance. He wore a long leather coat and wrap-around sunglasses, and his jeans were slightly flared. He opened the back door and got in. I smelled his aftershave, a sweet, heavy musk. The lenses of his glasses were reflective and when I looked at him I could see a small, distended image of myself. I found it disconcerting.

'Larry Nimble,' Bobby said. 'This here's Dr Lomax. Jerry.'

Larry Nimble made a slight downward gesture of his head, a terse acknowledgment. His skin was as pallid as that of a man who'd spent his life in the dim fluorescence of pool-halls.

I said, 'Thanks for coming.'

'Thank Bobby,' Nimble said. He had a deep, rich voice. 'I done it for him. I don't have a lot of time, doc. So say what's on your mind and I can be moving along.'

'You arrested my wife,' I said.

Larry Nimble nodded. 'I figured it was that when Bobby asked for this meet. Yeah. I busted Mrs Lomax and a guy called Dole.'

'You freed her the same night,' I said.

'Yeah. So?'

'She bought cocaine from you,' I said. 'How come you sprung her?'

Nimble looked at Bobby Stone and said, 'Duh? This guy serious?'

Bobby shrugged. 'I think maybe this is territory I don't want to enter. Hear no evil.' He got out of the car and slammed the door. I saw him pace up and down, hands in his pockets. The *Ralph's* sign burned behind him.

I turned my attention back to Larry Nimble. 'You want to explain?'

Nimble adjusted his glasses on the bridge of his nose. 'Are you wearing a wire?'

'A wire? Christ, no.'

He stared at me for a time, as if he wasn't sure he wanted to talk. Then he said, 'Bobby Stone says you're OK. Fine. Look, doc. I work a hard shift. I lay my life on the line day after day. There are people out there who'd take great pleasure in shooting me straight between the eyes. The way I figure it, I ain't gonna make it to no pension. Am I getting through?'

'Money changed hands,' I said.

'That's a fucking quaint way of putting it,' Nimble said, and laughed. It was a bass sound, a thud of a laugh, jazzy. 'Every day of my life is a hassle, doc. I get tense. I get migraines. I'm sick to my stomach. I'm bleeding inside. I drink two pints of low-fat milk and six cartons of yogurt a day. I gobble Zantac like it's going out of production. I don't eat solid food. I used to live on burgers and fries, but I ain't well, because this fucking work is eating me up. And I'll tell you something — the remuneration ain't exactly an incentive. So. You figure it.'

'Who paid you?'

'I only take cash, doc. No credit, and no promissory notes.'

I took my wallet from my pocket and

looked inside it. 'I have a hundred and twenty dollars, that's all.'

'It's less than my asking price. What the hell, Bobby says you're a good guy.'

I gave him six twenties. He stuffed the bills in his coat pocket without looking at them.

'We're going back to last March,' he said. 'Your wife and this guy Dole meet me at Joolie's, which is this dump on Sunset. I never saw your wife before. Dole comes recommended to me through another source. It don't matter who. They want to buy, I want to sell. Supply and demand. Capitalism. They want an ounce. I got that. No sweat. We go out to my car, the deal is done, and *jiminy fucking ker-ricket* — I bust them!' He laughed again and slapped his hands on his knees. 'I always get a kick outta their faces when that happens. Jaws slump about six miles. *Whoooooeeee* and down.'

'You booked them and took them in,' I said.

'That's it. Did some prelim paperwork. Then the lawyer turns up.'

'Resick.'

'Tod Resick, right.'

'And Resick runs errands for Nardini, right?'

Nimble paused. He slid his fingers beneath his glasses, massaged his eyelids. 'Sure,

221

Resick's the gopher for the big guy. He's like Nardini's fucking glove-puppet. Anyway, he makes it clear he wants to spread some bills. Take care of biz on the q. t. We settle. He's in and out like a fucking rattler through a hollow log.'

'How much?'

'Trade secret. Let's just say my ulcers were really giving me shit that night, OK? Your wife and this guy Dole, they get to go home.'

'And you killed the whole thing.'

'I killed it. But I was careless. I let some paperwork get away from me and it's sucked into the system before I can get it back. It don't matter. Anybody asks, I say it was a wrongful arrest. Nobody's ever gonna ask, though. This fucking city is awash in crime. We got it coming out the woodwork. It's a terminal condition. You think anybody's gonna lose sleep over a dope rap that's been thrown out by the arresting officer? Fuck no.'

I gazed a moment at Bobby Stone, who was leaning over the hood of the car. He'd pulled out a corner of his shirt and was using it to dab at a stain or mark on the metal. He kept the Cutlass shiny. He was compulsive when it came to his car.

'Tell me about Dole,' I said.

'What's to tell? I asked him his name, he told me, and I wrote it down.'

'Did you see ID?'

Nimble shook his head. 'I asked. He said he didn't have any.'

'You took him at his word.'

'Yeah. Look. Everything's rushed. It's bedlam downtown. Everybody's crazy. Shouting. Pushing. Swearing. People throwing up. Pissing their pants. Fistfights. You don't worry about niceties like ID. That comes later. You just want to get back on the streets because there's always another sucker to pop, and he's waiting out there in the dark. ID? Fuck that shit.'

'Describe him,' I said.

'Lookit, I think you've had your hundred-and-twenty-bucks worth.'

'It's the last question I'll ask,' I said. 'I give you my word.'

Nimble sighed. 'OK. About this high. Five-five maximum. Muscular little fucker. Gray hair sorta swept back. Blow-dried. He was a salesman type. Glasses kind of like that old rock guy used to wear. The dead guy, what was his name? Buddy Holly? You know, heavy frames. Oh, yeah, and he smoked a cigar that was about half the size of him.' He reached for the door handle, opened the door, stepped out. He bent down and looked in at me. 'Good luck, doc. Whatever it is you're doing.'

I said nothing. I was picturing the man called Dole. Muscular. *Gray hair sorta swept back. Glasses. Cigar.* I saw him, I conjured him in my mind. I thought of trick mirrors, Disneyland, haunted houses, holographs, cops who broke the law even as they pretended to maintain it. This was the world I'd entered.

I watched Bobby Stone get back in the car.

'You through, doc?'

'Yeah, I'm finished.'

'Was he helpful?'

'Yeah.' My ribs were aching again. I gazed through the windshield at Larry Nimble strutting towards the front of the market. I had an urge to go out and call him back and ask him more questions about the man who'd been arrested in Sondra's company; but I knew the answer, I didn't need to ask Nimble anything else.

Bobby Stone said, 'He's crooked.'

'So's this town,' I said.

'Ain't that the truth.' He smiled at me. 'You ain't gonna tell me, are you, doc?'

'Some other time, maybe,' and I opened the door. 'Thanks a lot, Bobby.'

I raised a hand in farewell and looked once again across the lot. There was no sign now of Larry Nimble. He'd faded into the texture of the same twilight where he'd first taken

224

shape. He might just as well have walked off into another world altogether.

I tapped the roof of the Cutlass with the palm of my hand and Bobby gave his horn a single short blast. I walked back to my car. The withering sun came off the big window of the market, a yellow rectangle.

Emily Ford hadn't lied to me about the coke bust. She'd told me the truth as far as it went. But truth was selective in her world. If Petrosian was way beyond the investigation of a mugging, why had he been sent to talk with me? And then the attacker himself turned out to be one of Emily Ford's personal courtiers . . . what did it all mean?

Only one thing, so far as I could see. *You think you can come up with just a wee bit more belief in me?* she'd asked.

No.

7.57 p.m.

The city finally edged into darkness. Lights burned in the high towers of commerce as cleaning crews swept through, or ambitious executives toiled after-hours in the hope of promotion and bigger offices.

I took the lock of Sondra's hair from the breast pocket of my jacket and held it in the closed palm of one hand. How light it was, lighter than any bird. I realized how worried she must have been, sick to her heart about the cocaine affair, wanting to tell me and not knowing how, accusing herself for her own act of folly, ashamed and despising herself for keeping a secret from me.

I wondered if I'd failed to detect little signs of stress in her, if I'd overlooked any peculiarities of behavior. I couldn't think of any giveaway tics, odd mannerisms, pro-longed gloomy silences that hinted at things hidden. I guessed if I looked back long and hard enough I'd encounter some small instance of unusual behavior: but my brain was lead, and I could only think of where I was headed and what I'd do when I got there — and how time was blowing away like filaments of some very fragile plant.

I reached my destination and slid the cellphone from the dash and put it in the hip pocket of my pants. Then I got out of the Honda and locked it. The house was Beverly Hills Absurd, a mock-Tudor-style building with exposed beams: Tudor and palm trees, olde England and cacti, an uneasy mix of worlds. There were six or seven cars parked in the long driveway: I noticed a Bentley, a Range Rover, an Alfa Romeo, a new VW Bug, red and shiny, a Lincoln Continental, and something sporty and low-slung I didn't recognize — a Morgan, maybe. Globed lights hung around the entranceway. I heard music from the house.

The curtains hadn't been drawn; I saw people standing around in a downstairs room in the manner of guests idly chatting over the first ice-breaking cocktail of the night. A small party was happening here, maybe a dinner. It wasn't a good time for me to call. But time, in my case, was neither bad nor good. It was a substance to which I was addicted, but the stash kept diminishing. I craved more of it, more minutes and seconds.

I walked to the door, rang the bell. I heard the chimes way inside the house, Westminster-style. The man who answered looked at me with an expression of vague recognition that yielded to surprise, then to a smile that may have been forced or genuine, I couldn't tell.

'Jerry? *Jerry Lomax?* What are you doing here?'

'I just want to talk. I won't take up much of your time.'

He looked at me through his curiously dated black-framed glasses. 'Sure. But you chose the wrong evening, Jerry. Can't it wait? I'm entertaining some people.'

'Then you can entertain me, Gerson,' I said, and before he could object, I slipped past him into the enormous marbled foyer of his four-point-something-million-dollar mansion in the world's most tacky suburb.

8.10 p.m.

Leo Gerson said, 'Whatever's on your mind, can't it keep?'

I ignored him and moved across the foyer. He caught me by the arm. He was strong for his size, but I managed to shrug him off.

'Jerry, how many ways can I say it? I have company.'

'I noticed. I need something to drink.'

'You been hitting the bottle?'

I wished. How I wished this was all some alcoholic hallucination. At least I'd know a time of waking would come. I'd be hungover, but I'd have Sondra beside me.

I saw a maid emerge from a room with a tray of canapés. I smelled cheese and garlic and anchovy. I went in the direction of the room she'd come from, the kitchen. My footsteps echoed on the floor. The foyer had a high ceiling from which a profusion of chandeliers dangled some twenty-five feet overhead. I had the impression of electric shards hanging in mid-air, like bad-taste Christmas decorations.

I said, 'I've no intention of gatecrashing

your soirée, Leo. I'll find something to drink in here.'

Visibly exasperated, Gerson came after me as I went into the kitchen, a large room of stainless steel surfaces, a stove with eight burners, and an exhaustive assortment of culinary implements hanging from hooks. I opened the refrigerator, a big Sub-Zero model, and rummaged inside. I found a bottle of peach-flavored mineral water, twisted the top off, and held the bottle to my mouth. I was dehydrated: tension had dried me out.

Gerson lit a cigar. He pointed it at me in the manner of some jungle republic dictator addressing a subordinate. 'I had you figured for a guy with more manners, Jerry. What's the idea, barging in all whipped up into a frenzy? Where's the fire, for Christ's sake?'

I wiped the back of my hand across my lips and said, 'Cocaine.'

Gerson ripped a paper-towel from a roll on the wall and rubbed the lenses of his glasses with it. He had red indentations on either side of his nose. The cigar dangled from his mouth. Smoke, rising upward, made him blink. 'What about cocaine? You been snorting some?'

I said, 'The *bust*. Remember?'

He showed no surprise. He put his glasses

on again just as a woman came into the kitchen. She was about twenty, very tall, and her pale blue dress was short and tight. She slinked up to Gerson and placed a hand on his shoulder.

'People are asking for you, Leo,' she said. She had a whispery, little-girl voice, the kind that seemed to cling to the air around her like static electricity to cashmere.

'Gimme a minute, Shantee,' he said. He growled his words; a man used to issuing commands. He patted the woman's buttocks, and she licked the lobe of his ear even as she looked at me, checking me out, trying to fit me into her frame of reference. Was I important? Could I advance her career, whatever that was?

Finally, she blinked at me in a dismissive way and said to Leo, 'Hurry back, Leo, I'm waiting for you,' and she eased her way out of the kitchen.

'Is she one of your artistes, Leo?'

'Come on, Jerry. You know damn well what she is. She's a wannabe who doesn't have the talent to go anywhere. She's deluded. She's dead meat in the making.'

Gerson tossed this line away in a callous manner. The young woman was mattress fodder in a city of good-looking wannabes who changed their names to sound exotic

— *Shantee*. They swarmed like wasps looking for jam, and some of them settled on people such as Gerson, who could give them a boost up the ladder of opportunity. Or so they imagined. But there was always a price — they had to be seen hanging on his arm at parties and they had to fuck him. They were more bracelet than human being. Leo, with his own record label and all the attachments of money, was a starmaker and a scalphunter.

'Is there something special you want to know about the cocaine bust, Jerry?' Gerson asked. 'I mean, it was months ago — '

'You took Sondra with you. You both got busted. You passed yourself off under an assumed name. To wit, Timothy Dole. You don't look like a Timothy to me. Or even a Timmy. Did you pull the name out of thin air?'

'Funny that. The name just rolled straight off the tip of my tongue.' Gerson grinned and drew hard on his cigar. He shrugged and said, 'But don't blame me, Jerry. I didn't drag Sondra against her will. She wanted to come.'

'What are you saying, Leo? That she asked if she could keep you company on this coke purchase?'

He blew smoke in my face. 'You know how she is. She gets a kick out of low-life joints.

She enjoys a sense of the edge. A cocaine buy in a dark back room turns her on, quickens her pulses . . . Ooops. Oh, Christ, am I telling you something you *didn't* know? What the hell. Your relationship with your wife has fuck all to do with me, Jerry. Talk to her.'

I had a rush of blood to my head. I gripped the lapels of Gerson's jacket, and drew him forward until his face was close to mine. I could almost taste his cigar. He seemed entirely unmoved by this physical contact. He stared at me from behind his glasses without blinking, and I pictured him negotiating a contract, making a deal with a singer or a musician, his brain an accounting-device, his heart hard as a winter turnip. *Take it or leave it*, he'd say. *I don't give a damn. There's plenty more talent crawling out the wood-work.*

'Jerry, this jacket was handmade in Jermyn Street, London, England, and cost me fifteen hundred bucks.'

'What are you telling me about Sondra, Leo?' I demanded.

'I'm only saying there's a wild side to your lady, friend. And that's something I figured you'd know. But obviously you don't, so forgive me if I happened to spill some ash in your fucking soup, jack.'

I shoved him against the edge of the stove.

He raised an elbow and forced it into my chest, and held it there. For a moment we stood in this ridiculous pose, my hands on his shoulders, his elbow in my ribcage. Something simmered in a small saucepan. It smelled of burned cherries. I didn't want to believe what he'd said about Sondra: how could I?

I released him and he took a couple of steps away from me.

'I know my wife,' I said.

'Jeez, don't get me wrong, sport. I didn't say she doesn't *love* you. She's *crazy* about you. She's got a photograph of you on her fucking desk, Chrissakes. Listen, she's an elegant lady. She brings a certain je ne say kwa to LaBrea Records. All I'm telling you is she likes these brief excursions into el mondo bizarro. It's no big deal, Lomax. It's like priests going to strip clubs or something. It's a break from routine respectability, an innocent little thrill — and, hey, who does it hurt? It doesn't mean she finds domestic bliss dull. She's happy. Only now and again she likes to get a whiff of what it is that lies out there. That's all.'

A wild side to your lady.

But I knew that, up to a point. Didn't I? Why deny it? I saw her as a teenager — surfing, catching a big wave, rising high on

234

the white foam, spray in her hair; I imagined her laughing and her heart racing with the thrill of the ride. I saw her smoking dope on the beach, then screwing a guy she hardly knew under a board-walk somewhere — a beach bum, maybe, a doper, or a lifeguard. I imagined her heartbeat accelerating, her senses honed to a blade's sharpness, as she spread her suntanned thighs for a stranger, her flesh tangy with brine. Yes, she had had a wild side, sure — but that was years ago; maybe some residual recklessness remained, but it was harmless, just the way Gerson had said.

And yet, I felt her drift away from me a moment, I couldn't bring her face to mind, she was a specter passing through my life. I had the deadening sensation I'd never see her again. Not in this world.

I finished the mineral water and tossed the bottle towards a big plastic trash-can with its lid open. I missed and the bottle skidded unbroken across the floor.

'You walked away from the bust without a blemish,' I said. 'You've got connections. Powerful ones.'

He blew smoke rings, perfect ovals. 'So what? The whole world comes down to who you know, Jerry. Tell me you haven't figured that one out.'

235

I didn't like him, and I didn't trust him, but I had a sudden urge to tell him everything, regardless of these feelings — how Sondra had been seized; she was being held somewhere and our time was running out. It was as if I wanted to tap into his powers, the clout he had in this town, whatever magic he might possess. *Help me, Leo, help me find her.* The temperature of my desperation was rising.

'Nardini was the one who greased your way,' I said. 'He must have cost you.'

'Did your wife tell you Nardini was involved?'

I ignored his question. Besides, I didn't want to hear myself say: *My wife didn't tell me anything.* 'How did Nardini get drawn into it, Gerson? What's the connection between you and him, and where does Sondra fit?'

'Look, Jerry, I got guests. Another time, huh?'

'What makes a high-flier like Nardini get involved in an insignificant drug bust involving you and my wife? Simple question.'

'OK. The answer's just as simple, Jerry, and if you're looking for complexity, you're about to be disappointed. The guy's my goddam *attorney.* I got a problem, I call him, he takes care of it. I asked him to get Sondra out of the bind as well. I wasn't going to leave her hanging out to dry, was I?'

Maybe. Maybe it was just that straight-forward. But I had the feeling I was missing something, or I was having a lie foisted on me. I couldn't read Gerson's expression. I couldn't tell if he was hiding something.

Guy's my goddam attorney . . . I call him — what was *wrong* with that? What the hell was I looking for here? I had an answer from Gerson, and it was logical. Sondra liked the excitement of a dope deal in a sleazy club, she liked the *thrill* of stepping away from her everyday world. Nardini was only doing what attorneys did for their clients. OK. Fine. That was it.

I ran the palm of a hand across my face. My skin smelled of the steering-wheel of the car. I was grubby. The city had engrained itself in my flesh. And now I'd made a complete fool of myself, coming to Gerson's home and behaving like a lout. I thought of the moment when I'd pinned him to the stove and I was embarrassed. I was buckling. The pressure was an avalanche.

I said, 'I'm sorry, Leo. Crashing in on you this way . . . *Jesus.*' I shook my head slowly in disbelief.

'I don't know what's troubling you, Jerry. But you're too stressed. You're out there, way

237

out there. Maybe you should write yourself a prescription, something to alter your mood.'

I shook my head. 'Yeah. Maybe I should.'

'Physician heal thyself,' he said.

'Did Sondra . . . ' I stopped mid-question. Gerson looked at me. 'Yeah?'

I didn't want to ask the question. But I needed to know the answer, even if it meant revealing a gap in my knowledge, that there was an aspect of my wife's life I really didn't know about. 'Did she ever . . . did you ever see her use cocaine?' Gerson's cigar had gone out. He plucked it from his lips, producing the sound of a rubber gasket popping. 'If she ever used it, Jerry, I never saw it. She liked the drama of the buy, sure. But if you want to know whether she ever snorted coke herself, it's a question you need to ask her. Clear the air, Jerry, if something's bothering you.'

He walked with me to the kitchen door, opened it, stepped behind me into the big entranceway where the chandeliers hung. I felt Gerson's palm on my back. He was steering me gently across the floor. He wanted me out of his house. He wanted to have his party in peace. I was an interruption, the uninvited loony he was ushering to the front door.

'I bet you've been working too hard,' he said.

'Yeah,' I said. 'Maybe.'

He patted me on the back a couple of times in a solicitous way.

A door opened on the far side of the foyer and the maid I'd seen earlier appeared. I glimpsed the room beyond, the partygoers with their drinks, a collection of men and attractive young women in fashionable casual threads. Somebody stroked a piano. A few well-fed faces turned in my direction.

Gerson kept guiding me to the door, as if he had a guest in the house he didn't want me to see, somebody I knew, somebody whose presence might have surprised me. I sensed that at one level this was manic thinking, another aspect of my erosion. Just the same, I couldn't free myself of the feeling that he was pressuring me out of his house a little too hastily, so I changed direction.

I moved towards the party room. The door was beginning to close, and the maid with the tray was walking back in the direction of the kitchen.

'Jerry,' Gerson said. 'It's a private party. You weren't invited.'

The door was almost shut by the time I reached it. I put my hand flat against it. Gerson came up behind me. I had a sudden sense of displacement, as if I weren't in Leo Gerson's house at all, but elsewhere

— trapped in a piece of theater, where all the guests were extras muttering nonsense. And then another sensation eclipsed this disorientation, as if I'd seen an unexpected signal on the radar screen in my head.

I pushed the door open with one hand, the other I placed against the side of my face where, for some reason, my skin had begun to tingle.

I thought: *It's Sondra I sense. She's here. She's in this room.*

She's at this party.

It made no sense.

I crossed the threshold anyway, because sense didn't figure in my scheme of things, and I found myself looking around the guests with an expression of bewilderment on my face. I must have resembled a man in the grips of extreme dementia.

A woman was playing a grand piano in the corner.

'Chances Are' was the tune. *Though I wear a silly grin.*

The wallpaper was flamboyant red and gold and the pattern vibrated. The guests were drinking champagne.

Gerson said, 'Come on, Jerry. I'll show you out.'

I scanned the faces. No Sondra. I'd been wrong.

But instead there was Jane Steel, looking at me from a corner of the room. Her expression was one of embarrassment, as if I'd caught her in a moment of theft or an act of treachery. She had a glass in one hand. The man who stood beside her, in an expensive dark-blue brushed-suede jacket, was Joe Allardyce. He gave me the kind of smile that said, *I wish I was a million miles from here.*

Just for a moment I didn't want to move, I didn't want to say anything that might cause a scene and disturb the peace of Gerson's party. But then I thought of Sondra and what the hell did the niceties of this gathering matter? I was beyond polite. I stepped across the room to Jane, who raised her glass to her mouth but didn't drink.

'This *is* a surprise,' I said. 'Come here often, Jane? Is this the kind of crew you hang out with? Are they all gun freaks like yourself?'

'Jerry, I can explain — '

'What's to explain? You move in certain circles I'd never have guessed, plus you play with pistols — you're just a bundle of little surprises, Jane. Got any more for me? And here's Joe, too. Well, this is intimate. This is nice. The three of us. Jane and Joe and Jerry. Like a clapped-out vaudeville act.'

Jane said, 'Joe invited me.'

Joe said, 'That's right. Is there a problem, doc? Is there some code that a patient doesn't ask his shrink's secretary out for a harmless evening?'

'I thought you were never asked to parties, Joe,' I said. 'I thought you were blackballed. The world is against you, et cetera.'

'I still got a couple friends left, Jerry.'

'I'm sure you have. Good friends. Great friends.'

Gerson stood at my side, a hand on my elbow. 'Keep the voice down, Jerry.'

'Am I talking too loud?' I said. Of course I was. I knew it. I was spinning out of control again. Any moment now, I'd punch somebody in the face. Or I'd break something.

'Jerry, please.' Gerson looked forlorn.

Joe Allardyce said, 'I asked your secretary if she wanted to keep me company. It's no big deal. We're not seriously dating, doc. There's nothing going on behind your back.'

'It doesn't feel that way,' I said. 'I think there's all kinds of shit going on behind my fucking back.' I reached for Jane's wrist, caught it. A slick of champagne spilled over her fingers. The piano continued to play. 'How Long Has This Been Going On'. Great choice of tune, maestro.

'Jerry, don't prejudge the situation,' she said. 'I don't want you to misunderstand.'

'What might I misunderstand?'

'Joe and me being here together, don't get the wrong impression.'

'What impression am I meant to get, Jane?'

She drew me to one side; Jane Steel, British and discreet, hated the idea of a scene. *Let's talk quietly in a corner of the room: let's be hushed about this.* 'You don't look well, Jerry. You look pale.'

'I feel pale, Jane.'

She said, 'It started this morning, whatever it is. Didn't it? You got that phone call — '

'You're trying to tell me you don't know what's going on?'

'All I know is you're in some kind of trouble. You don't want to discuss it, fine. I understand that. That's your prerogative.'

'Prerogative,' I said. 'Lovely word. Very fair of you, Jane. Very *balanced*. I have your permission to mind my own business.'

'This is foolish, Jerry,' she said. She forced a smile. 'And so unlike you. People are looking.'

'Let them look,' I said. I stared at her face — rounded, cheeks a little plump, lips full, dark hair immaculately brushed — and I thought of picnics and green meadows, and a rainy cloud forming around an English summer sun, and sudden umbrellas. It seemed to me that Jane Steel had a certain innocence she couldn't keep from appearing on her face. She didn't know what had happened to Sondra; she hadn't a clue. I could see this in her eyes. Her concern was all for me, and it was genuine.

But I'd been fooled by appearances before. Too easily.

She said, 'I know I probably shouldn't accept invitations from patients, Jerry. I just felt sorry for Joe. And when he asked me to this party, I accepted. He looked so . . . sad. It's as simple as that. If I broke a rule, I'm sorry. This is strictly a one-off. It won't happen again.'

I had a sense of collapse. My energies disintegrated. Pain cut through me; my ribcage felt as if it had been hacked by a butcher's cleaver. I needed to get out of this place. My head was overloaded with a cast of characters whose roles were elusive: Joe Allardyce and Jane, Leo Gerson, Tod Resick, Nardini, Emily Ford and her two hacks, the mysterious Stam. Their names were shards shifting inside the tunnel of a busted kaleidoscope.

I stepped away from Jane and back to Gerson, and I told him I wanted fresh air.

'Great idea,' he said.

I glanced at Jane, who'd returned to her position beside Joe Allardyce; they gazed at me with worried expressions. I wondered if it was their first date. Or if it had happened before, if intimacy had taken place. Had Jane been carrying on this liaison right under my nose? Was this yet another instance when my instinct had abandoned me? Still, what the hell did it matter to me if she dated the clients? She wasn't going to give away trade secrets to Joe Allardyce. She wasn't the kind to discuss private cases, individual patients, personal details.

I walked out into the foyer and towards the front door; and Gerson came behind me, making solicitous noises. 'You want somebody to drive you home?' he asked.

'I'm fine, I'm fine.'

'Sure?'

'Yes, yes, sure.'

Then I was outside and Gerson was saying, 'Go home, Jerry. Rest. Do yourself a favor.'

Yes, yes. I walked down the driveway and along the block.

Halfway to the car I thought about trust, and how worried I'd been about trusting Emily Ford — but now a sharper dilemma had arisen, a more demanding problem: how could I trust *myself* and my own deteriorating senses, for Christ's sake? How could I put any faith in my own radar when it was receiving faulty signals? I'd been so goddam *sure*

Sondra had been at the party. So *certain* —

And I'd been wrong.

I was spaced. There was a prairie in my head.

I needed to be strong. I couldn't afford to be victimized by my own imagination. I didn't need cerebral terrorism, to be bushwhacked by my own demons.

What I needed was my wife.

When I reached Jane's Honda, I noticed somebody in the passenger seat.

8.27 p.m.

The figure was motionless. I couldn't make out any features. Man or woman, I couldn't tell. Light fell across the Honda from a streetlamp, but didn't illuminate the inside of the car. I opened the door on the driver's side and the interior light kicked on. The stench of brandy was overpowering. It filled the warm space of the interior like a toxic nerve gas. The figure's head was slumped forward.

I touched it tentatively and it rolled a little to one side. I saw it was Harry Pushkas — eyes shut, mouth open. Blood ran from just above his scalp-line and down his right cheek. I looked for the source of the wound as I shook Harry's arm and urged, 'Wake up, wake up!' He wasn't responding. I felt his blood on my fingers and the palm of my hand. I said it again, 'Harry, Harry, wake up!' and I gripped the shoulders of his jacket — that old navy-blue shapeless double-breasted garment he wore every day of his life — and shook him vigorously.

Nothing, nothing. I placed a fingertip to his left eyelid and pushed it up.

The eye that looked back was mournful.

And dead. Very dead. I searched for a pulse, found none.

I sat down behind the wheel. Then I felt sick. I pushed the door open and hung my head from the car and a thin substance that had the taste of sour peaches came up from my throat. Eyes watering, I gazed along the street. I half-expected Harry to stir suddenly. *I think I haff had a little too much brandy, dear boy.* No such thing happened. I felt weird and flat, like a seltzer left too long exposed to the air. No bubbles. Just still and stale. I shut the door, sat back in my seat.

Then, without thinking where I was going, I started the car and I drove a few blocks. Then I reached another leafy street, and found I couldn't drive any further. I parked outside a half-built house surrounded by a security fence and *Keep Out* notices. Scaffolding clung to brickwork. I saw the skeleton of a roof.

When the phone rang I answered it as if I were on auto-pilot. *Harry's dead. Harry's dead in this car*, I thought.

'He was a sorry old drunk,' the voice said. The tone was unctuous. 'Don't feel bad.'

I didn't respond. It took me a moment to make links and connections. Where I was. What I was doing here. I'd been looking for Sondra five minutes ago. I'd been certain she was at Gerson's party. I'd had an experience either psychic or psychotic, sensing her presence when she was nowhere near.

'He was a sad old alkie who quit living the day his wife died, Lomax. He's no loss. Don't waste time on grief. You don't have time to waste, anyway.'

'You didn't know him,' I said.

'What is there to know? One alcoholic's story is much the same as another's. Hard times on a steep slope. Broken hearts and splintered families. Rock bottom. Ho-hum. But you brought this on yourself, Lomax. It was never my intention to dispose of your dear old friend. And it wouldn't have happened if you'd been straight with me, instead of trading cars and trying to slip away. We'll always find you in the end.'

'You're a bastard,' I said. 'Life means nothing to you. You wipe people off the face of the earth and it doesn't touch you, does it?'

'You underestimate me, Lomax. I'm not a beast. But sometimes you need to be hard. You develop a shell and it's waterproof, it's a place under which you feel no emotions.'

'And the end justifies the means in your book,' I said.

'Oh, Christ, let's not turn this into a high-school debate. The truth is, you fucked up. You tried to cheat me. You were supposed to be straight with me. But no, you couldn't do it that way, you had to pretend you were some kind of goddam prince on a charger, running here and there looking for clues to the location of the high tower where your princess is imprisoned. I understand your actions, Lomax. Believe me. In your position, I might well have behaved in the same way. I'm not heartless. But you must see how totally pointless it is for you to even *think* about getting the upper hand. It can't be done.'

'So you punish me by killing an old man,' I said.

'In a phrase.'

I wanted to reach down the phone and strangle the owner of the voice. I wanted to look in his eyes and see all life go out of him. 'Let me speak to Sondra.'

'She's out cold. She's sleeping off her mind-altering intake.'

'Wake her,' I said.

'You're droll at times, Lomax, the way you think you can issue commands and have me obey them. I worry about your relationship with reality. The situation here isn't conducive to you giving orders. Have you got that? Is that coming through to you loud and clear and static-free? *Dr Lomax does not give orders. He takes them.* Try saying that to yourself.'

'Fuck you,' I said. I was pounding my face against a concrete wall, and getting nowhere.

'I understand finding old Harry in your car is something of a blow, but let's have a little decorum, shall we? You're supposed to be locating something for me. Remember? My question is — have you got it?'

'I want to talk to my wife,' I said.

'You're a broken record, Jerry. In the words of the immortal bard, M. Jagger, 'you can't always get what you want.' '

'Put her on the goddam *phone*,' I said.

'You're not getting the hang of this, are you? Take a look at the old guy sitting in your car. Now I want you to picture your wife in his place. You got that? OK. Think back. The cleaning lady in the bath-tub. Remember? The lock of hair. OK? Remember that also? The drugs we gave her? Following the script, Jerry? Listen close, listen hard. We could have killed your wife a hundred times over. Think about that. We could have tortured her. We could have used a red hot poker and stuck it in her eyes. We could have given her an OD and dumped her in a canyon somewhere like a junkie hooker who had a sorry encounter with some low-grade serial-killer type. We could have mutilated her or tied her to a bed and gang-banged her. Anything we liked, we could have done. You are getting all this, I trust? What I'm saying is — don't develop a bad attitude, don't make it any harder than it already is. I've been kind to you. I've allowed you a certain latitude. Other men might have acted with less charity. Correction. Other men would have acted with absolutely *no* charity.'

I stared along the street. The lamps. The soft yellow glow. I tried to pretend Harry wasn't in the passenger seat and the air didn't smell of the booze he'd drunk before he'd been killed. I figured a small-caliber gun. One shot into the brain. Very little mess. Painful? Maybe for an instant. I had no idea.

I had a question I needed to ask. It hung in my head like a huge icicle. I dreaded having to utter it. 'How do I know she's alive?'

'Take my word for it.'

'Sure. Absolutely — '

'You have any other choice, Lomax?'

I said, 'All you have to do is wake my wife and let me speak to her and you get what you want.'

'Ah, but have you *got* what I want, friend?'

I glanced at Harry; I was still half-expecting a practical joke. Once, he'd gone to great lengths to write a research paper about the effects of aspirin on the pineal gland of baboons, and he'd published it in a respectable medical journal. All fake, every word of it, every statistic. He loathed the establishment, any establishment — medical, psychiatric, political. They were all bastions of pomposity to him. He was a lapsed Communist who'd learned the hard way in the streets of Budapest that his ideals were no match for Stalinism. He'd survived the street battles, the tanks and the guns — now he lay dead in a car parked on a street in Beverly Hills, where a faint mist created by pollution was forming between the streetlamps.

'Lomax? Are you listening to me? You know what I'm talking about. I want the stuff you locked away. Have you got it for me?'

The stuff locked away. 'What stuff?' I asked.

'You're pushing me, Lomax. Don't. Be warned. I bend only so far.'

'What stuff?' I asked again.

'You're not thinking. I only have to nod my head, a very simple gesture, and somebody will slit your wife's throat and hang her upside down on a meat-hook and she'll bleed to death like a pig. Or I can have her taken out into the desert and shot and buried where bodies are never found. So let's quit being coy. I want the stuff you keep in a safe-deposit box at a certain bank.'

I lost the connection suddenly.

There was static crackle on the line, a break

in transmission. His voice became a series of disconnected words and sounds. *Sten . . . got . . . get . . . placent.* I turned the ignition key and drove down the street. Thoughts rushed me like hordes of wild birds — how did he know about the safe-deposit box? Who had that information? I hadn't told anyone.

So how had he found out?

Jane Steel — maybe she knew, maybe she'd seen a bill from my bank for the rental of the box, maybe it had come in the office mail and she'd opened it the way she opened everything.

Jane Steel. But why? Because she was afraid? Had she been threatened? I couldn't imagine her selling the information like a mercenary, but what did I know? I'd been surprised to learn about her interest in guns, and Emily had mentioned something about how Jane's gun permit and visa had expired. Maybe there were even more hidden surprises, levels of Jane I hadn't begun to divine beyond the love of guns, the lack of a work permit, and the assignation with Joe Allardyce.

I pressed the Off button and killed the static. The phone rang again immediately.

Emily Ford said, 'Where are you?'

'Meet me,' I said.

'Where?'

'I'll call you back in a few and let you know. And bring me whatever you've got on Jane Steel.'

I drove until I found myself in a side street near Laurel Canyon. Was I being followed? I wasn't sure. I thought it likely. But they were good at it, they had a magic touch, access to invisibility; I saw nothing in the rearview mirror.

I parked outside Harry's house. I pulled his body as gently as I could from the car and dragged him on his back across dry grass. Then I propped him against me and staggered up the steps to the porch of his small wood-frame home. His cats sat on the porch-roof, purring. They were called Palota and Fortuna, after streets in Budapest. They were all glistening black fur and silent grace.

I took the doorkey from Harry's pocket and I got him inside the living-room; gasping under his weight, I lowered him to the sofa. The room was cluttered with books, thousands of them. The air smelled of moldering cat food and mildew. *You're home, Harry. You're home.* I saw a photograph of Harry on a bookshelf, a black-and-white shot taken around the time of the Russian invasion of Budapest; he wore a beret and had a rifle strapped to his back. Young and tough, vital and filled with hope — and now this: killed, not by the Stalinists he hated, but by an accident of friendship.

He was dead because he knew me.

I said, '*Viszonlatasra.*' Goodbye: the only word Harry had ever taught me in Hungarian. I wanted to mourn him somehow; later, when all this was finished, I'd think of him again, and there would be a wound in my heart.

I walked back to the Honda.

I punched the button for Directory Assistance. I gave the operator the name of the person I wanted and she patched me through.

I heard a man's voice say, 'Bo Sonderheim speaking.'

'I need your help, Bo,' I said.

'Who is this?'

'Jerry Lomax.'

Bo Sonderheim uttered his banker's cheerful little chuckle, the one reserved for clients with healthy balances and sound investments. 'Ha, Jerry. Don't tell me you need access to overdraft facilities at this time of night?'

It was his idea of a joke. I figured bankers had their own humor magazine filled with inoffensive little jests.

'I do need access to something, Bo,' I said. 'Only it isn't money.'

9.04 p.m.

I drove the Santa Monica freeway at just under 100 m.p.h. When I reached the bank, Bo Sonderheim was already in the big parking-lot, the headlights of his Ultima burning. He got out when he saw me arrive and walked towards the Honda. His usual friendly appearance had lost some of its blandness; he seemed mildly irritated, yet laboring not to show it. I was a good customer: why alienate me?

'This is kind of weird,' he said. 'I guess there's a first time for everything.'

'I guess there is,' I remarked.

'A matter of life and death was what you said, Jerry.'

'I mean it, too. You got a key that can unlock this place?'

'It's not that easy, Jerry. This isn't like the old days when your friendly bank manager could come down and let one of his favorite customers inside the bank after hours. Life's not that simple, unfortunately. This is more involved.'

'How involved?'

'I have to have a senior representative of

257

the bank's security personnel here,' he said. 'Without him, I can't get inside my own damn bank at this time of day.'

'Did you contact him?' I asked.

'He's on his way,' Sonderheim replied.

'How long will it take him?'

Sonderheim looked at his watch. 'He should be here momentarily.'

I was burnt-up with impatience, fevered. I imagined some security officer grumbling as he left his home, maybe driving at a speed to please himself. *Stupid goddam customer wants something from the bank at nine at night.*

I stuck my hands in my pockets. I watched traffic go past beyond the parking-lot. Again, I wondered if I'd been followed. Maybe. In truth, I couldn't tell. I felt like a yo-yo on the end of a string — sometimes the player spun me through the air or rolled me along the ground, other times, the player rested and left me alone. I was a toy, a piece in a board-game. Somewhere along the way I'd ceased to be human. I had no free will. My actions were all predetermined. The only destiny I had was one I hadn't crafted for myself.

'What have you got in your safe-deposit box that's so urgent you need it at this time of night?' Sonderheim asked.

'It's confidential,' I said. 'Sorry, Bo.'

'Something to do with a patient, I guess.'

I nodded.

Sonderheim peered across the parking-lot. I looked at my watch again.

A car came into the lot, a dark Land Rover. A man, stumpy and aggressive, emerged, slammed his door, walked to where I stood with Bo Sonderheim. He had a security-man's face, skin etched with lines of suspicion developed over the years. His eyelids were tiny hoods, half-moons. He looked at Sonderheim and then at me.

Sonderheim said, 'This is Doctor Lomax.'

The security guy said his name was Parlance. He didn't shake hands. His voice was gravelly. 'This couldn't wait, huh? This has to be done now? Rush rush rush.'

'I'm afraid so,' I said.

'You any idea what this entails, Lomax?' he said.

Sonderheim made a conciliatory noise, a soft throat-clearing. 'Rick, Jerry's an old and valued customer.'

Parlance was unimpressed. He stared at me with raw belligerence. What did he care about customer relationships? His was a world of electronic security devices, circuits, codes. 'I had to contact our central security office and ask for special access, which means they have to rouse a computer expert to make certain adjustments to the system, so that we can go inside this building without bringing half the goddam cops in this town screaming here in their wah-wah wagons. What I'm saying is, this is untidy, this is a nuisance, and not just for Sonderheim and me, but people you don't even know, people sitting behind consoles — '

'A key would have been simpler,' I said.

Parlance looked at Sonderheim. 'A key? Did he say key? Is he serious?'

Sonderheim tried a smile. 'Jerry enjoys a little joke.'

'A key, a key,' Parlance said, shaking his head in disbelief. 'Life is complicated, Lomax. Life is way beyond Chubbs and nifty little Yales and dead-bolts.' He moved towards the bank building. 'Let's go in, get this over with.'

We climbed the steps. Sonderheim punched numeric keys on a board attached to the wall. I listened to the bleep sound each key made. He must have punched fifteen or sixteen before a security light went on in the foyer and he was able to open the door. Inside, the place was hushed, weird, and had the ambiance of a museum after-hours.

'Get the business over with,' Sonderheim said. He took a small cellphone from his coat pocket and spoke into it. 'We're in.' He severed the line and looked at me. 'The system reactivates in five minutes. You better move it, Lomax.'

I went downstairs with Bo Sonderheim to the vault where the safe-deposit boxes were stored. I accessed mine, opened it, looked at the white envelope. This time I didn't hesitate. I removed the envelope and stuck it in the inside pocket of my jacket. Then I shut the box and replaced it, thinking how like a tiny coffin it was, the whole vault a miniature morgue.

'Through?' Bo Sonderheim asked.

I patted my pocket. 'Through,' I said. I looked at my watch again.

We went back upstairs. Parlance was waiting close to the door. We all went outside. On the steps, Parlance said, 'I suggest you try to keep regular hours in the future, Lomax.'

'I'd like that,' I said.

I thanked them, and I turned and walked towards the Honda. I heard Parlance say, 'That guy helps sick people? He needs some of his own medicine, you want my opinion.'

Droll.

That was when I saw the Pontiac slide into the parking-lot at about twenty-miles an hour. It slowed to a crawl just in front of the bank entrance. I saw Parlance stare inquisitively at the sight of the car; he slipped a hand inside the pocket of his jacket. The Pontiac was still. Fumes pumped out of its exhaust. The air smelled of burning sewage. Parlance descended a step, his hand still in his pocket. I was about thirty yards away.

That was when the first shot was fired.

A crack, a burst of light, an assault on the ears. Instinctively I dropped to the ground behind the Honda, and heard a second shot. I raised my face to look. I saw Bo Sonderheim go down like an axed tree and my heart bucked in my chest. He lay on the steps, holding his leg and crying out in pain. The gunman had fired from the passenger seat of the Pontiac, and now Parlance, exposed, was firing at the car. More flares, gun blasts.

Parlance rushed down the steps and ducked behind his Land Rover. I heard glass break. The Pontiac wheeled past the Land Rover and more gunfire issued from the passenger window, and Parlance returned the fire; I imagined a war zone, riot squads, buildings burning. All around the lot commercial buildings, hives by day, were empty and silent.

Poor Sondheim, who'd come down to the bank at my request, a favor to me, lay screaming in pain, and I couldn't do a damn thing about it because if I moved I'd be caught in the crossfire between the Pontiac and the Land Rover. I reached up, opened the Honda's door a little, but now the Pontiac came in my direction, belching out great palls of rubbery exhaust fumes, muffler dragging on concrete and creating bright sparks.

Parlance must have busted the tailpipe with one of his shots.

I thought: *If I could get in the Honda and drive away I might escape.* But the Pontiac cruised towards me, clattering over speed-bumps with dangerous indifference; the gunman fired from the window and his shot struck the back bumper of the Honda and I could feel the force of the bullet reverberate the length of the chassis and through my bones. I was kneeling, half in and half out of the car; I rolled over on my side and lay close to the car even as I pondered the idea of getting up and sprinting across the lot and running down a side street where I might lose myself.

Parlance fired two quick shots from the cover of the Land Rover. One struck the roof of the Pontiac, the other smashed the rear window. The big car spun, a complete shuddering circle, then came to a halt. The doors on both sides opened. I saw, from a tight ground-level angle, Big Skull step out, gun in hand; the other guy, the fair-haired one, emerged from the driver's side clutching his left arm. He must have been hit. The sleeve of his shirt dangled loose and his arm looked useless.

I heard him say, 'Sonofabitch.'

Big Skull stared in the direction of the Honda. Seemingly indifferent to the gunman in the Land Rover about fifty yards away, he called to me, 'Jerry, old pal, just give us what you got from the bank and I'll stick my gun safely back in its little holster and peace will return to Happy Valley. Whaddya say, Jerry?'

I lay pressed to the ground. I heard the pair approach the Honda. I could see their feet on the other side of the car. They were within five, six feet of where I lay. The Land Rover started across the lot and was collecting speed as it headed towards the Pontiac.

'Aw, fuck,' Big Skull said, and gazed at the moving vehicle. 'Some guys don't know when to quit.'

Parlance fired his gun from the window at the Pontiac and the two men flattened themselves on the ground and Parlance kept coming at them, firing as he drove, his aim wayward. I heard bullets bite asphalt. I heard the pock as concrete cracked. The Land Rover continued for about fifty yards, then turned back; Parlance, obviously enraged by the shooting of bank personnel on bank property, was driving towards the Pontiac again.

Big Skull fired into the Rover's windshield.

The four-wheel drive vehicle skidded, swerved, struck an electric pole, causing a live-wire to sag and create a wild blue and yellow sizzling effect, so that the Rover seemed to have been outlined in lethal neon.

I thought of Parlance inside, voltage killing him with the certainty of an electric chair.

Like a kid at a firework show, Big Skull said, 'Wow.'

I rolled quietly away from the Honda, got to my feet and ran to where Bo Sonderheim's Ultima was parked. The keys, mercifully, were in the dash. I drove towards the street and when I glanced in the rearview mirror I saw Big Skull and his friend rush towards the Pontiac — but I had a better car and a headstart, and I was out of their range before they could even get their rusted, half-wrecked clunker out of the lot.

Behind my eyes the sparking image of the Land Rover still burned, but dimmer now, like the lights of a midway losing power. I thought of Parlance and Sonderheim, one dead, the other seriously wounded. And it was as if everything I touched, however lightly, however briefly, was destined to perish.

I was a curse; a carrier of violence.

9.30 p.m.

A knife, a razor-blade; I imagined sharp steel drawn across Sondra's throat. I could see blood rush from a severed artery: how long before she'd die? Dead thoughts. Morbid passages in the mind. Dark blue fugues. My hand trembled. My shirt was glued to my skin. The beat of my heart was arrhythmic. I was composed of loose fibers, strands I couldn't stitch together.

I called an emergency number on my cellphone as I drove. I told the sympathetic guy who answered that there had been a shooting, and a man may have been seriously wounded, and I gave the address of the bank. An ambulance would be despatched and Sonderheim rushed to an emergency room.

Then I removed the envelope from my jacket. I opened it and took out the cassette it contained. I thought of the voices trapped on magnetic tape, waiting to be freed. I thrust the tape towards the slot of the cassette-deck, missing the first and second times because my hand wouldn't be still. I finally inserted the cassette on the third attempt and there was an instant hiss from the speakers.

Then I heard myself say: *August fourth,* *nineteen ninety-six.*

I thought: *I don't want to listen to this. It happened, and you remember it, you don't need to listen to it.* But you do. Refresh your memory. Reacquaint yourself with what you're giving away.

I heard my own voice again. I never liked the sound of it. It seemed nasal. *Subject is in a state of hypnosis. Can you hear me, Emily?*

In the dreamy voice of someone in a trance-condition, Emily Ford said, *Yes, I can hear you.*

Can you remember some things for me, Emily?

Silence.

Go back to March nineteen ninety-five. Can you do that?

Yes.

March seventeenth specifically . . . Where are you?

I'm in a courthouse.

And what's happening?

Silence.

A man is standing at a table.

You've seen this man before?

Yes.

Is he Billy Fear?

Yes.

Is there a judge presiding?

267

Justice Randolph Hartley.

What is he saying?

He's saying, he's saying . . .

What, Emily?

He's telling Billy Fear he's dismissing the case against him. That can't be true. That cannot be true.

Why?

Because Billy Fear is the killer and everybody knows it and Hartley is setting him free on account of evidence illegally gathered by the cops, no no nooooo way —

Relax, Emily. Take a deep breath.

I want to scream, because everybody knows Billy Fear is guilty.

Relax, Emily. Please.

I remembered how she scratched the air with her hands bent into claws, as if she were tearing at Fear's face — or Hartley's, I wasn't sure which. I'd caught her wrists and held them and watched her head move from side to side on the pillow, a rigid gesture, her muscles locked. I worried about a possible seizure, because her skin darkened and a pulse throbbed visibly on the right side of her head and sweat covered her face. Her eyes were wide open. I kept saying, *Relax, relax, relax.* The trance imprisoned her. She didn't want to come back from it. She was frozen in the buried past by the sheer force of her feelings. She tried to rake my face and I twisted her hand to one side to defend myself. Only under hypnosis did she remember the trial. In her conscious state, the trial and the discovery of her dead parents were bolted inside a cabinet she couldn't or wouldn't open.

She became still. *Hartley's looking at me.*

In what way, Emily?

He's sorry. He knows Fear's guilty, but he can't do anything. His hands are tied. The law's been broken. He can't break it again to send Fear to prison. Those incompetent detectives screwed up. They didn't get a warrant to search Fear's goddam trailer. There's even a suspicion they planted incriminating evidence. They broke the law. Now Hartley's staring at me with this look of pity.

What are you feeling?

I can't put a name to it, no one name: it's hatred and helplessness and terror and astonishment and I'm sick in my stomach because I want to do something, I don't know what. I don't hate Hartley, he's helpless, but I hate Fear. Hartley's standing up. It's finished. It's done. Fear's acquitted.

What is Fear doing?

He's smiling, oh, he's smiling, and he hugs his lawyer, then he punches the air with his fist, I can't watch him, but now he's turning his face and he's grinning at me.

The tape was silent, then another short period of hissing, followed by a click. I reached out to eject it, but instead I pressed the *Pause* button. I dialed Emily's number on my cellphone; she answered immediately.

'Where are you, Jerry?'

'On La Cienega,' I said. 'It's time to meet up.'

'Where do you suggest?'

I'd been giving this careful thought. My house was out of the question. It was certain that somebody would be watching it. Likewise Emily's home. I said, 'You know the Pacifica Center on La Cienega?'

'I know it.'

'Meet me at the offices of LaBrea Records,' I said.

'Now?'

'Faster than now, Emily.'

'I'm out the door,' she said.

'One thing. Make absolutely sure you're not followed. Be devious. Be inventive. Use one of your guards as a decoy. Think of something. When you arrive at the Pacifica Center, go inside *Look & Listen*. Walk to the back of the store and get inside one of the elevators. Take it to the tenth floor. I'll be waiting.'

She hung up.

I pressed the *Play* button and heard myself say: *August eleventh, nineteen ninety-six. Subject is in a state of hypnosis.*

How are you today, Emily?

OK.

Relaxed?

Yeah. Sure.

I want you to go back. Early April nineteen ninety-five. Let's say April fourth. Where are you?

In my parents' old house.

What are you doing?

I'm just walking through the rooms. They're empty now. All the furniture's been removed. Men are painting the walls. The house is going on the market.

What room are you in?

My parents' bedroom.

And what do you see?

I see . . . I see where fresh paint covers the wall, that place where there were bloodstains from before . . . my mother . . .

What are you feeling, Emily?

Sorrow. Injustice. The world is all wrong.

And what do you want to do about that?

I can't make up my mind.

But you're thinking. You're working something out in your head, right?

I never stop trying to work it out. All the

*time. It haunts me. She was lying on the
. . . bedroom floor with her face blown off.*
You think about Judge Hartley, too?
Sometimes.
Do you fault him?
Silence.
*I think he lacks courage. He's a prisoner of
procedure.*
And Billy Fear?
Yes. I think about Billy Fear.
*What do you feel about him on April
fourth, nineteen ninety-five?*
Nothing has changed.
You hate him?
That's not the correct word.

I killed the tape and parked in a street
behind the Pacifica Center, then walked to
the entrance of *Look & Listen*. I strolled
through the audio-visual assault-course; my
mind was elsewhere, distanced. Frantic
figures danced on TV monitors. A gorgeous
chocolate-colored girl on screen licked an
ice-cream cone with her long pink tongue;
subtlety was dead in our world. Speakers
boomed. Zombie sales clerks wandered
around as if on castors.

I moved towards the elevators, pressed the
Call button, then I rode to the tenth floor.
The corridor was half-lit. The offices were
mainly empty, although I noticed a couple of

272

lights in the bright white studio where LaBrea's art department was located. They worked round the clock in that space, young men and women — graphic artists — filled with a sense of their own hip importance.

I looked at my watch, although I didn't want to: 9.47.

I stood by the elevator. I heard it fall in the shaft, a door open way below, then it was rising again. Emily stepped out. She clutched my hand in the manner of somebody who expects to find her companion's flesh stone-cold and in need of warmth. A tight grip.

She said, 'Talk to me, Jerry. Tell me where you've been. What's happening.'

'Let's go inside Sondra's office,' I said.

We moved down the corridor.

Sondra's room was big, cluttered with all kinds of promo materials — posters, glossies, life-sized cutouts — and stacks of CDs and stereo equipment. I felt her presence strongly in this place. I saw a half-smoked Camel Light in an ashtray on her desk; the butt was lipstick-stained. That might have been the last cigarette she'd smoked before Sweetzer told her she was pregnant. A coffee-mug with the logo of LaBrea Records sat on a pad of Post-It notes. All kinds of messages and schedules had been thumbtacked to a cork board on the wall — call this person, call that, a ragged assembly of numbers, dates, names. I was moved by her absence, by the traces of a life interrupted. I ached.

From the store ten floors below I could hear the thud-thud of music; how did Sondra put up with that all day? Maybe you reached a point where it was background noise. Emily Ford stood by the desk, one hand lightly touching the surface. She held a briefcase in the other.

I heard myself say, 'Leo Gerson was Sondra's partner in crime. He came up with the pseudonym Timothy Dole. Nardini's man Resick apparently bribed the undercover cop, and Sondra and Gerson just strolled away. You didn't hear this from me, by the way.'

'I couldn't do a thing about it, even if I wanted to. It's hearsay.' She sat down on the purple-velvet sofa; I remembered the day Sondra had chosen it from a furniture catalog, *I love purple velvet, it's so goddam regal, I'll feel like a queen in my office.* Emily's black overcoat parted. She stretched one long leg out and, reaching down, lightly massaged the muscle in her left calf.

'Cramp,' she said. She worked the muscle a moment. 'Well, I explored a few avenues looking for this guy Stam.'

'Any luck?' I said.

'Nothing.'

'He's good,' I said.

'He's got his act down, sure.'

And I'd been fooled by it.

She said, 'You asked about Jane Steel before. Why? Do you think she's involved?'

'It's a possibility.' I was conjuring up connections, stretching membranes to where they might just snap. Jane Steel and Stam in some kind of collusion. Was that conceivable? Anything was possible.

She took a blue cardboard folder from her briefcase and opened it. 'Here's some background on Steel I didn't mention earlier. Born Harrow, Middlesex, July fourth, nineteen fifty-five. Independence Day, you'll notice . . . She entered the US in April nineteen ninety-six. Originally she came on a tourist visa. She somehow managed to change this to a one-year work-permit along the way. Apparently she's forgotten to renew it, or else she's worried that an extension might not be granted, which sometimes happens. You've got an illegal alien working for you, Jerry.'

'Anything else?'

'Only what I already told you. Gun-permit is out of date. A surprising oversight, given the fact you consider her Little Miss Efficiency. And now you think she might be implicated. How? She broke into your floor-safe? Is that what you mean?'

'Maybe,' I said. 'The contents of my goddam floor-safe were of interest to a few people . . . You included, Emily.'

She blinked. 'Of course they were of interest to me, why wouldn't they be? I'm not denying it. We discussed all this.'

'I didn't think you'd stoop to violence, though,' I said.

She gave me a baffled look.

'Don't even think about bullshitting me, Emily. You've got a nice set-up inside the LAPD, haven't you? Very tidy. You get Sy Lancing to mug me — which was crude and, as it turned out, ineffective. I guess you figured he'd steal my briefcase, my wallet, carkeys . . . plus the key to my office. Was that the idea, Emily? Armed with the key, you could dispatch one of your private guards to my office and he'd get the safe open somehow. Or maybe you'd use a pro.'

'I wanted the records,' she said. She shrugged. I admired her for not even trying to deny the scheme.

I said, 'Bad strategy, especially from somebody sworn to uphold the law. But I liked the toy knife, and how you used Petrosian to contain the situation. Tidy.'

'I wanted the records, for Christ's sake,'

she said again. 'But I didn't want you to get hurt in the process.'

'I am deeply touched, Emily,' I said. 'Sy Lancing was the one that got hurt. You should have sent in more muscle.'

'OK, I underestimated you, I didn't think you were such a hot-shot,' she said. 'I'm sorry. I'm deeply apologetic. I knew those guys were coming down from Washington. I panicked, I guess. I wish I hadn't. It was a poor stunt, and it was bolted together at the last damn moment.'

'Unfortunately, it's more than just the contents of the floor-safe that we need to worry about,' I said. I thought: *You don't need to tell her the truth. You can lie if you like.*

But I couldn't. She deserved to know. It had been a secret too long. I'd carried it alone, and I was tired of it.

'Worse? How?' she asked.

'There's more material,' I said.

'What kind of material?'

'Of a confidential nature. I think that's the expression.'

'Where?'

'In a safe-deposit box.'

'Was it also stolen?'

'No. I have it. The point is, nobody else was supposed to know about it. But it hasn't worked out that way.'

'And you think Jane Steel knew about this box?'

'I guess she did. The rental bill for the box comes to my office. She couldn't have missed it. She opens all the mail.'

'How did she know this box contained something confidential?'

'I haven't figured that out yet.'

'It's a leap, Jerry. You jump from her *knowing* about the box to knowing what it *contained*. How?'

'I don't know how. Let's say she aided and abetted Stam in the matter of getting into the floor-safe. How they worked it, the practicalities of it, the mechanics . . . I don't know. Then somewhere down the line, when they decide the material from the floor-safe isn't powerful enough, she tells him about the safe-deposit box. She surmises there might be something juicy tucked away in a bank vault.'

'Surmises, Jerry?'

'Whatever. Stam mentions this box to the guy who keeps calling me — the contact guy — and that puts the pressure on me. *Open the box. Get me the material you've got stashed, Jerry. We've got your wife.*'

'Why don't you call Jane Steel? Tell her what's bugging you. Confront her.'

'I don't think she's home,' I said.

I walked restlessly to the other side of the room, paused beside the stereo equipment and the stack of CDs that were mainly LaBrea freebies — demo CDs of rock bands, CDs that had never been released for one reason or another. Some were probably bad. Others might have been made by bands Gerson had axed. I ran a fingertip down the glossy spines.

I glanced at Emily and I thought: *She doesn't need to know. Spare her this. Why should you?*

'What kind of material are we talking about, anyway?' she asked.

I didn't answer.

'It's connected to me,' she said. 'Right?'

I thought how vulnerable she looked; how unaware of the blade about to fall. But I wasn't about to buy all the way into that look. A woman perfectly capable of orchestrating a mugging and sending one of her own private force to investigate wasn't exactly defenseless. A woman who'd spent much of her professional life in single-minded pursuit of criminals, and yet was prepared to use criminal means herself when she thought it necessary, wasn't lacking the capacity for duplicity.

'It's material you didn't keep with my main file, is that it? Material you wanted

279

to hide away, right?'

'Right.'

'My God. You edited my records years ago, didn't you?'

'I just decided that this particular item belonged in a more secure place than my floor-safe. That's all.'

'Why, Jerry? What's so special about this *item*? Have you been protecting me from something?'

'As much as I could,' I said.

'Why?'

I wasn't sure why. Duty? A certain affection? On account of an oath I'd taken once when I was young and gullible? Or because I'd traveled the private highways of her mind and sympathized with her and how she'd acted? That sympathy had eroded to some extent, but for some contrary reason I still had an urge to comfort her. *Explain that*, I thought. *The vagaries of the heart*. Feelings were beyond cartography. They could be explored, but never fully mapped.

I stared at her. I was conscious of the clock on the cassette-player. It was a bright blue color. The minute counter changed soundlessly. A digital reality. A microchip kept track of time and sent messages along the arteries of a mother-board. In this digital reality there were no feelings, no emotions, no regrets. I wanted to enter this world and live my life within the confines of it. Silence and nothing, no pain, no threats of death.

I took the envelope that contained the cassette out of my pocket. Emily crossed the floor towards me.

I removed the tape. I'd marked it *Side B* in felt-tip pen, and dated it *September 7, 1996*. I held the cassette towards the slot and Emily covered my hand with her own, stalling me, preventing me from putting the cassette into the deck.

'That's the item?' she asked. 'A tape. A goddam tape.'

'Yes.'

'And you're going to play it?'

'You have to know what's here,' I said.

'Don't make me, Jerry. Don't make me do this.'

'If you don't listen, you won't understand what I have to do and why I have to do it.'

She looked at me for a time, then she said, 'Sometimes I have these ... areas of experience that are sort of blacked-out, things I can't see. They're like sounds coming from a room I can't quite find. The experience has a dreamy feel, and I've grown comfortable with it. And I want it to stay that way. But you're going to change all that if you play the tape, aren't you?'

Yes, I thought. *Everything changes for you, Emily.*

'Just listen,' I said. I pushed the tape into the slot and let my finger hover close to the *Play* button.

She turned away from me. I caught her by the shoulders and brought her around to face me and I held her for a time.

Then I reached out and punched the *Play* button.

9.52 p.m.

I heard my own voice say *testing, testing* and then the date.

The patient is in a state of trance. Can you hear me, Emily?

Yes.

I want you to do something for me. I want you to go back to August sixth, nineteen ninety-five. Can you do that?

Yes.

Where are you at around two in the afternoon?

It's hot, it's very hot, I'm in what looks like a trailer park. It's called something Glades. OK. Whipperwill Glades. There are weeds growing all over.

What else, Emily?

I'm wearing blue Levis and a matching jacket.

Fine. What other things do you remember, Emily?

I go inside this trailer. I'm very quiet. Walking on tiptoe.

Whose trailer is this?

A pause in the tape.

Emily pulled away from me. She stood with

her arms folded, her back pressed against the shelves of CDs. She stared at the floor. A muscle worked in her jaw.

'Stop it, Jerry,' she said.

'Why? You don't know what's coming.'

'I have a bad feeling,' she said.

'Listen. Just listen.' I put my hand on hers. Her flesh was cold.

She said, 'I just had this flash . . . like *déjà vu*. Only I don't know what I was *déjà vu-ing*.' She shivered, and I drew her closer to me. I didn't want her to hear this recording without my support. I didn't want her to think I was using this tape as the ammunition of revenge for the abortive mugging. She'd erased the experience — and now she was about to be exposed to it, and it was as toxic as a radioactive substance.

He's sitting on a couch, there's a crocheted rug tossed over it. He's got a can of tomato soup in one hand and a spoon in the other; he's eating the soup straight out the can, cold. He's wearing a maroon T-shirt, sleeveless.

Tell me what happens, Emily.

I don't speak. He looks up and sees me. But he's wasted, totally wrecked. I don't think he even sees me. Or he thinks I'm a hallucination.

And then what?

284

I have . . .

What do you have, Emily?

'Stop it now, Jerry,' she said. She tugged her hand free of mine and reached for the *Stop* button, but I caught her fingers and pulled her back against me. I encircled her with my arms, imprisoned her against my own body. She struggled a moment.

'Listen,' I said.

She shook her head furiously. 'No.' She tried again to break away from me. I held her all the more tightly.

I have a gun in my pocket. The gun belonged to my Dad. I take the gun out.

What happens?

He looks at me and laughs and then he spoons more of the cold soup to his lips.

And what do you do, Emily?

I just go up close to him and..

And what?

'Jesus Christ, Jerry! Stop the goddam tape, I don't need to hear this!' She reached out and punched the *Stop* button, and as I caught her by the arms and tried to move her away from the cassette-player, she suddenly swung up her fist and struck me directly on the bridge of my nose. I could feel blood run from my nostrils and tiny starry sparkles appeared in my vision. She turned, made a move for the tape, trying to haul it out of the deck, but I grabbed her hand and twisted her wrist. Blood falling from my face splashed over her fingers. She raised a knee quickly, directed it at my groin; I swiveled away from the thrust of her kneecap and she caught me on the side of the hip. Then she lost her balance and we fell, clutching each other, to the floor.

'Goddam you, Jerry. God fucking damn you.'

'Emily, Emily,' I said. 'I don't want to fight with you.'

'Then don't play the fucking tape!'

She pulled a hand free and spread her fingers like weapons, directing them at my eyes. I managed to turn my head a little, and felt her fingernails, missing my eyes, stab my cheek in little jabs of pain. This fighting, this grappling, this squalid warfare on the floor — how could I make it stop? She was strong, and energized by a force I'd never seen in her before. I caught her shoulders, pinned her to the Navajo rug, rolled on top of her, using my weight to keep her in place. She stared up at me. Blood dripped from my face into her eyes and she blinked. My blood gathered in small flecks at the corners of her mouth.

All at once she was still. I placed my hands flat on either side of her face, feeling the structure of bone. There was an enormous distance in the dark of her eyes. She was like a kite that had suddenly collapsed, a darkness folded within itself.

Then I rolled away from her, and I stood up and punched the *Play* button. Emily's voice filled the room.

And I shoot him in the face.

Like that?

Oh yes.

You think he deserved to die?

Deserved? Billy Fear deserved it all right.

She looked at me. I wasn't sure she saw me. She uttered a silent *No*. I heard the tape hiss, then a period of quiet, but I knew there was more, because I'd listened to this tape a score of times — more than that — before I'd decided to bury it in a box at a bank.

I pressed the *Stop* button.

'Oh, Christ, *Christ*.' She gazed at me. 'This is crucifying.'

'You had to know.'

She shut her eyes now and I couldn't hear any sound from her. It was as if she'd suspended the act of breathing. I slipped the cassette from the deck and put it back in my pocket, then I went down on my knees and touched the side of her face, shoved a strand of black hair away from her ear. She looked devastated and lonely. She looked as if she were emerging from years in a *gulag* of amnesia. And she didn't like the outside world. She preferred the prison, the isolation.

'You're giving that tape to the kidnappers,' she said.

'You see any other choice, Emily?'

'Why didn't you go to the cops with it years ago?' she asked.

'Maybe I felt you'd been through too much already. Maybe I didn't believe you deserved to be punished for shooting Billy Fear.'

She was staring at me, but seeing through me. 'I wanted that job in DC, Jerry.'

'I know.'

'But I'm not exactly the right person for it, am I? I killed a man. It doesn't matter that he deserved to die. That's not the point. The Attorney-General of the United States shouldn't have blood on her hands.' She made a gesture of enormous frustration, banging tight fists together, knocking knuckle against knuckle. 'I worked and I worked. I drove myself hard, year in, year out. I passed up on the chance of leading a real life. Now do I just give up? Do I just walk the hell away from my dream? Is that what you expect me to do? I don't get to Washington. I fade into goddam obscurity.'

She was never going to DC. It had been a misplaced dream from the beginning. She had too many enemies. She was too vulnerable. She'd been too severely damaged. She was one of the walking wounded.

I helped her to sit upright.

'So I drop out of sight, quit my work, go off quietly into the dusk? Is that what I do? Say 'Welcome' to oblivion?' She raised an eyebrow, passed a hand through her hair. 'What will they do with the tape, Jerry?'

'Probably nothing. They'll have what they wanted in the beginning. The threat of exposure is enough to make you take your name out of the picture.'

'But the tape will always be out there somewhere, always hanging over me, I'll be waiting for it to resurface somewhere down the line, the dread will never go away — '

My cellphone was ringing. I grabbed it from my pocket. Emily held my arm very tightly, as if the sound of the telephone suddenly brought the whole world into the room, all the fears and terrors of what lay outside, all the doubts and anxieties that permeated the night.

I heard Sondra say, 'I'm sick, Jerry. Real sick. Come get me, please . . . '

My heart was suddenly pumping Freon. I shouted her name into the handset two or three times, but it was a futile gesture because the line had already been disconnected.

Sick, I thought. The drugs had affected her

. . . what else? Her voice had sounded lifeless and very far away. I tried not to panic. I looked at the blood I'd deposited on the receiver.

I shut the phone off. I turned to Emily, who was standing motionless beside the cassette-player. She seemed to be gazing inward, checking the contours of her mind, her memory. Maybe she doubted the veracity of the tape. Maybe she was thinking that her unconscious had taken the reality — the slaying of Fear — and built a fantasy of participation around it. She wished she'd killed him, and so she'd concocted a story of her own involvement. But that didn't work, because the tape contained tiny details that had never been released in any newspaper story. The color of Billy Fear's shirt. The profusion of weeds around his trailer. These weren't the kinds of trivia that you encountered in press reports, and certainly never on TV news. Murder was commonplace, anyway; who had time to be interested in the color of a slain man's shirt? The death of another junkie. Nobody gave a shit. The nation barely had time to register murder any more. The cities were running with blood. We were blasé, we didn't want to know.

She suddenly hauled the cassette-player from the wall and tossed it a couple of feet in the air, and I tried to catch it, but I didn't react in time and it clattered to the floor, dangling black wires as it fell. The back panel broke off and some computerized bits and pieces slid out. Emily made a sound like someone in sharp pain, and then began to pick CDs from the shelf one at a time, casually dropping them on the floor, one after another; picking one up, dropping it, picking up, dropping. Shock. A breakdown of sorts. How else could her system deal with what she'd learned? What she'd lived with for years, without knowing the experience inhabited her? That the memory was there, and festering?

I caught her hands but she jerked herself away from me and went on pulling the flat, glossy boxes from the shelves. She was working faster now, hands a flurry. 'You could issue my tape as a CD, Jerry. You could get that sleazoid Gerson to put it out on his label — '

'Emily, please — '

'Emily, please, Emily, please, Emily, *please* . . . Well, fuck you, Jerry, fuck you!' Hysteria had altered her voice; it was higher, each vowel shortened like a gasp. Her face had changed too; it had become rigid, and her eyes were manic, like those of somebody emerging from a collapsed

291

building — shocked, irrational, unseeing. 'Think up a neat title, put a nifty photo on the box, maybe a tit shot and some see-through lace, something sexy, wham-bam, a hit, a fucking big hit, Jerry!'

I struck her with the flat of my hand against the side of her face, as lightly as I could; she seemed not to feel it. I wished I had a hypo and a bottle of liquid Demerol. I'd fill the syringe and inject her, sending her into temporary oblivion, a trip on the fast highway out of her pain. She was surrounded by the CDs on the floor, and hauling more of them from the shelves all the time, her hysteria speeding up her actions.

She started tossing CDs through the air like Frisbees.

'There. There. And there. And here's another one!'

They whizzed past me, struck walls, the desk-lamp. This was madness. Everything in the room had broken free of its moorings. Gravity was defunct.

I grabbed her arms and held them against her sides. She was breathing hard. The look in her eyes was poisonous.

'Calm down, cool it,' I said. I thought of Sondra: *Come get me, please.* The dream had no ending. The nightmare was without limits.

'Fuck calm,' she said.

'Emily. Come on. *Calm.*'

'Shove calm up your fucking ass,' she said.

She bent her head and opened her mouth, then plunged her teeth into the back of my hand. I moaned with the pain of it. I saw the deep impression left by her teeth in my skin.

'Shove calm, Jerry . . . ' And she slid slowly from my hold to the floor, where she kneeled, shoulders slumped, among the slick CD boxes. She was crying in a strangulated way, holding back each sob instead of releasing it.

She covered her face with her hands. Her body trembled. I touched her shoulder lightly.

I said, 'I don't have any choice, Emily.'

Maybe she whispered through the spaces between her fingers. Maybe she said, *I know, I know.* I wasn't sure. Instead, my attention was drawn to the upturned CDs. I reached down and picked up one of the boxes that had fallen face down in the heap, and I looked at the photograph on the back.

A picture of a band called *Fibber McGee.*

I'd never heard of them.

There were four faces in the photo, and I recognized one. He was holding a guitar. His face had slightly haunted eyes.

I knew him.

10.03 p.m.

The fire inside her suddenly flickered and died. Drained of energy, she slumped against me, and I helped her to the sofa. She was very light, delicate; she might have been composed of fragile materials, paper stretched over slender struts of balsa-wood. She lay down on her side and looked at me as if I were very far away.

'I'm tired. I'm so damned *weary*. Just do what you think is right, Jerry.'

There was only one right.

I walked to the desk. I skipped over the heap of CDs on the floor. I opened the telephone directory. I found the name I wanted, wrote the address down in a small notebook, stuck the book in my pocket. I looked at the photograph of the band that called itself *Fibber McGee*, as if to make absolutely sure I wasn't mistaken.

I wasn't. It was a face I knew very well.

I said to Emily, 'Rest. Stay where you are and try to rest.'

She looked at me, but her gaze was focused inward. Maybe she was sifting the wreckage of her life, wondering how it might be salvaged, how the torpedoed ship of her ambition might be raised up from the place where it had been sunk. I didn't know. I didn't stop to ask. I didn't have time.

I wondered whether some little spark of optimism remained inside me even now: some absurdly faint hope that I might somehow salvage something out of all this, maybe rescue Sondra, and at the same time save Emily Ford from *total* ruin. If I allowed myself to think like that, I was deluding myself. The world didn't work that way. Nothing was that neat. Everything was ragged round the edges, and impenetrable at the center.

I hurried from the office. I calculated it was going to take me five minutes to reach my destination. It was already past the deadline. Just. My cellphone would ring at any moment. *You're running late, Lomax.*

I left the building, ran to where I'd parked Bo Sonderheim's Ultima. I stared into the dark as I drove, noticing how streetlights turned into shapeless gashes of light against the smudges on my glasses. It didn't matter. I could see where I was going, and that was all I needed. I passed the abandoned, fire-damaged shell of a warehouse a few blocks from Hollywood Boulevard. I saw boys and girls trawling the sidewalk for custom. Their faces, hard-bitten and sad, exploded in the lights of my car. City of Lost Angels. One hopeful boy, long-haired and slim, stepped forward and I almost collided with him. But I spun the wheel at the last possible moment, catching a glimpse of his face, whiter than any mime's, the eyes like a couple of tiny mirrors reflecting the beams of the car. An accident, I didn't need that, I didn't need anything that would slow my progress.

Fibber McGee. One in a multitude of bands that hadn't made it anywhere. Doomed to silence and neglect in half-price trays in record stores, or to those sad cardboard boxes in Salvation Army shops. Maybe the CD hadn't even been released by LaBrea, because the band had broken up. Maybe there had been acrimony and betrayal, or Gerson, the tastemaker, had decided the band's sound didn't quite belong in the Now, that it wasn't going to get bodies dancing and cash-registers ringing. So Gerson killed the album. He was the executioner of careers.

The cellphone rang. I picked up, said nothing.

'It's past the deadline, Lomax. Are you trying to play games with me again? Running and running and hiding and hiding. When will you learn that there's no escape route, Lomax? No back staircase. No concealed doorways or hatches. Change cars, change your clothes, change your name, dye your hair and change your whole damned appearance, there's no hiding-place. I know what it is — you're stoned on adrenalin. You're buzzing. You need another blast. Just say the word and I'll put something together for you without any trouble. More fireworks for the good doctor.'

I wondered if he knew where I was, if his associates had tracked me. I said, 'You think I get a kick out of people being killed? I figured you'd know me better than that. *You're* the one with a taste for blood. Violence gives you a hard-on. You're a sick shit.'

He laughed. 'Sick shit? Doesn't sound like a professional diagnosis to me, Lomax. Say I hire you as my shrink and then I submit your bills to my health-insurance company — can I claim I need psychiatric treatment on the grounds that I'm, excuse the imprecise expression, a *sick shit*? We don't need to guess what the insurance company would say, do we? Let me tell you what I think, Lomax. You're too involved. You can't make detached judgments. You need to be aloof in your line of work, and you've lost it, doctor. You've let it slip away. I don't blame you. You're only human.'

I heard him light a cigarette, then inhale

deeply. It was the first knowledge I had of any of his habits. I said, 'Look, we had a deal. I got what you wanted from the safe-deposit box. As soon as I stepped out of the bank with the goods, your guys launched a goddam assault and tried to take it away from me. The way I see it, you made an attempt to renege on the deal. You planned to rip me off. There was never any bargain.'

'I want the goods,' he said. 'I just wasn't sure you'd play according to my script — '

'Your script is the only one. You've got my wife, for Christ's sake! You think I was going to turn my back on her? Tell you to piss off, you're not getting the goods, you can do what you like with her?'

He was quiet for a moment. 'I never intended to keep your wife. Believe me. I want the material. We're all under some kind of pressure in this situation, Lomax. It's not only you. I have to deal with certain parties who think my approach might have been more . . . let's say, direct. But that doesn't concern you. As for the deal, it's valid. It's always been valid. Regrettably, a little too much haste was shown at the bank, things got out of hand . . . '

Out of hand, I thought. *Too much haste*. But I was interested in only one thing. 'Tell me about my wife's condition.'

'She's sleeping — '

'Wake her. Do that for me.'

'I really don't intend to wake her, Lomax. You see, I have this wonderfully sweet image. Call me romantic. She wakes up in her own bed with her husband lying beside her, and all's well in the world and God's up there looking wise and benign. And Emily Ford disappears from public life, and all my friends and associates, who do not like the idea of her candidacy because it runs counter to their business interests, can breath a collective sigh of relief. You're following me?'

'She becomes a backwater lawyer somewhere,' I said. 'She gives up chasing big-time criminals.'

'Oh no, she gives up on law *entirely*, Lomax. Maybe she teaches in a Montessori someplace. Or we find her some work in a roadhouse, slinging eggs over easy and sausages on the side to fat truckers who'll pinch her little ass. We'll see. We may be charitable ... I don't know. It's not my decision.'

'Whose decision is it?'

'A question I can't answer. You're talking about locked rooms and shuttered houses and plush, quiet offices that are totally off-limits to you, Lomax. They might as well be on another planet.'

'I don't want Emily Ford subjected to any physical harm. No threats. Nothing like that. I want to hear you say that.'

'Take it as said.'

'Take your word, you mean?'

'What else do you have in the end, Jerry?

Nothing, I thought. *I have nothing else. No guarantees. No pledge in writing*. I was still dependent on his word. His promise. I said, 'I still want to talk to my wife. Give me that much, at least.'

'And I told you I don't want to wake her. Besides, you heard her voice about fifteen minutes ago. You know she's fine.'

'I know she was fine fifteen minutes ago,' I said.

'And she's still fine now.'

'You say.'

'I'm not going down this road with you again, Lomax. Are you ready to finalize? Are you ready to make the transfer?'

Yes, I was ready. I said, 'No more gunmen, no more assaults?'

'I promise you. I'll call you back in a few minutes with final details of where and how. Be good, Lomax, and all will end well in this city of angels and enchantment . . . oh, almost forgot. One last question. Is the Ultima a car you'd recommend?'

He hung up.

OK, so he knew I was driving Sonder-heim's car. But did he know my location? I was weaving down side-streets past rows of apartment buildings, most of them shabby. I pulled over to the side, braked, waited ten seconds, fifteen. The rearview mirror was dark. Nothing showed. No car behind me. No evidence of anyone. But I couldn't be sure. I could never be sure. I didn't know how many people were detailed to watch me. I didn't like uncertainty. Suddenly, I wanted a life in which all the important things were predict-able.

I drove on, then slowed and checked the address I'd written in the notebook. 224 Pineon. It was a Sixties building. Each apartment had a tiny balcony overlooking the street, and each balcony had a bleached-out canvas canopy. I saw stained-glass discs hanging in a couple of windows, a crystal or two, a couple of bumper stickers with old Clinton jokes on them. I guessed there was a pool out back. The smell of chlorine floated through the neighborhood.

I parked the car and shut my eyes for a fraction of a second, feeling the weight of eyelids. The dead and injured appeared to drift through the dark spaces in my head — George Rocco gunned down, Harry in the passenger seat of my car, Bo Sonderheim lying motionless outside the bank he managed, Parlance electrocuted in his Land Rover, and even Billy Fear, killed with an open soup-can in his hand inside a wretched trailer in a place called Whipperwill Glades Trailer Park.

I shook myself from this morbid torpor. I got out of the car and walked to the front door; through a glass panel, I saw a row of mailboxes. The door wasn't locked. It opened into a kind of ante-chamber where another glass door — this one locked — gave me a view of a poorly-lit lobby, receding into shadows.

I was faced with a bunch of buzzers, each of which had a name attached. I couldn't get beyond this locked lobby unless an inhabitant of the building buzzed me inside. I checked the names. Apartment # 28. If I rang this buzzer and announced myself through the intercom system, there was no chance of getting in, I knew that.

Gaining entrance required ingenuity. Or brute force.

I hurried back to the Ultima, parked half a block away, and opened the trunk. I rummaged inside, found the tire-iron, smacked it once in the palm of my hand as if to test its heft. I returned to the building, stepped into the vestibule, whacked the glass panel once; the pane broke and a section fell away. I reached inside, half-expecting an alarm to sound, but none did; I turned the handle, opened the door, then walked quickly along the corridor. I climbed a flight of worn stone steps to the second floor; dull yellow paint peeled from walls.

I found Apartment 28 and rang the doorbell even though the door was open a few inches.

'You the cab-driver?'

The man who asked the question was hauling a couple of suitcases towards the door with some difficulty, and had his back turned to me. But there was no mistaking the voice: I'd heard it dozens of times. I'd listened to it drone on about dreams, anxieties, the terror of supermarkets, cold sweats in the produce section, the angst that lurked beneath the watermelons and the mangoes; I'd listened to it describe what it was like to suffer the feeling that fluorescent lights were about to fall on you, or that the great sandy spaces of a beach concealed an unspeakable menace.

And there was no mistaking the ponytail that hung down the back of his neck.

'Leaving?' I asked.

He turned. His expression was one of

astonishment. He flicked his head, a nervous gesture I'd seen him make a hundred times before, and the ponytail swung away from his neck a moment. 'I'm pushed for time, Jerry,' he said. 'Plane to catch. You know how it is. They don't wait for you . . . is the iron just for show?'

'I don't know yet.'

He shrugged. 'I'm sorry I misled you. OK? I feel bad about it. I'm sorry I cancelled my appointment, too, but I had more pressing concerns. Pity. I was beginning to enjoy our sessions.'

'Why the big pretense?'

He looked at me carefully. 'How did you get my name?'

'From a LaBrea CD,' I said.

'Old things just keep coming back to haunt you.'

'Don't they,' I said. 'Also Gerson used your name when he was busted for a coke buy. Another connection.'

'He used my name with the cops? That fucking bastard stoops so low he gives low new heights.' He looked at me carefully. 'You been in the wars, Jerry? You've got some blood on your face and your clothes look less than debonair.'

'Forget my appearance. Do I call you Tim Dole or Phil Stam?'

'I don't give a damn. I'm leaving, see the suitcases?'

'Wait,' I said.

'Or you'll hit me with the iron?'

'I might get round to it,' I said.

'But you're the nonviolent type, Jerry.'

'I used to think so. But I'm under pressure, Tim. And I can't predict what I'll do next. I might swing this iron. I can't say.'

'Unless I speak.'

'Quickly,' I said.

'What are you in the dark about?'

'The part you played.'

'It's a sad story. I was a thirty-six-year-old struggling musician. Funny how those two words seem to have been made for each other — struggling and musician. Like ham and eggs. Anyway, I put a band together four years back, Gerson liked our demo, he fronted us a shit-load of money. Then he did one of his famous overnight U-turns. Decided he didn't like our songs. Wanted his cash back. I'd spent my share. The other band members managed to cough up — but not me. I owed Gerson more than I could raise. I tried to back out. Ah, no way, we had a contract with some weird lawyer-speak small print I hadn't read too carefully in all the excitement of signing.'

He looked at his watch, then ran a hand

through his hair and caught the ponytail, bringing it forward and examining it as if for split ends. His pale-gray eyes had always struck me as sad and honest, which was probably why he'd managed to fool me for as long as he had. Or maybe on some subconscious level I wanted to be fooled, because I needed to think people sought my insights, my experience, my touch. The vanity of a man and his profession. Had I ever really helped anyone?

'Did Gerson put you up to this?' I asked.

'Jerry, I like you. I enjoyed being your 'patient'.' He hung quote marks around the word 'patient' with little pincerlike gestures of his fingers. 'I got into the role. I made up all these fears. These great anxieties. I even took the medication. Wow. I liked that, too.'

'The point, Tim, the point. Did Gerson give you instructions?'

'The point is, I fear for my life. There's some heavy people involved in Gerson's set, Jerry.'

'Like Nardini?'

'You expect me to say I can implicate the Great Nardini? I don't know anything about Nardini except what I read in the newspapers.' He smiled, but without any joy. He held his hand forward, palm down. 'See how I shake, doc. I'm running. I'm the fugitive kind. I kid you not.'

'So who gave you your instructions?'

'I don't like to snitch,' he said.

'And I don't like the idea of physical violence,' I replied.

'The role of hurtee is particularly unappealing,' he said.

'Then speak,' I said. 'Spare us both.'

'OK. Gerson mainly. But a couple of times a guy called Resick would make an appearance. A lawyer type. His main function seemed to be to remind me I owed vast sums of cash to his client — viz., Gerson — and the debt would be wiped out if I did what I was told and asked no questions.'

'And you were to infiltrate my office, impersonate somebody in need of help.'

'Yep. I was to come off as a basket-case, a guy only loosely connected to reality.'

'You did it well.'

'You led me by the hand, Jerry. You asked the questions, I answered. You seemed so . . . *eager*, man, I didn't want to disappoint you.'

'And the reason behind all this was the file.'

'The file. Right on.'

'How did you get into the safe?'

He held up his hands; they were his principal mode of communication. His long, bony fingers were stiff. He had unusually big knuckles. 'With these, Jerry. With these God-given, guitar-plucking, fine-tuned hands, I got into your safe.'

'Without any inside help?'

'I didn't need any.'

'Jane didn't help you?'

'Your secretary? No.'

I was relieved to hear this about Jane, but I still felt puzzlement, anyway. 'How did you know there was a floor-safe?'

'Gerson told me, Jerry. Told me exactly where it was.'

Gerson was like a shadow spreading all over my life. How did Gerson know about the safe? I wondered if he had a hold over Jane, if he'd forced Jane to tell him. I flashed on the party in Gerson's house, the presence of Jane and Allardyce, and wondered if there was some collusion between the three of them, if they were parts of a larger connivance whose design was just beyond my range of vision.

'So, it was basically a matter of waiting for the right opportunity, Jerry. Hey, I'm missing my plane, man. I'm getting flustered and fluttery. I need some more of those nice calming drugs you gave me.'

'And when was the right opportunity?'

'Lunchtime yesterday. It was a piece of cake getting inside the office, Jerry. Your locks suck. As for the guy in the lobby, an earthquake wouldn't shake him, I swear it. I opened the safe. It took me less than three minutes. Unhappily, it was a wasted effort. The file wasn't there. Which caused Gerson apoplexy. I thought he was going to blow like a fucking geyser.' He held his hands up again. 'These babies didn't always strum a guitar, Jerry. The Devil once found work for these bad boys.'

'You were a thief,' I said.

'I was misguided in my youth,' he said. 'No offence, Jerry, but I have to fuck off out of here. I want a little distance between myself and Gerson, OK? I don't want to be at his beck and call if something else crosses his mind and he comes looking for me. I don't want to be his goddam prisoner. I want a simple life in another town. I'll shave my head and wear a saffron robe and hang out in provincial airports if I have to. Now, excuse me. With any luck, I might make the plane. Maybe.'

He bent to lift up his bags.

I said, 'Did you know about the kidnap?'

He straightened up again and looked at me. 'What kidnap?'

I told him.

He looked surprised. 'I swear I didn't know, Jerry. I wouldn't get involved in anything like that. I met your wife a few times, and she was always real nice to us back when we thought we were stars. She was also nice when we discovered we weren't. She's a good woman. I often wondered how she could stand working at LaBrea. I guess she likes the job.'

She likes the job. She likes the buzz. The wild side. My Sondra.

'What else do you know?' I asked again.

'That's it.'

I gazed at his face. He'd fooled me before. But I had the feeling he was weary of acting; that he was too afraid to pursue that particular career.

'You can still catch that plane, Tim,' I said.

'Yeah, maybe.' He picked up his bags and struggled towards the door, groaning from the weight of them. 'I called a taxi about half an hour ago. You can't get a cab in this city any more. None of the drivers know their way around LA. They're all from Macedonia or someplace.'

'One last thing,' I said. 'How do I find Resick?'

'Not in the phone book. Guy's unlisted.'

'But you know the address, Tim.'

He looked at me with concern. 'Leave it alone,' he said.

'The address, Tim. That's all I want.'

He hesitated, then he shrugged and told

me, and looked sorry that he had.

'I'll help you with the bags,' I said. I took one, a black leather carry-on bag, and we walked towards the elevator. We rode down to the lobby in silence. We walked in the direction of the front door, the dark street.

Before we made it, Big Skull loomed up out of nowhere. A huge mirage. His fair-haired friend was standing just behind him, with a red-stained bandage on his left hand and the sleeve of his shirt rolled way up his left arm. His bracelet dangled from his wrist.

'Hot dog,' Big Skull said. His eyes popped as he smiled. 'Lookeee here. What have we got? Tim the spy and Supershrink carrying bags.'

The fair-haired man said, 'Looks to me like somebody's planning a trip. We got here just in time, you ask me.'

I tightened my grip on the tire-iron, which I held pressed flat against my thigh. I set down the black leather bag I was carrying. Dole was standing motionless; this was his nightmare — he wasn't going to walk away from the trap in which Gerson had imprisoned him. There was no escape. He belonged to Gerson.

Dole made a nervous little sound somewhere between a sigh and a sob. 'Guys, listen, let me walk out of here, you never saw me, who's gonna know?'

Big Skull said, 'We'll know.'

Fairhair said, 'Yeah, we'll know. We'll have to live with the fact we've been derelict in our duties if we let you walk, Dole. See the problem?'

Dole said, 'Hey, we can talk, come to an understanding.'

Big Skull looked at me, bug-eyed and spooky, like an extra in a movie populated with aliens. 'As for you, doc, you got something we were supposed to get from you back at that bank, only you appeared to split before we could get our hands on it. You got it with you now?'

I shook my head. 'I have a deal, and it doesn't include you.'

The fair-haired guy stared at his bandage as if he were fascinated by it. He said, 'We never heard about any change of plan.'

Big Skull blinked in an uncoordinated way. 'Get the goods, that's what we were told. That's why we went to the bank. Nobody's told us any different since then.'

'Then you've had a serious breakdown in communications, guys, and I suggest you call your controller and get this all straightened out.' I gripped the iron as hard as I could, because I knew where this was headed, and I didn't like the prospect. I felt flushed with the idea of violence; I was poised on a dark ledge. The combined IQs of the two guys probably made them candidates for the baboon house; nevertheless, they were bright in the one place where it mattered to them — the realm of savagery.

Dole said, 'I'll just leave you guys to — '

Big Skull suddenly headbanged Dole. One backward dip of the strong man's head, and then a fierce swift arc as he brought his face forward and cracked his forehead against Dole's brow, shuddering bone on bone. The musician went down at once, and as I was about to say something to Big Skull — complain, protest, whatever — I saw that Fairhair had the brass knuckles on his right hand and was preparing to swing his fist towards me.

I raised the tire-iron very quickly and hit him a vigorous blow to the side of his head, a serious shot he couldn't avoid. Bone crunched. Blood streamed from his ear and out of the ragged slit the iron had hacked in his jawbone; he fell back against the wall, head dangling at a terrible angle. Big Skull reacted fast to the situation, drawing his gun out of his spine holster, but then I brought the iron down again with a speed and strength I'd forgotten I ever had. I pounded the back of his hand and the gun went flying away; then, as he raised his hand to his mouth as if to lick it for pain-relief, I struck him again, hard to the side of his neck. He half-dodged the blow, but not quite. He lost his balance and dropped to one knee and, struggling for breath, glared up at me. 'You fuck,' he snarled, and I swung the iron two-handed, a mighty swipe like with a golf-club or baseball bat, and hit him across the nose, breaking the bone, splitting the upper lip, shattering the teeth. He hunched forward, his spine curved, and blood poured out of him. He held his hands cupped just beneath his face as if he might catch the blood. I thought about hitting him one last time, but I didn't, the fight was done. The big swing with the iron had stretched the muscles in my ribs and sent pain through me, and when I moved my lungs ached, but I felt good and vibrant. I hadn't become soft and West Coast altogether, there was still something steely in me that didn't mind fighting, something cold, something born in storm and snow.

I ran from the building, reached the Ultima, got inside. As I wheeled away from the sidewalk, I was amazed to see Big Skull staggering out of the apartment building, moving with God knows what kind of effort.

Each step he took was a struggle. His face was black with blood, but he was grinning and I couldn't figure why.

'Hey, doc. Don't forget your free gift!' And he threw something silvery that sailed through the open window of the car, flew past my face, and landed on the passenger seat. Then he collapsed on the sidewalk, going down on all fours like a motionless bear.

I drove past him. I heard him cough blood. I also thought I heard him laugh a loose, fractured kind of laugh.

The box on the passenger seat measured about twelve inches by nine, roughly. It was wrapped in silver paper. I picked it up in my right hand as I drove. It weighed a few ounces. I shook it, heard nothing.

I set the box in my lap. Did it contain another lock of Sondra's hair? Another reminder? I pulled the car to the side of the street. Quickly, I ripped the silver paper away. I reached in, encountered some tissue paper. Wet and sticky. I pulled my hand out of the box and saw, by the light that fell from the streetlamp, that my fingers were dark with blood.

Sickened, I let the box slide from my grasp; it dropped on the passenger seat and its contents slithered out on the fine tan leather. I stared at it.

The mess on the seat. The soft, shapeless mess.

What was this? All my medical training dissolved.

Recognition wasn't instant, but when it came I felt a pain as severe as that created by a serrated knife thrust into my heart. I covered my mouth with a hand, and at that moment my environment changed weirdly: the streetlamps dimmed, the sky tipped sideways, I was detached from my body and floating out over the city; a capitulation of senses, an eclipse of reason.

10.30 p.m.

I drove about a quarter mile, perhaps more, I wasn't sure. I parked outside an all-night convenience store, where a bunch of young people milled around the payphones. The kids wore long, baggy shorts or jeans that were too big and hung slackly from hips. Drug deals were being made, surreptitious encounters, bindles and tiny bottles passed from hand to hand. The city had become totally alien to me; it existed on levels I couldn't map and each level was darker than the one before. It was a place of strange designs, crazed schemes, contradictions.

And clocks. Weird clocks. Time running out too fast. Everything speeding away from me. The universe emptying.

I held the cellphone to my ear. I listened to the buzz of the number I was calling. I expected an answering-machine, because it was late. My chest was tight. I had a series of strange rainbow flickers, shimmering things in my visual field that were the harbingers of migraine.

I didn't look at the box, although I was conscious of the torn silver wrapping-paper lying on the floor on the passenger side. It caught the light and gleamed. The blood on my fingers was black, or a red so deep it had no name. Out of nowhere, I remembered a game we played in Buffalo as kids, ringing doorbells and running away laughing, fleeing the anger of some householder. I felt like the guy who'd opened his door because he'd heard the bell, only he'd found nobody on the doorstep; he was baffled, irritated by his own bewilderment, and the night was alive with secrets —

'Yeah?' The voice on the line was sleepy.

I said, 'Marv? This is Jerry Lomax.'

'Jerry? What time is it? Is something wrong?'

'I think something's really wrong, Marv.'

I glanced at the shape on the passenger seat now, this stunted, lifeless creature denied a world. I felt panic and sadness and anxiety and my brain chugging like one of those old steam engines my father had driven. The contents of the silver-wrapped box — like Consuela, like Harry, another stake driven into me. Another turn of the screw, this one an almighty twist.

'Talk to me,' Marv said. 'I'm listening.'

'Sondra's miscarried, Marv. She's miscarried.' I didn't know how many times I said the words, nor how many times Marv

318

Sweetzer said, *Now wait, now wait.*

Hard pressure lay just behind my eyes. The bloody thing on the seat. The box. The silver wrapping-paper. Miscarried. Wrapped up, delivered to me by somebody driving a Pontiac. Sick fucks. Did they abort her deliberately? Did they force her? Or had she miscarried because of stress or fear? I didn't know.

Did it matter how?

My sadness was for her. More for her than for me. And for this child, and that small town I'd imagined, where he or she might have grown up, where the air smelt of woodsmoke on fall afternoons.

I heard myself say, 'She may be ill, Marv. She may be in need of hospitalization. It's been years since I interned, I don't remember the procedures, what we're supposed to do in a situation like this. I only delivered one kid in my life, I never dealt with a miscarriage before.'

'Jerry. Listen to me. Run this past me again. From the beginning. Take your time.'

I repeated myself.

Sondra's lost the baby. The fetus. Sondra's aborted the fetus. I didn't know how much blood she'd lost. Was she ill? Was her life in danger? What was I supposed to do?

'Sondra's miscarried, you say.' Sweetzer

319

had a rich baritone voice. Women liked it. It comforted and reassured them. They trusted themselves to Marv.

Comfort and reassure me too, Marv. The way you comfort your female patients. I need you now.

'She's lost the fucking *baby*, Marv,' I said.

Marv Sweetzer was silent a moment before he said, 'If I didn't know you better, Jerry, I'd say you'd been dabbling in those psycho-drugs you hand out to people.'

'What's that supposed to mean?'

'This fetus. This baby. I must have missed something, Jerry. How the Sam Hill is it possible for Sondra to lose a baby if she isn't pregnant?'

'Isn't — What the *fuck* are you talking about, Marv?'

'Quit cussing at me, Jerry. I hate cussing. I'm telling you what I know. She was in my office last Monday and she wasn't pregnant then, so how could she be pregnant now? How is that possible?'

It was a damn good question. I shifted the position of my hand on the phone. I was sticking to plastic. Oozing sweat. 'She isn't ... wasn't pregnant. Is that what you're saying to me?'

'I'd bet my reputation on it.'

'Dear God,' I said.

320

'She'd love to be pregnant, Jerry. But she just isn't. I'm worried about you.'

I cut the connection. I got out of the car.

If I sucked down some bad air, filled my lungs with gunk, walked up and down with my hands rattling coins in my pockets, maybe everything would return to normal, or whatever passed for normal now. Then I'd get back inside the car, and there wouldn't be blood and sodden tissue paper and a small, damp cardboard box on the passenger seat.

Sondra hadn't been pregnant.

She'd been *unpregnant*.

I went inside the store, blinked in the searing totality of fluorescence, that most unnatural of lights. I bought an *LA Times*. The clerk didn't react to the bloodstains on my hands and face. He was maybe only nineteen and he'd seen everything. A couple of young kids jostled me just for the sport of it, a teenage assertion of self and power. I sidestepped them, walked back to the car, opened the newspaper.

I scooped the soft remains of the half-formed thing back inside the box, then placed the box inside the open newspaper. I folded the paper over.

I got out of the car again and walked to the dumpster at the side of the store. I tossed the package in. I heard it fall, heard it strike bottles and make them clink. The day that had begun with a sense of new life in the making had ended in a night where death was everywhere.

Sondra wasn't pregnant. *Why did you tell me otherwise, my love? Why did you do that?* I listened to the roar of the store's air-conditioning unit, watched the kids work the payphones, saw two airplanes float out of the night sky as they drifted down towards LAX. For a second, I expected a collision. But none came.

Dreams were only dreams. Mine hadn't been prophetic. I'd predicted nothing.

I'd been blind, even in sleep.

I returned to the car.

The interior smelled of metal and plastic and wet leather, and something that would turn foul eventually, like old meat or spilled milk, or the world we lived in, overflowing with the sorry treacheries we committed almost daily.

10.43 p.m.

I drove through the canyons with the windows of the car rolled down and warm night air circulating. The road behind me was empty. Dense foliage loomed up on either side: an illusion of rustic life. I needed the comfort of illusion. I longed for simplicity, no more elaboration.

My cellphone rang. I picked it up, listened.

'I'm sorry about the unpleasant nature of the delivery.'

'Fuck you to hell,' I said. 'Let's just get this over with. I want to get on with my goddam life.'

'I know, I know,' and his voice was grave, considerate. 'If it's any consolation, your wife's OK. She's weak, sure, but she'll be back on her feet soon enough. Nice to think she'll recuperate at home with you. She's going to need a lot of TLC, Lomax. It's a tough break — losing a baby.'

'It's tough all right,' I said.

So he didn't know I'd contacted Marv Sweetzer. His intelligence system had let him down. He was under the impression that I believed Sondra had miscarried, which was what he wanted. All day long, he'd been building a little universe for me, and he'd directed the events that had taken place in it, but this one time his concentration had lapsed. He hadn't taken into consideration the possibility that I'd call Sweetzer.

I wondered where they'd gone for the unborn child, how they'd acquired it. I guessed it wasn't difficult if you had the cash or the brute force. And people like Resick and Gerson had plenty of both.

I thought of Sondra's terrible perjury. The why of it. But I didn't want to follow this line of inquiry through, because I didn't like where it was leading. I remembered making love to her on the deck of our house, and how she'd said, *I'm not glass, Jerry. I won't break.* How conscious I'd been of the baby inside her, and my fear of causing distress or damage.

It was the worst lie she could have invented. She knew how hard we'd tried to have a child, and I couldn't believe she'd use that great *yearning* against me.

No, no, I didn't want to think she'd lied.

I needed to believe she'd been forced into this situation.

I conjured connections, delicate as a pattern in old lace: Nardini bought Gerson and, incidentally, Sondra out of a cocaine bust; and then Gerson introduced Sondra to Nardini, because she was the wife of Emily Ford's psychiatrist. And Nardini had to stop Emily's ascent to power by whatever means, since she was a menace to the people whose interests he protected and represented: the corporate scam artists who made dirty money clean again, or who hid fortunes in unassailable bank-accounts in countries the size of Rhode Island and evaded taxation; the pushers of merchandise — whether useless swamp with allegedly great investment potential in Costa Rica, or cocaine from Medellin, there was always, *always* a buyer; smooth, hard men who rigged juries, bought judges, and lived where the law couldn't touch them; and then down a few levels from the hushed boardrooms and private dining-rooms and fancy cufflinks and Hugo Boss suits were the gophers, the guys with dirty hands, swindlers, con-men, pimps, hookers, and killers — the tiny wheels that made the big wheels turn.

What the hell was the hold they had over Sondra? What obliged her to go along with them? It *had* to be more than just a cocaine bust. Surely Sondra would have told me about that, rather than participate in an elaborate charade, a cruelty involving a fake kidnapping, and dubious phone calls that required her to act as if she were in pain or drugged.

I preferred this kind of reasoning to the notion that she'd perpetrated an enormous falsehood. In my version, she was no liar: she was a victim. She hadn't deceived me. She was the instrument of other people's deceptions. I could live with this explanation, even if a shadow at the back of my mind troubled me. But I didn't want to think about that. It wasn't the time for doubt. Faith was what I required.

I loved Sondra. I wanted her.

'Are you still there, Lomax?'

'I'm here.'

'Dole tell you anything of interest?'

'We didn't have time to talk before your people showed up.'

'I heard about that,' he said. 'I'm impressed. You can take the boy out of Buffalo, but you can't take Buffalo, et cetera.'

'That's right,' I said.

Between trees, I had a view of the city way below; it filled the valley, a vast expanse of lights and lives. I checked a street sign. I was on Grierson Drive. I was looking for 3245.

'So, Jerry, are you ready to play the last card? We're well past the deadline, and my people are becoming impatient.'

'I'm ready,' I said.

'I'm going to give you very specific instructions. Follow them to the letter. To the letter: let me underline that.'

'What about Sondra?'

'She'll be returned to you, Jerry.'

'Isn't she bleeding?' How easily I played this game of prevarication.

'Not now.'

'Did you call a physician?'

'I told you. She isn't bleeding any more.'

'The blood just stopped on its own, is that it?' I asked.

'What is this, Jerry? All you need to know is that she'll be given back to you when we make the switch.'

'Just make sure you move her carefully.'

'Wrapped in cotton, I assure you.'

'Use plenty of it,' I said.

'There's a payphone across the street from Book Soup on Sunset. You know the place?'

'I've been there,' I said.

'Go to the payphone. Wait five minutes. Then call this number. 545 6098. You want to write that down?'

'I'll remember it,' I said.

'Say it back to me, Jerry.'

I did so.

'A man will answer. He'll give you an address in the neighborhood. You'll go there.

When you get to this destination, you'll learn more.'

I looked from the window again. *3245*. I drove straight past, and parked about a hundred yards down the street.

'OK,' I said. 'The payphone first.'

'Go easy, Jerry,' he said.

I killed the ringer on my phone, stuck the phone in my pocket, got out of the car. There were no other pedestrians. I reached the driveway, which was about two hundred yards long and lined with soft lamps and eucalyptus trees, the leaves of which caught the light in such a way that they resembled misshapen antique coins. At the end of the drive, the house was perched, a little precariously, on a promontory that overlooked the city. It was one of those hyper-modern homes, a layered, angular affair on steel stilts. The windows were oval, and lit, creating an impression, in the dark, of cats' eyes.

An unwelcoming place, and I didn't want to go near it. I imagined tripping a sensor, setting off an alarm, bright lights, sirens. I had no way of knowing what security there might be here. Plenty of it, I was sure. Everybody in this city lived in fear of violence and home invasion. It was a mind-set: lock up your possessions, protect them with guns and alarms.

I stepped onto the driveway, noticing that the high, wrought-iron gates had been left open. I thought this an odd oversight, but I didn't pause to analyze it. I took a few paces along the drive before I realized that I was exposed to anyone watching from the house.

I slipped into the trees and found myself moving across short grass.

The lights in the windows illuminated small purple flowers here and there and they reminded me of the image I'd had many hours ago when, in the full flight of despair, I'd tried to force myself to create a vision of Sondra. I'd stood at the window of my living-room and imagined I could project my mind over the city like a distress flare. The spectral impressions I'd received were of a purple field and a pale-green room. I wondered about this — was it just coincidence or had I experienced a weird excursion of my senses into a region beyond the normal —

My brain was at the races.

I looked at the house: the yellowish lights in the windows, the shiny stilts supporting the structure at the edge of a sheer cliff, the enormity of the city below, rushing to the horizon. No sign of life. No evidence, except for the lights, that anybody occupied the place.

I kept going, concealed by the trees. Overhanging leaves rustled as I brushed past them. I tore a leaf from a branch, held it between thumb and index finger and rubbed it nervously, releasing a scent of eucalyptus oil. I kneeled in the grass. I emptied my pockets at the base of a tree. I was about forty yards from the house. I listened to the night, the endless drone of the city that sounded like a great turbo in the distance.

The trees thinned out. Anybody behind one of those windows could see me. I ran towards the house, thinking I'd retreat into the shadows, conceal myself in the spaces under the stilts, which were ten or twelve feet high. The house seemed for a second to float unsupported in space, a travesty, a whim.

I made it as far as the stilts.

I heard footsteps on a wooden walkway above me. I drew back, making myself small in the dark. I was between two parked cars. Then the thought discharged inside me, like an accidental explosion: *It's the safe-deposit box that's weighing on your mind.*

I held my breath.

There were several people on the walkway overhead. Voices. I heard the flick of a lighter, then smelled smoke from a cigarette drift down through the dark.

'We're leaving at midnight,' one of the

voices said. It was a man's voice, a little gruff, and I knew it immediately.

The next speaker was a woman — I knew her, too. 'You're way past your deadline,' she said. 'We can't wait here for ever. Enough's enough.' She sounded angry. I could imagine her petulant little mouth hardening.

'I'll send the material over to your hotel,' another voice said. 'I'll have it within twenty minutes.'

This was a voice I'd become all too familiar with in the last twelve hours. I heard him exhale smoke.

'Then you get the file,' the woman said.

'Deal's a deal,' the first man said.

'Between the file and the material you expect to get . . . ' The woman stopped. I listened to her footsteps on the stairs. She reached the bottom. I saw her through shadows. Her blond hair was bright in the dim underside of the house. Brunton was directly behind her. They were walking towards one of the cars. I stepped back, hidden.

Carrie Vasuu said, 'She's dead in the water.'

'Dead and buried,' Brunton said. 'The file would have been enough — '

'Overkill is always a better policy than underkill,' Carrie Vasuu said. 'Whatever. A copy of the file's been e-mailed to DC.'

The Washington pair had Emily's file.

I wanted to hear more. How they procured it. Who they sent it to. Eavesdroppers never hear enough. But they didn't say any more. They got inside one of the cars, a Jaguar, and they drove away. I listened to the engine fade down the driveway. The butt of a half-smoked cigarette flashed past me, then the man who'd tossed it away turned and went back up the stairs. I listened to him climb.

I heard a door close way above me.

I moved through the space underneath the house, passing between the steel stilts that held the structure upright. A crazy house to build in an earthquake zone. Somebody with a death wish. I came to the stairs that led to the wooden walkway where I'd heard Brunton say *We're leaving at midnight*.

I climbed quietly, light from a window above falling over me as I moved. I reached the walkway. I saw other walkways overhead, an elaborate arrangement of them.

The view of the city was bewilderingly *complete*. A billion lights out there, and a billion black spaces. Everything in motion, like atoms, sub-atoms. Darkness and light, on and off, off and on.

The safe-deposit box was the only secret I'd kept from her in our marriage. *Correct?*

Yes. What am I worrying about?

I went quietly along the walkway. I waited for a board to creak, but it didn't. The house was well-made. Solid and sound. I was breathless, and the dazzle of the city made me vertiginous. I saw a door a few feet ahead. An oval glass pane was set into the door, matching the windows. I backed against the wall and slid towards the glass. I peered inside the room.

A white leather sofa. Two chairs that matched it. Logs burning in a fireplace, although the night wasn't cold. A couple of paintings, vivid streaks of red and yellow oil applied to canvas. I smelled tobacco, and saw a very thin curl of smoke drift over my shoulder. I swung round quickly.

'Lomax,' he said.

He wore gray sweatpants and a black T-shirt with a nautical logo: a yacht, wavy lines suggestive of a sea. He was tall and he'd shaved his head. He was suntanned. He clearly lived much of the time outdoors. He carried an air of sailboats and long days on the ocean. He wasn't how I'd imagined him to be — and yet I couldn't recollect ever having conjured up a detailed picture of him.

'We haven't met formally,' he said.

'You don't seem surprised to see me.'

He shrugged. 'You were asking enough questions and getting enough answers to reach some conclusion. So, no, I'm not altogether surprised to find you here. Welcome to my home,' and he reached past me, opened the door, ushered me inside the room.

I entered. He was working at being casual, relaxed. 'Drink?'

I shook my head.

He smiled and looked at his watch. It was a thick metal disc with a confusing number of mini-dials. I imagined it functioning on ocean floors or inside a lunar capsule.

'I was in the neighborhood,' I said.

'Indeed you were. You want to sit?'

'All I want is my wife,' I said.

'Won't drink, won't sit,' he said.

'I told you what I want,' I said.

'You've got a stubborn streak, Jerry. Sometimes good. Sometimes not so.' He sat on the white sofa, crossed his legs, looked at me in a friendly way. 'You shouldn't have come here.'

'I know that.'

'In your shoes, I would have followed the instructions and gone to the payphone on Sunset. Sometimes the trespasser sees too much. Or hears too much.'

'It happens,' I said.

'You saw my guests leave?'

I nodded.

'And what did you hear?'

'Nothing. I wasn't listening.'

'I don't believe you, Jerry.'

'Let's get to the business,' I said. 'Sondra.'

'First tell me what you heard,' he said.

'Are you stalling me? Is my wife here or not?'

'I wish you'd sit. You're making me uncomfortable.'

'I don't want to sit,' I said. Out of nowhere, it bothered me again, it erupted and troubled me. I thought: *No, I've never told her.* I was certain. I trusted my memory.

I said, 'I just want to get out of this place. With Sondra. Is she here? Why can't you answer a simple question?'

'First, tell me what you heard.'

'Will I get my wife back quicker if I do?'

He said nothing. He looked at me inscrutably.

I said, 'All I caught was a couple of garbled sentences. Did they mean anything to me? Maybe. If I believed in unholy alliances and unlikely clandestine liaisons. If I was a conspiracy freak.'

'Are you, Jerry?'

'I have good days and bad ones,' I said. 'Sometimes I think we're ruled by a sick confederation of Mensa members and NRA devotees who have a secret base in Montana.

Other days, I just think we're governed by dolts and deadheads in Washington.'

'I expected a serious reply.'

'Fine. I get the sense of standing at a fork in the road where government and crime converge. Where they have mutually beneficial arrangements.'

'Far-fetched,' he said.

'You asked, Resick. It suits certain vested interests in Washington to make sure Emily Ford doesn't become Attorney-General. She's made enemies out of too many people: the Civil Liberties Union; the warm fuzzy center of the Democratic Party; a potent caucus of far-right-wing types who think her programs don't go the whole way, because she doesn't advocate the chopping off of hands for petty theft. She represents a potential embarrassment to a President who's trying his best to be liberal, even as he knows he has to please extreme law-and-order sorts . . . '

He leaned forward, opened a silver cigarette-case, lit a cigarette. 'Go on,' he said.

'The rest is obvious, Resick. Organized crime — call it any name you like — doesn't want her in the hot-seat either. Absolutely no way. She's going to be too tough on them, even if she keeps only half of her promises. They don't want to squirm. They hate that

336

feeling. They enjoy the *status quo*. They have exactly the same goal as our friends Brunton and Vasuu: send Emily Ford into total oblivion.'

Resick rose from the sofa. 'Intriguing theory,' he said. 'The trouble with conspiracies is how damn difficult it is to prove they exist. You can dig in all the wrong places. Evidence turns out to be misleading. Or, like JFK's brain, it vanishes entirely. I wonder why people adore the idea of conspiracies.'

'That's not my field of expertise,' I said, 'Now I want my wife.'

'And you have what I want?' he asked.

'I have it.'

'Show me,' he said.

'I want to see my wife first.'

'You think I'll go back on our deal at this stage, Jerry?'

'I can't give you what you want if I don't get Sondra. Is this a stand-off?'

'I don't believe in stand-offs,' he said. He stood up, cracked his knuckles. 'Tell me this much about the material. Is it worth your wife's life?'

'It's what you want,' I said. 'It fulfills your every dream, Resick. And I feel like shit giving it to you. Now give me back my wife.'

'Do you have the stuff on you?'

I gave him a look: *Do-you-think-I-just-flew-in-by-paper-airplane?*

'OK. Is it near by?' he asked.

I said, 'I can get it. Are you stalling for some reason, Resick?'

'No.' He appeared nervous suddenly. He tossed his cigarette into the fireplace.

'We had a deal. I want it finalized,' I said.

'Just be patient, Jerry.'

'Patient? Look, we're way past the deadline. Which you imposed. *Your* idea. *Your* timetable. Now you ask me to be patient. What are we waiting for, Resick?'

He moved to the fireplace, picked up a poker, stabbed the logs. They caved in, sending a weak flame up into the chimney. I watched him — what was he worried about? Why was he so obviously procrastinating? Or did I only imagine this? The way I was imagining Sondra once asking: *What do you keep in that box at the bank anyway, Jer? Letters from old girl-friends?* I had a bad feeling. I couldn't entirely pin it down. It was a queasiness of sorts.

'You're fucking *stalling*,' I said. 'I don't believe it. Has something happened to her?'

He shook his head. 'She's fine.'

'Did you harm her with those drugs?'

'Drugs?' he said.

'That was all play-acting, right?'

'Pure theater,' he said.

'How did you get her to agree to do it? What kind of goddam spell is she under?'

'I didn't do anything, Lomax,' he said.

'I don't believe that. I want to see her, and I want to see her now. She's here, isn't she? She's in this house?'

I walked to the door. 'I'll find her if she's here.'

'Wait,' he said.

'I'll find her,' I said again.

'No, wait,' he said.

I was tired of the obfuscation, the maze I'd been funneled through. I was weary of deception and anxiety. I felt like I'd been on a rack all day, stretched by a sadist who loved his work.

'Lomax,' he called after me.

I moved along a corridor. I had no idea where I was going. The house was another mystery. More and more levels. I opened doors all the way down the hallway. Rooms, rooms. One with a big piano, lacquered red and shining like a waxed apple. Another with a single bed and a floor-mat, a monastic little cell. Another with a dining-table and chairs and unlit candles in silver sticks. Rooms and more rooms. Empty spaces. What if she wasn't here at all and this conviction I had was just a repeat of the brainstorm that had happened at Gerson's?

'Wait, Lomax!' Resick called out again.

I was hurrying away from him. He came after me. Then I was rushing, storming through the house, climbing stairs, searching the levels for my wife. Still Resick pursued me, only now he'd quit calling out to me because he knew it was a waste of time.

Rooms, more rooms: one filled with plants and humidifiers spraying the air, one stuffed with packing-crates, one with a desk and a PC whose monitor displayed a series of ethereal shapes revolving in cyber-space. I kept going — another flight of stairs — how many levels did this weird house have, how many rooms? I saw an empty sauna, a shower, a big bathroom tiled black and white . . . rooms collapsed into other rooms . . . Where was Sondra? Where was she if she wasn't here?

I heard Resick behind me. He reached out and grabbed my shoulder, trying to slow me, but I slipped his grasp and kept moving. Even when he went down on his knees, and tried to tackle me from the back like an ungainly football-player, I sidestepped him easily and heard him clatter into the wall.

I was running, gasping for air. I saw from a

window how high I was above the city — I had to be on the uppermost level of this house now, it couldn't go any higher, it wasn't possible. The final corridor, the last stretch of rooms. I kept opening doors.

And there she was.

Sondra. My Sondra.

My wife. The woman I loved.

She was sitting up in a big bed. She had a cigarette burning in her hand. She had a sheet drawn up over her, but her shoulders were bare.

She looked at me with an expression I'd never seen before — a chill distance in her eyes I couldn't measure — and said, 'Is it that time already?'

A door on the other side of the bedroom opened and a man appeared. His hair was thick and black and he was dressed in a green silk robe. The cord was loosely tied. He looked at me, stuck his hands in the pockets of his robe. I knew who he was. Suddenly, I knew everything. The knowledge was as cold as an arctic wind. I shivered and had to put my back against the bedroom wall because I was certain I was going to fall down without some support.

Nardini said, 'Jerry Lomax.'

He went to the bed and sat.

Sondra reached out to the bedside table

and picked up a glass half-filled with red wine. She drank, watching me over the rim, her hair only a shade darker than the wine. She wasn't wearing her wedding-ring.

'Cheers, Jerry,' she said.

11.10 p.m.

Dennis Nardini rose, went out of the room. *Diplomatic of him*, I thought, and the thought was a bitter one, an acrid cloud in my head. He shut the door. I could hear him in the corridor with Resick, voices raised arguing.

I went towards my wife. She set her wine down on the bedside table. Her look was challenging. It was: *So-what?* It was: *You never knew me.* It was: *I don't love you.*

'How long?' I asked.

'Six months.'

'Since the coke bust?'

She looked away from me. 'Since that night.'

'Why didn't you tell me about you and . . . ' I faltered. My insides were tumbling. My heart had gone before. I was hanging on barbed-wire in a wintry field and the earth was black and wet.

'I thought about it. I wanted to. I wasn't sure how.'

'This isn't . . . Jesus, this isn't a terrific way to find out,' I said.

She dropped her cigarette into the

wine-glass and it sizzled briefly. I wanted to hold her and say, *I love you, come home with me, we'll move on from this terrible place, we'll seek out that archetypal safe town in the hills and raise a child, a real child this time.*

'Six months,' I said. 'I didn't *know*. How could I not goddam *know*?'

'You weren't looking, Jerry. You were busy with your patients. All their crap. All their pains and delusions. You just quit looking.'

She fidgeted with the hem of the sheet. I realized for the first time that the room was scented by her body, but the aroma was altered by another element: Dennis Nardini. The smell of a man. Of sex.

I shut my eyes, sat on the edge of the bed. I wondered when shock would dissipate and pain kick in. The walls of the room were the color of a lime. A green room. In my imagined room, the walls had been a paler shade of green. Like a bleached leaf. Purple grass and pale green walls.

'This plan,' I said. 'Who dreamed it up?'

'Dennis,' she said.

'Aided and abetted by you?'

'Yes.'

'Willingly.'

'Not at first,' she said.

'But you came round to his way of thinking.'

'It made sense.'

'Bravo,' I said. I couldn't keep the hurt out of my voice. I tried, but it forced itself through. I imagined her and Nardini lying here or in other beds in other rooms, fucking and planning, planning and fucking, locked and rocking in each other's arms. The intimacy of that image was a bayonet into my heart.

'He used you,' I said.

'Only to get at your precious Emily Ford,' she said.

'Precious?'

'Oh, come on. You spent so much time with that woman I felt we were living separate lives. She drained you. She squeezed you dry. You worked on her problems constantly. It went beyond therapy. You became *attached*, Jerry, the cardinal sin in your profession. And the more attached you were, the more you cut me loose.'

'I was only doing my job,' I said. 'Are you suggesting I was having an affair with her or something?'

'I'm not suggesting anything, Jerry. All I know is, your life orbited exclusively around her problems. You came home, couldn't sleep, sat up into the small hours making goddam notes. And even when she quit being your patient, you still buried yourself in your work.

It had become a habit with you by then.'

I couldn't remember devoting so many hours to Emily and her problems, to the moral dilemma of her life, that conflict between right and wrong, between conscious and unconscious, memory and amnesia. Maybe I'd done so without realizing that I was neglecting Sondra. Hunkered down inside Emily Ford's life, I'd forgotten to pay attention to matters of a more personal emotional resonance.

The stuff on my own doorstep.

Sondra lit another cigarette. She'd given up smoking because of the baby, I recalled. *The baby, lovemaking on the deck, and then nothing. Now less than nothing.*

'Nardini's a fucking crook,' I said.

It was a reflex statement, born out of hurt, and she smiled when I said it.

'You don't know him,' she said. 'He intrigues me. His world fascinates me. He moves in exciting circles. He isn't sitting in some office, listening to dull people whine about their emotional inadequacies. He isn't pushing pills to gullible Hollywood wives who have too much time on their hands.'

'That's how you see my work?'

'It's beside the point how I see your work. Look, this is hard to say. I don't love you, Jerry. That's the only point. It's *more* than not loving you . . . I used to think it was a form of pity. You were somebody I felt sorry for. You poor man, you had all the cares of the world on your shoulders. But then I realized, no, it's nothing to do with the burden you carry, it's the fact I dislike you, I began to despise you, I couldn't even stand to be in your company, I'd met somebody else who meant more to me than you ever could, and you diminished to the point where my contempt for you became a kind of abstract constant, like a dull toothache that never quite goes away.

'I hated coming home. I hated small things about you. The fussy way you breathed on your glasses before you cleaned them. The sounds you made when you slept. Truly petty things, like the way you folded the newspaper when you'd read it . . . It was an accumulation of stuff.'

I don't love you, Jerry . . . I couldn't even stand to be in your company . . . was there any statement more devastating that a man could hear from the woman he loved?

Hurt me some more, Sondra. Pile it on. Kill me. But do it quickly.

I reached for her hand, a gesture of hope. She drew it away. I closed my fingers on the empty space where her hand had been. I gazed at her and she looked at me with the defiance of somebody saying: *Get used to this, because this is the way things are.*

She was too far gone. I saw that.

She loved this Nardini. She was besotted. That was the hold he had over her: Love, in one of its many varieties. I felt like cracked glass. I was standing on a fault-line on the earth and it was about to break open and I'd vanish inside some deep, hot place.

I looked at the wine-glass, the cigarette butt floating on a disc of red liquid. I wanted to go punch the window out, let night air enter the room and dilute the smell. I experienced the zigzag lines again, the migraine electricity, and my mouth was dry. I needed to lie down in a darkened room and sleep for a week. Then, when I woke out of my dreamless state, amnesia would be hard at work, deleting passages of my memory, excising all the bad things. Later, I'd take off somewhere; I'd pack a bag and drift up a jungle river on a ramshackle raft in search of whitewater.

I'd forget who I was, and the woman who'd been my wife, and the cruelty of this whole pantomime. The inhumanity of it.

'You knew about the safe-deposit box,' I said. 'I must have told you about it.'

'You don't even recall *that*, do you? You're so wrapped up with those freaks that come to your office that everything just kind of slips past you. Sure, you told me about the box, Jerry. You told me the day you opened it. You said you needed a safe-deposit box because you had material you didn't feel secure keeping in your office. Words to that effect.'

'I remember vaguely,' I said.

But I wasn't sure. I wondered what else had drained out of my mind. What else I'd overlooked because I was buried in the problems of others. I must have lived some of my life at a tangent to everyday concerns, overlooking not only the obvious, but nuances, too, hints, slips of the tongue, behavioral clues. How many times had she lied to me and I'd missed it? Saying she was working late, when in reality she'd been with Nardini? And then all those weekend music industry conventions, those business retreats — how could I have missed a giveaway, a bad excuse, a slyness, an evasion in her manner?

She said, 'It was at the time when Ford was your patient. So I knew that whatever you stuffed in that box was connected to her. And I knew it had to be big, because you were more worried than I'd ever seen you before. You were jittery. You were prescribing downers for yourself, for God's sake. You were becoming secretive. Paranoid. The sound of the goddam phone made you jump. Remember?'

I didn't recall being jittery back then. But I was jittery now. I got up from the bed. I wasn't sure where to turn, what to do.

I heard Nardini and Resick talking just beyond the door. I watched Sondra blow smoke and I thought how I still wanted her, how love created clowns out of otherwise sensible people. If she got out of that bed and said she'd changed her mind about Nardini and wanted to come back, I'd take her home, and I'd be glad, my heart would come to life again. I stood without moving, half-hoping she'd say just that, *Nardini was a lustful fling, I just wanted his big cock inside me. I wanted to fuck him, suck his dick, I wanted him to screw me from behind, I wanted him to shackle me and fuck me until I bled, whatever. But it's over, let's get on with things, forgive me.*

And I'd forgive and be glad even as I knew I was being dumb.

'Give Dennis what you kept in the box, Jerry,' she said. 'Just do it. End this thing and let us all move on.'

Move on where, I wondered.

I listened to Nardini and Resick in the hallway. Nardini was saying, 'You shouldn't have let him run free through this goddam house, Tod, it's out of hand.' And Resick said something that sounded like, 'I'm not the one screwing his wife.' This dispute seemed to take place in another world, one that bore no relation to my life and marriage. Two men squabbling. My wife's lover and his sidekick, his junior partner in crime. They were arguing about timing, the fact that I'd been allowed the liberty to discover Nardini in a compromising situation with my wife.

I looked at her. 'I wasn't supposed to find out about this, was I?' I asked. 'It was meant to be a straight exchange. I give them whatever I've got on Emily Ford, and you come home with me. Right?'

'Right,' she said.

'And then what? How was it meant to play out? You'd have continued to meet Nardini secretly.'

'Yes.'

'And?'

'Dennis and I . . . we'd wait for the appropriate moment before I walked out on you entirely to be with him. Meantime, we'd take things one day at a time.'

'Yeah, right, like some fucking twelve-step program, huh?'

'It's pointless to talk with you, Jerry.'

'But you'd pack a suitcase at some point in the future and walk out on me because Nardini loves you and you love him?'

She nodded her head slowly. 'Along those lines.'

I was supposed to play along, thinking my marriage was still a happy one, that my wife loved me. And all the time, she'd be listening for the phone to ring, to hear her lover's voice say, *Come to me now.*

'This isn't you,' I said. 'You're not Sondra.'

'People change, Jerry. They choose a different path.'

'Does he love you?' I asked.

'Yes.'

'Has he told you?'

'He's said so, sure.'

'He's used the words,' I said. 'He's said 'I love you' because it's expedient.'

'You're trying to undermine him,' she said. 'You're hurt. I understand that.'

'Thank you for your understanding,' I said. 'And fuck you.'

I stared at her. I wanted to strike her. The urge to do violence was strong and unexpected. If I remained in her presence, I'd hit her. I knew that. I'd hit her more than once. Maybe I'd take her neck between my hands and squeeze.

Kill her.

I turned, opened the door.

Dennis Nardini looked at me.

I had an insight into what Sondra saw in

him: a dark attraction, a secret promise in the eyes, a hint of fire, an intimacy that was menacing. He didn't flinch from me, there was none of that embarrassment predictable in situations of exposed infidelity, no quiet apology: *I stole your wife, I'm sorry, these things happen.*

Dennis Nardini was the kind of man who never apologized to anyone for anything.

I said, 'You can have her.' The words were like arsenic in my mouth.

I made to walk past him. He laid a heavy hand on my arm.

'You're forgetting, you have something we want,' he said. The voice was pure gold liquid, something sweet and honeylike tapped out of a tree trunk. It was rich in a way that suggested power, a world without limitations. I imagined Sondra swooning and drowning in such a voice. I imagined him whispering in her ear, *Spread your legs for me, my love. I want to be deep, deep inside you. As deep as you can take me.*

I looked at Nardini. 'I don't have a goddam thing you want,' I said.

Nardini smiled. It was a smile you might imagine at the end of a chic cigarette holder. It was a smile made for tossing aside elegant witticisms; and to conceal ruthlessness.

'You know the price if you don't produce,' he said.

'I used to know,' I said. But it was a half-hearted remark.

I'd never really grasped what it was that made the human heart work the way it did, the modulations, the upheavals. I'd dispensed advice and pills in equal measures, but truth had always eluded me. My life had been misguided, my work a fiction.

I took a few steps down the corridor. I was aware of Tod Resick watching me with an expectant look.

Nardini said, 'So now you don't want to produce, Jerry?'

'I don't care,' I said.

Resick had a gun. I'd been expecting this. The last examination. The final test. He gave the gun, small and black and lethal, to Nardini.

'This is what I'll use,' Nardini said.

I said nothing. I wondered if he was serious. I couldn't tell. The inside of my head felt like a bar of rusted iron.

'This is the gun I'll kill her with,' he said. 'Look at it.'

I said, 'I see it.'

'You want me to use it on her?'

I moved a few steps away from him.

'She thinks you love her,' I said.

'I'm not responsible for what people think,' he said.

Sondra appeared in the bedroom doorway. She wore a man's robe, dark-blue terry cloth, bulky. She looked both beautiful and vulnerable. I had a sense of a volatile device ticking under the floorboards, inside a closet, or down in the shadows where the steel supports held the house in mid-air. I imagined an explosion and the whole structure thrown from the cliff's edge.

Nardini studied the gun in his hand. *Use it, don't use it. Heads or tails.* He seemed to be deliberating.

Sondra laughed a nervous laugh. 'What's with the weapon, Dennis?'

I said, 'He's wondering if he has to shoot you.'

'Bullshit,' she said. She looked at Nardini. 'Put the gun away, Dennis.'

'I think he's committed to the gun, Sondra,' I said. 'I think it's part of the master plan.'

Nardini's stare was as hard as a diamond. 'We can finish this cleanly if you give me the stuff, Jerry,' he said.

'I say shoot her,' I said. 'Shoot her.'

Did I mean it? Or had I become so engrossed in the charade that I no longer understood the role I'd been assigned to play

— the sucker, the cuckold, a man wrecked and wronged and twisted out of shape?

'Hey,' Sondra said. 'Shoot who?'

'Give me what you've got, Lomax,' Nardini said to me.

'What if I told you the safe-deposit box was fucking empty?' I said.

'You'd be lying,' he said.

'You don't know that.'

'Your wife said it contained records, important records.'

'Well, she was wrong,' I said, and I gave the last word a bell-like resonance. 'She was guessing and she guessed plain fucking wrong.'

Sondra laughed a little derisive laugh, one I'd never heard from her before, one I didn't like. 'The box had material about Emily Ford in it,' she said. 'Don't let him tell you anything different, Dennis.'

Nardini stepped towards me. 'Why do I believe your wife and not you, Jerry?'

'Because she's a damn good liar.'

Nardini smiled and said, 'Are you bluffing?' He looked at Resick. 'Does this man play poker, Tod?'

'He doesn't have the cards,' Resick said.

'Maybe, maybe not,' I said. I had a fluttery sensation in my chest.

'We'll see what he's got,' and Nardini

grabbed Sondra and held the gun to her head.

She twisted her face, looked at her lover. 'Dennis, what is this?'

'This is how I get what I want,' he said.

I walked away, kept walking.

I heard Sondra say, 'This is a joke, right? This is, like, some kind of prank, Dennis?'

'Say goodbye to your wife,' Nardini called out.

'Goodbye,' I said without looking back.

No turning around.

Keep moving.

'For God's sake,' Sondra said. 'Dennis, put the gun away!'

'It's no joke, Lomax,' Nardini shouted at me.

But I wasn't turning back. I'd be damned if I did.

'It's no goddam *joke*,' Nardini said again. 'It was always serious.'

Sondra said, 'Dennis, get that gun out of my face.'

I kept moving. But slower now.

I heard a metallic click. And then I couldn't go any further.

This was the place where I walked into the boundary of myself. This was where I ran into pity and mercy, the benign sisters of the soul who turned up when I didn't want them. I wanted to be as hard and cruel as everyone else in this house. But I didn't have all that inside me.

Not even now.

I turned to look at Nardini. 'What you want is outside,' I said.

Resick said, 'Well, well. The man folded his hand.'

Nardini lowered the gun. He pushed Sondra towards me. She swung round and looked at him, and although she uttered a kind of half-laugh, she was baffled and scared by this turn of events, this new current on which she was swept along. She'd mismanaged her heart. She'd counted on love, but she'd strung the beads all wrong on the devotional abacus. Her valentine card was defaced with ugly graffiti.

We went outside. We descended by the bizarre arrangement of wooden walkways. I heard the hum of the city again. The night was tinted orange-yellow. Nardini and Resick and Sondra walked after me towards the eucalyptus trees. A straggle of four.

You don't have to do this, I thought.

But I did.

I stopped at the third tree from the house and fumbled around in the half-dark until I found the envelope. I gave it to Nardini. He opened it and took out the cassette.

'This has everything I want?' he asked.

I nodded.

'This one small tape has it all?' he said.

'Yes,' and I looked at the cassette in his hand.

'I suggest we listen to it,' he said.

'I've heard it before,' I said.

'You don't understand, Jerry. I *insist* we listen,' he said, and he smiled. We moved back towards the house, where Nardini opened the door of a scarlet Porsche, and slid into the passenger seat. He turned the key that dangled from the ignition and the panel lights came on. He slotted the tape into the cassette-player.

I didn't want to hear Emily's voice. I didn't want Nardini to hear it either.

I thought: *Nardini's scum. Pure scum. Numb and unfeeling. A cold-hearted monster.* It didn't matter that he'd been my wife's lover, that he'd enjoyed her body, or that he'd created an intimate world with her, one I was barred from. None of it mattered. I was beyond narrow considerations of self and jealousy. I was thrown into another place, a blood-red place where I remembered the hatred I'd felt before, the rush of it, the consuming intensity. I couldn't avoid doing what I did next; I was compelled, gripped by a force outside my experience, and the opportunity was presented to me, everything came together: the sight of the gun in the pocket of Nardini's robe, a moment when it was unguarded and I could reach for it and pluck it out without interference. I projected my hand through space, across the short distance between the attorney and myself, and I pulled the gun from the pocket and I raised it and — just as Emily Ford had done on a hot afternoon in the trailer where Billy Fear lived — I shot Nardini in the head once, twice, I wasn't counting, and he slumped, half-in, half-out of the car, and then I turned the gun on Resick and I shot him in the chest. He was whipped back against the side of the Porsche, and his blood ran down the glass of the window.

I took the cassette from the deck and pocketed it. My hand didn't tremble. I'd never killed before, and yet I felt strangely whole, collected. I wiped the small gun clean in the folds of Nardini's robe. I dropped the weapon at Sondra's feet.

'What have you done, Jerry? Jesus Christ, what have you *done?*'

She looked at Nardini. She went down on her knees beside the car and cried. Her crying changed in intensity. I stared at her. She and Nardini had given me a child, and then they'd taken it away again. There was no baby, no future of the kind I'd imagined.

They'd vandalized my dreams. They'd crippled me.

'I was never here,' I said.

She placed a hand under Nardini's head, a gesture so sad and tender I thought I'd break.

I said, 'You can call the cops and explain all this. It shouldn't be beyond you to come up with something convincing.'

She put her face close to Nardini's, and when she raised her eyes to look at me her forehead and cheeks were colored with his blood.

'You killed him,' she said.

I began to walk.

I heard her scream after me.

'You sonofabitch, you killed him!'

When I reached the end of the driveway, I heard a sound from the house. It was like stone struck and cracked by a sledgehammer, or dynamite exploding in the distance, or the faraway backfire of a car, or a gun-shot. It was all of these things.

I hesitated. I wondered if Sondra had fired a shot in my direction, wild and desperate and hopeful.

I heard her cry out again, and her voice was animal-like with grief, a keening. *You fucking bastard, Lomax. You miserable, heartless, fucking bastard.*

I wasn't listening.

I reached the car and drove through the canyons. A chill lay suddenly on the night air. I shivered and rolled the windows up. I traveled in a dazed state, like a man burning out after days of speed and sleeplessness, crashing through the surface of one reality and into another. I wanted neither.

I parked outside my house and remained in the car for a time, hands on the wheel, mind nowhere. The street had changed. It had become unfamiliar. I didn't like the place. I stepped from the car.

She was standing under a shade tree. She came out of the shadows as I approached.

Saturday, 12.01 a.m.

I put an arm around her shoulder because she looked sad and contrite. 'Have you been waiting out here long?' I asked.

'I wasn't keeping track,' she said.

'I know what you did,' I said.

'How?'

'A process of elimination, I guess.'

'They pressured me, Jerry. As soon as you got that phone call and flew out of the office, they said they'd give my name to Immigration. I was desperate. They backed me into a corner. They said I'd be deported. I didn't want that. I like it here, I enjoy working for you.'

'Jane, it doesn't matter,' I said. 'It's OK.'

'I stole a file, Jerry. That matters to me. I gave it to people who had no right to it. I broke the rules of confidentiality. Trust.'

Oh, Jane, I thought. *You're not alone.* Trust was powder, ashes blown away and scattered.

I said, 'Take next week off. Let's cancel all the appointments and close the office.'

'Is that what you want?'

363

'You don't know how much,' I said.

'Will you go out of town for a while?'

'Probably.'

She turned her face so that lamplight fell against it. I thought how young she looked in this merciful orange light.

She said, 'Allardyce — that was more poor judgment on my part.'

'You like the guy?'

'Not in a way that suggests we have a future,' she said. 'I feel sorry for him. He has that kind of face.'

'Go home, Jane,' I said. 'It's late.'

She said, 'You'll be OK?'

'Sure I will.'

She turned away. I called her back. 'One thing,' I said. 'How did you know the floor-safe combination?'

'Jerry, you entrust me with bills, petty-cash, banking, correspondence, so there's very little I don't know about what goes on inside the office. And very little I don't know about your personal habits and preferences . . . I figured there was a good chance you'd use the same number for the safe combination as for your bank PIN. Because you're a creature of habit, Jerry. Why remember two sets of numbers when one will do?'

'Predictable,' I said. 'Is that what I am?'

She nodded. 'Much of the time.'

'Is that good or bad?'

She smiled and moved slightly, and her face passed out of the lamplight and back into shadow. 'Both,' she said.

12.10 a.m.

I entered the house, switching on lights as I moved. The place was familiar and yet not familiar: a dream environment. Strangers might have lived here — Jerry and Sondra Lomax, married couple, future uncertain. I tried to relate to the everyday things around me: the brown leather sofa, the low-slung coffee table a few yards from the TV, the books stacked on shelves; I wasn't comfortable with any of this stuff. I knew it all, but it had changed in my absence. I looked at the bound journals, *American Journal of Psychiatry, Journal of Clinical Psychology*. I couldn't remember ever having read them.

And the photographs on the wall above the fireplace — the pictures were unarguably shots of myself and Sondra, but the man looked less like me and more like a distant cousin, someone with a mild family resemblance, someone who lived far away, and every now and then mailed a photograph of himself to me in California.

Sondra, the soul of the house, was gone.

I walked into the bathroom. The floor was still damp from where Consuela had lain. Wet towels lay in a pile. In the tub was a single strand of her hair. I stared at it for a time.

I went into my office. I checked my answering-machine. No messages. I sat at my desk and placed my hands, palms down, on the plain wood surface. I was very still. I thought back to the dream of people falling out of the sky, but it had faded to the point where it was no longer mine; it was distant, it was as far removed as everything else in this house. The doorbell rang; my first thought was Sondra. She'd come home. She wanted a fresh start. She wanted to mend the damage. *We'll talk*, I thought. *We'll talk everything through*. Maybe we could make believe none of this had ever happened. This was California, and dreams came true in the land where nothing was real, didn't they?

It was Emily Ford who stood on the doorstep. She stepped inside. She followed me into the living-room. I told her the bare bones of what had happened. I skipped the flesh of details. She listened without expression.

She said, 'So Nardini's dead.'

'Yes.'

She sighed. I couldn't interpret the sound. Relief? A tiny passing touch of regret? No, she had nothing to regret. Nardini had been her enemy.

I took off my jacket. It smelled of gasoline fumes and dirt. I slung it across the back of a chair.

She said, 'And Sondra, what about — '

'No, don't ask,' I said. 'I don't want to talk about her.'

I felt loss. It was all around me. It would linger in this house a long time.

Restless, I walked into the dining-room. The plates from the dinner we'd shared just before Sondra had announced her 'pregnancy' were still on the table. Consuela had been interrupted before she'd had time to clean up. The dead candles in their holders were left-overs from an old dinner-party in another era.

I want to be a good mother, Jerry. I want that so badly.

Yes, Sondra. You wanted that. Once upon a time.

I remembered how she'd spoken in her sleep.

My love.

I hadn't been the love she'd addressed in her dream.

I entered my office and sat at my desk.

I gazed at a photograph of Sondra. The light from the lamp glossed the glass and hid her features. She looked innocent, without guile, a lovely young woman of the kind you sometimes see when you're flicking the pages of an old high-school year book and you come across The One Most Likely To Succeed, and you wonder what happened to this promising girl; whether her beauty had taken her anywhere, bit parts in low-budget movies, say, or a repertory theater in a provincial city, or whether she'd been wrecked by the erosions of time, withered by marriage and childhood and bored out of her beauty by barbecues and cocktail parties, and now she was bitter and dried out by life in some dusty place like Amarillo or Las Cruces.

I turned the photograph face down. I didn't want to look at Sondra. It was an immature action, but I wasn't interested in behaving like an adult.

I smelled something burning.

I walked along the corridor to the kitchen. Emily was standing at the counter with a big ashtray in front of her: magnetic tape, which she'd unraveled from its container, burned. It didn't burn easily. It shriveled and twisted, like an organic thing resisting death; it threw up small flames that flickered briefly before they went out. She had to keep applying matches to the pyre.

'What are you doing?' I asked.

'Burning a tape I took from your jacket,' she said.

'You didn't have the right — '

'Why not? It's as much mine as it is yours, Jerry.'

I didn't like the idea of a small larceny, Emily rummaging through my jacket. I said, 'That cassette was my property. You didn't have the right to destroy it without my permission.'

'Did you have the right to record it without mine?' she asked.

I didn't feel like arguing. I had no energy left. She poked the smoldering tape with a fingertip and a small blue-yellow flame rose from the ashtray.

'This is for the best,' she said. 'Nothing goes back to normal after all this, does it?'

I agreed. Everything was different now. The whole world had changed. I couldn't see a future. Whatever half-drawn map had guided my life in the past was no longer a reliable document.

I watched Emily. She was enchanted by flame. She stuck the end of a cheap ballpoint pen into the tangle of scorched tape, provoked a few more licks of fire, then drew the pen back. She was miles away. I understood she wanted to be thorough. I thought of an alchemist inclined over an alembic, waiting patiently for the results of a distillation.

She was burning her history. Erasing her past. I wondered if she was thinking of Billy Fear as the tape smoldered. If she was remembering details now. Maybe it had come back to her in bits and pieces: the gun, the way she'd shot Billy in the face, the thick heat in the trailer, the roar of flies.

I looked at the dry bloodstains on my fingers. I went to the bathroom, washed my hands; pink liquid flowed towards the drain. I splashed water on my face, buried my head in a towel. I felt unplugged from myself. The events of the long day had depleted me. I was fading around the margins. I didn't look at my reflection in the mirror.

I heard Emily Ford's voice in the kitchen and I wondered whom she was talking to; my first thought was that she was conversing with herself. Then I realized she was speaking on the telephone.

I walked to the kitchen doorway.

'I hope I didn't wake you,' she was saying.

Whoever was on the other end of the line said something to make her laugh.

She said, 'The city that's too paranoid to sleep. I like that.' She noticed me, smiled absently, almost as if I were a passing waiter, a lackey.

She didn't break stride in her conversation. 'Mort, that pair of dufuses you sent out here.

Carrie somebody and Brunton. I have to tell you, they don't project a whole lot of warmth and human understanding . . . '

Mort Wengler, White House Chief of Staff, Emily's man on the inside. I felt cold. The tiny hairs on the back of my neck shivered as if touched by a passing breeze that had blown from a frozen place a long way off.

I watched Emily. I heard the confidence in her voice. She was self-assured, cheerful, a lift in her voice. 'You've already heard about the psychiatric treatment? Don't tell me that pissant stuff worries you. God, that was run of the mill, your basic depression. After the tragic murder of my parents, I owed my central nervous system some downtime. Right? Am I right? Don't tell me you haven't had to ingest a Valium now and then?'

I sank deeper into cold.

She'd burned the tape and she'd risen from the ashes reborn. Instead of recognizing the crime in her past and adjusting her world accordingly, instead of sitting in some quiet, cloistered place to analyze her past actions and figure out how they might relate to her future, she'd denied her history. It was something that had never happened, an hallucination, or a bad dream.

A man dies in a trailer-park, and it doesn't matter.

Had she intended this from the beginning? Had this been her aim all along — that she'd get her hands on the evidence somehow and she'd destroy it and she'd be liberated from her past?

No. She hadn't known about the cassette. She'd seized a chance, that was all. She'd jumped on it. She'd played the cards the way they'd fallen, and they'd fallen beautifully for her.

I thought of the tape in Nardini's hand. I fixed on that moment when he'd slid inside his car and reached for the slot of the cassette-player, and how I'd seized the gun from the pocket of his robe and shot him.

I thought: *You protected Emily Ford one time too many.*

'Maybe I'll fly up tomorrow,' Emily said to Mort Wengler. 'I mean, if that's what you want, Mort . . . ' She glanced at me, but again she wasn't really seeing me. 'Yeah, OK. We'll talk through some stuff. Clarify anything that's troubling you. Fine, fine.'

She puckered her lips, made a kissy sound, then she put the handset down. I went out on the deck and looked at the city. I felt an unbearable sadness. I imagined lives behind the lit windows of other houses, broken loves and great tragedies; joys too, but even the joys made me sad.

A strong breeze blew out of the darkness and rattled shrubbery. I shut my eyes and remembered the sound I'd heard outside Resick's place — that crack and how it split the air. And I thought of Sondra and how she'd shouted, *You sonofabitch, you killed him!*

Emily came out on the deck and placed her hands on my shoulders. She rubbed my muscles lightly. 'You're tense,' she said.

I felt padlocked, stiff.

'Somehow Mort's already got a copy of your original file,' she said. She sounded up, buoyant, someone with a life to look forward to. 'He wouldn't say who sent it to him.'

I didn't speak. I listened to her voice and I thought about the woman who'd thrown a cassette-player and scores of CDs around a room, who'd lost control of herself. And I thought: *She's two people. Emily Ford isn't just one person.*

'I'll fly up to Washington and I'll sit down with him and we'll go through the whole damn file together,' she said. 'I don't imagine there's anything in it I can't explain, is there?'

I made no answer.

'Well? Is there anything, uh, *completely* detrimental in the file?' she asked. 'I know we discussed this before, but I want to be sure I can defend myself if anything *awkward* comes up.'

I still said nothing.

'Cat got your tongue, Jerry?' she asked. 'Moody old silence descended on you? Ah, you're angry with me, right?'

'I'm not angry,' I told her. But I thought: *I've failed her. I haven't fixed her. She isn't complete. She isn't mended. She's broken in two halves. Erratic, volatile here; zealously ambitious there. You flopped on the job, Lomax. You screwed up. You failed to glue Emily Ford back together again.* She belonged in a psychiatric unit, not in high political office.

'Did you *honestly* think I'd let this opening pass, Jerry?' she asked. 'Did you expect me just to walk the hell away from my dream, and blow Washington off? Did you really think obscurity would be enough for me?'

'With the benefit of hindsight, no. You're an opportunist. Among other things.'

'Which are?'

'You're manipulative. Self-centered. Driven. Devious.'

'Some people might regard those as compliments,' she said.

I gazed back across the lights. The city sparkled. I felt fatigue eat through me like a tapeworm, growing stronger the more it devoured me. I thought of Sondra down there somewhere in the chasms of the night. I thought of her grief.

Emily continued to massage my shoulders. 'You didn't imagine I'd fade away into the distance, did you? A door opened unexpectedly for me. I heard the fucking *hinge* squeak and it jolted me awake, believe me. You had the tape and Nardini was dead and God was up there saying, *Go for it, Em baby, go for it, this is your moment, and it's not coming your way again.* So I just kicked the door wide open. I just battered it down and stepped into the room and suddenly, wham, I'm back on track again. I'm rolling, dearheart. I'm traveling. Burning up the miles. I'm *this* close to getting what I want. Who was the fool who said there were no second acts in American life? Boy, was he wrong.'

I couldn't take her touch any more. I didn't want to feel her fingers work my muscles. I said, 'You murdered a man. You shot a man in cold blood, Emily.'

'Talk to me about killing somebody in cold blood, Jerry.'

'What I did was different,' I said.

'How? Explain.'

Where to begin. I wasn't sure there was a starting-point. Or if there was, I couldn't find it at the moment.

She said, 'Was it justice you were after? Was that why you killed Nardini? Or was it something way less admirable, Jerry, like rage and jealousy and hurt? Were you just responding like a common garden cuckold?'

I felt a weird shifting of balances.

She'd killed for retribution.

And I'd killed for — what? What had I *really* murdered Nardini for? Hatred because he'd bent my world out of shape? Because my wife loved him and not me? Because she'd entered into an abhorrent pact with him and I'd been used and discarded and had no further role to play in her life?

Or was it for the protection of a former patient who certainly didn't merit it?

A single motive, or a tangled skein of them: which? I wondered if I could ever free one string from another, if I was destined to spend the rest of my life trying to cut through this fibrous knot of mystery.

I looked for honor in what I'd done.

I found none.

Emily dropped her hands to her side and said, 'Tell me I'm a terrible human being, Jerry. Tell me I'm unfit for high office.'

My voice was quiet. I spoke with no real conviction. 'Unfit. Unstable. You'll crack under pressure. You'll snap and go off the rails.'

'Unfit and unstable never stopped people in the past from holding high office,' she said. She smiled at me. 'Prove I'm a killer, Jerry. You know you can't. Even if you wanted to. And I'm not sure you do.'

I said, 'I should have let Nardini have the tape.'

'But you didn't,' she said.

'I should have let him keep it. Then he'd have had power over you. And he'd have known how to use it. My problem is, I don't know what to do with that kind of power.'

She said, 'You'll get over it. I'll think of you when I'm in Washington.' She chucked me very lightly under the chin. I resented the gesture, the mock playfulness of it. It meant: Take it on the jaw, Jerry. It's not the first mistake you ever made. Is it, *dearheart*?

I looked into her eyes, which were as hard and brilliant and baffling as the city itself. I smelled the faint chemical scent of burnt tape drift from the house and out across the night, and I wondered if a second act might be possible in my life, too.

Or when.

Or if this was as far as I was destined to travel, a lonely man on a high redwood deck overlooking a crazy, teeming Californian city whose inhabitants were sick and needed me, a qualified psychiatrist, to guide them back to mental health.

God help them.

'Well?' she asked. 'Truce?'

'Why not,' I said.

And then the thought came to me from nowhere, and I was surprised by the ease with which I considered it: I wondered how much effort it would take to push her with enough force to snap the handrail, so that she'd fall from the deck and go on falling until she lay shattered on the sidewalk.

What reserves of strength did I have? Or would I have to dig very deep at all?

I'd watch her drop, unable to intervene in any way. The powerless observer. The hapless bystander. I'd watch her fall in much the same way as I'd seen the airplane passengers drop out of the sky in my dream. And then she'd lie way beneath me, broken on stone.

'No hard feelings?' she asked.

'None.'

'Good,' she said. 'I prefer it that way.'

I heard a plane roaring in the dark sky over LAX.

I placed my hands on Emily Ford's shoulders. She interpreted the gesture as one of amnesty from me, appeasement. We understood each other. I appreciated her goals. I knew her needs. She was confident I wasn't going to judge and condemn her. She was certain of me.

All bone, she weighed practically nothing.

She'd crack in pieces like porcelain when she struck the gray concrete that stretched out in pools of street-lamp and shadow below.

THE END

MY FATHER'S HOUSE

Kathleen Conlon

'Your father has another woman'. Nine-
year-old Anna Blake is only mildly
surprised when a schoolfriend lets drop
this piece of information. And when her
father finally leaves home to live with
Olivia in Hampstead, that place becomes,
for Anna, the epitome of sinful glamour.
But Hampstead, though welcoming, is not
home. So Anna, now in her teens, sets out
to find a place where she can really
belong. At first she thinks love may be the
answer, and certainly Jonathon — and
Raymond — and Jake, have a devastating
effect on her life. But can anyone really
supply what she needs?

GHOSTLY MURDERS

P. C. Doherty

When Chaucer's Canterbury pilgrims pass a deserted village, the sight of its decaying church provokes the poor Priest to tears. When they take shelter, he tells a tale of ancient evil, greed, devilish murder and chilling hauntings . . . There was once a young man, Philip Trumpington, who was appointed parish priest of a pleasant village with an old church, built many centuries earlier. However, Philip soon discovers that the church and presbytery are haunted. A great and ancient evil pervades, which must be brought into the light, resolved and reparation made. But the price is great . . .

BLOODTIDE

Bill Knox

When the Fishery Protection cruiser MARLIN was ordered to the Port Ard area off the north-west Scottish coast, Chief Officer Webb Carrick soon discovered that an old shipmate of Captain Shannon had been killed in a strange accident before they arrived. A drowned frogman, a reticent Russian officer and a dare-devil young fisherman were only a few of the ingredients to come together as Carrick tried to discover the truth. The key to it all was as deadly as it was unexpected.

WISE VIRGIN

Manda Mcgrath

Sisters Jean and Ailsa Leslie live on a small farm in the Scottish Grampians. Andrew Esplin, the local blacksmith, keeps a brotherly eye on the girls, loving Ailsa, the younger sister, from afar. Ailsa is in love with Stewart Morrison, who is working in Greenock. Jean is engaged to Alan Drummond, who has gone to Australia, intending to send for her when his prospects are good. But Jean shocks everyone when she elopes with Dunton from the big house . . .